BAD BOSS

STELLA RHYS

BAD BOSS

Copyright © 2017 by Stella Rhys

This book is a work of fiction. Names, characters, places and incidents are either products of the author's imagination or used fictitiously. Any resemblance to actual events or people, living or dead, is entirely coincidental.

Cover Design: Vivian Monir
Editing: Wendy Chan, The Passionate Proofreader

1

SARA

Holy shit.

I panted in the backseat of the cab, still running on the adrenaline of tonight's potentially disastrous decision-making. It could be the biggest mistake of my life but fuck it, I'd done it.

I'd finally walked out.

I was supposed to be Stable Sara with Excel sheets for everything from her taxes to her groceries to her budget for next year's Christmas gifts, but tonight I had officially reached my limit and quit the dream job I'd given my entire adult life to despite everyone imploring me to stay. *But the company's so famous, so* iconic. *You've put in so much time already. Why not stick around? Shouldn't you consider yourself lucky to be there in the first place?"*

I scrunched up my face as I freed myself from my blazer.

Yeah, no. Not so much.

If lucky meant nine years of chasing nonexistent promotions, being tricked into working thousands of overtime hours without the pay, getting thrown under the bus for anything the higher-ups did wrong, and spending the past three months on a piece that my editor had *no intention of crediting me for* – a fun fact I'd discovered just today

– then sure, I was lucky. So lucky that I wound up permanently deleting all history of my research, contacts and writing, leaving the office in a blaze of glory that set my bosses back three months of hard work.

So... bridges?

All burned.

There was definitely no going back. And while it was exhilarating now, I knew that by morning, once reality set in, I'd be horrified. I'd worked with the company since I was eighteen. My office-centric life was all I knew. Being *overworked* was all I knew. In fact, I had no clue what to do with my time if I wasn't strapped to a desk, and around 8AM tomorrow, I'd probably remember all that and have a very thorough meltdown.

So for now, I was going to ride the high.

"You said Lower East Side, miss?" the cabbie called back to confirm.

"Yes, Ludlow Street, right below Houston."

Also known as the corner of Drink My Ass Off and Dance Till Four, I declared silently, yanking out my hair tie and shaking out my topknot.

I was in a rare mood.

I was feeling bold... *liberated*. Practically drunk off the thrill of having *no* responsibilities tomorrow. For the first time in my adult life, I had no one to report to, not a soul to be on call for, and I felt *good* about it, which was something I knew wouldn't last, so... why not take advantage of tonight and do something crazy?

Well.

I bit my lip. I had answers for that.

A bevy of them that had to do with spur-of-the-moment decisions having deep and lasting consequences, and how I should really, *really* know that better than anyone else. But before I could get into that buzzkill with myself, a storm of texts pinged in my phone.

Perfect timing. I reached into my pocket, knowing without looking that the messages were all from my best friend.

LIA: Helloooo why must you text me and then disappear??

LIA: Wait so I don't get it are you really going to make it tonight? How did you get out of work??

LIA: Did you finally duct tape your boss to her chair like I told you to

ME: Hi. I did... in a way. I'll tell you when I get there. It's a long story that you're not going to believe and I'm going to require a drink first. Maybe three.

LIA: Yesssss story time so excited

LIA: Also Lukas knows the owners here so... open bar :)

ME: YESS. I'm 5 min away. Rooftop at the Victorian Hotel?

LIA: Yep rooftop terrace! Just give them Lukas's name at the door. Should I have a drink ready for you?

ME: No but if you can find a hot guy who looks like he'd be killer in bed please grab him and tell him all about me

I WAS HALF-KIDDING but that didn't stop the flurry of shocked emojis before Lia's next message came in.

LIA: Whaaaaaaaaaat?

I snorted as I watched the ellipsis repeatedly drop off and return as my best friend tried to decide which of her many questions to ask first. I knew what she was thinking – when did I get the balls to have a one-night stand? Wasn't I the chick who kept the same mild-mannered, borderline vanilla friend with benefits over the course of the past five years?

Yes. Yes, I was.

His name was Jeff and he was my copy editor at the magazine I just quit and figuratively set on fire. I chose him because he was already at the office and he was cute enough without being distract-ingly hot. He was pretty good without being great. He wasn't strong enough to make me break much of a sweat during sex and show up to my next meeting disheveled – which sounded horrible, yes, but that was the point.

Jeff was just enough to satisfy my libido, but not enough to launch my hormones into crush mode. He got the job done so I could get *my* job done and finally earn myself a spot on the masthead like every one of my bosses kept promising I would. For that company, I'd adapted myself to an active but deeply mediocre sex life.

And all for nothing.

Those dicks, I scowled as Lia's text finally came in.

> **LIA:** *HOLD ON I'M SO CONFUSED. WTF is happening can you tell me in one sentence please??*
> **ME:** *FINE*
> **ME:** *Basically I just snapped and quit June Magazine in a way that might get me blacklisted from publishing entirely so before I launch into disaster control tomorrow, I'm going to make up for all the years of bad sex I had for that company by finding the hottest guy at the bar tonight and having him do EVERYTHING to me.*

Once I hit send, I let out a heavy *whoosh* of a breath. I didn't realize it till a second after sending the text, but apparently my mind was made.

I was indulging tonight.

In everything.

Fuck it – for just one night, I was going to let myself have whatever I wanted, however I wanted – as hard and fucking *sweaty* as I wanted.

In ten hours, it would be 8AM, but till then, every one of my rules would cease to exist.

Any fantasy I had, my wish was my own command, because I was both Cinderella and her own fairy godmother at the hotel rooftop ball. Tomorrow, it was back to reality.

But tonight, I was making every second worth it.

2

SARA

"Lia, we're officially in the same building – can't this wait till I meet you up on the roof?" I pleaded, my phone pressed between my shoulder and my ear as I handed the bouncer my ID. Once I slipped past him, I found myself in the sleek and seductive lobby of the hotel's quieter side entrance, waiting alone for perhaps the slowest elevator known to man.

"No, Sara, it cannot wait, because you strung me along all night with your cryptic-ass texts and now that I *finally* know what the heck is going on, I'm drunk and I'm excited and I'm ready to butter up some hotties for you so they're nice and warm by the time you get up here!"

"Oh, that just sounds... so creepy, Lia."

"Did it?" She made a sad little sound. "I guess so. Lukas is giving me the weirdest look right now. But whatever, it's not *your* night, Lukas – I'm talking to Lukas right now – it's *Sara's* night. Right, Sara? I'm talking to you right now."

I had to laugh at what an adorable shitshow my best friend turned into after just a few glasses of wine. "Sure, drunkie, it is."

"Exactly. So listen. I was talking to this guy just now who is a solid nine – don't look at me like that, Lukas – and he is a *total* sweetheart. Like, such a nice person."

"Uh-huh."

Lia's voice faded out as I opted to check my reflection in the mirrored doors of the elevator.

All things considered, not bad.

Despite the fact that I'd been ugly crying in the women's bathroom at work two hours ago, my mascara was still fairly intact, as was the light blush I'd applied early this morning. Tilting my face to the side, I admired the natural sheen on the cheekbones I'd inherited from my mother – sky-high and eager to reflect any shred of light in the room. Lia fondly called them dirty attention whores. My cheekbones and my "ass that won't quit," apparently, were the guiltiest parts of my body.

Oh, Lia. I had to interrupt her when she got to the part about this super nice guy's three rescue cats.

"Lia – listen," I started carefully. "I appreciate your tip, and I love you very much, but I don't think a cat dad sweetheart is what I'm looking for tonight."

"What? Why?"

"Is this a serious question?" I jabbed the elevator button again out of pure restlessness. "And do we really need to be having this conversation right now?"

"*Yes*, Sara, it's a serious question, because I'm drunk, and when I'm drunk, I have comprehension issues, which makes every question a serious question," Lia explained with frustration, simultaneously charming and annoying the shit out of me like only she could do. "Now explain to *me* why you don't want the nice guy I picked for you when I already told him *all* about you, and please tell me why you keep trying to get off the phone with me all night!"

"*Because,*" I hissed. "For starters, I just spent the past however many years having a bunch of okay sex with a guy I was the bare minimum of attracted to, so tonight I specifically don't want that kind of sex. I want good, *sweaty...* kind of *mean* sex with a man who'll just pin me down and... *fuck* me so hard he breaks the headboard.

And to answer your second question, I want to get off the phone because I don't want to talk about the mind-blowing sex I'm going to have tonight, I just want to *have* it. Thinking about it is turning me on to the point of torture right now and being on the phone with you while I'm this insane level of horny actually feels kind of weird, so will you please just let me get in the elevator, Li?" I asked, exasperated as I dragged my feet inside. "Because it's here, I'm in, and I –
"

Fuck.

My heart seized as I turned around to see the world's most stunning fucking force of a man stride in behind me, wearing a ridiculously expensive-looking suit, an incredibly crisp white shirt, and just enough of a smirk on that perfect mouth to let me know that he'd heard.

Everything.

"Um." I raked my awkward smile between my teeth as we made two seconds of eye contact so scorching hot I could have ripped my clothes off right then and there. Swiftly hanging up on Lia, I peered over at the stranger.

Good Lord.

He was a walking statue – tall, stoic, and carved from stone. His thick brown hair was slicked back just enough to give me an unspoiled view of sculpted cheekbones and a jaw so razor sharp I wanted to run my finger on its perfect edge. I cleared my throat.

"Hi."

He glanced over, hitting me with the piercing blue of his eyes just as he leaned in to hit the button to his floor.

"Hi."

That voice. I could taste it. It was low and sexy, smoky but smooth, and it matched perfectly with the rest of his unreal gorgeousness. One flick of my gaze over his body and I could already see that he was long and lean, several inches over six feet tall with a solid, muscled build. Even under that tailored jacket, I made out the strength of his broad shoulders, the tapered V of his chest. He was power and sex wrapped in an Italian suit, and it had me picturing him in some shiny

Manhattan office, conducting business as usual while getting sucked off under his desk.

Okay, Sara.

"So..." I chewed my lip, my heart pounding when he lifted his gaze to meet mine in the doors. "Were you..." *sent from Heaven? Just kidding.* "Were you there for the entirety of that conversation? Downstairs?" I topped my question off with a nervous little laugh that went unreturned.

Damn it. The statue was already bored with me. He was utterly expressionless, without so much as a twitch of emotion on those exquisite features. But just as embarrassment started flooding my cheeks, I spotted a little glint in his eye.

"No." He took his time to reply. "Just long enough to hear about how hard you want to get fucked tonight."

Oh.

My God.

"Right," I started slowly, biting down hard on my lip. "In my defense, I just had a bit of a catastrophic day, and tomorrow's probably going to be worse. So I'm giving myself basically the next ten hours to do whatever I want."

"Ten hours." He eyed me curiously. "That's not a lot of time."

I was as flustered as it got so I attempted a casual shrug.

"That's okay. I'm a simple girl."

My pulse heightened as I watched the sharp lines of his features move, forming the sexiest little frown between his brow. Was it...? It was. It was teasing me.

"I'm not so sure that's the word I'd use to describe you."

My pulse picked up but I played it off. "No? Why is that?"

"Simple implies easily explained."

"Which I'm not?"

He hesitated for half a second then gave a laugh. It was a low, velvet sound that had me instantly addicted.

"No. I already have... more than a few questions about you."

God, why did it feel like he was talking dirty to me? He offered few words but every one made me absurdly hot. Even his pauses turned me on. I couldn't help but prod him for more.

"What kind of questions?" I asked, trying to downplay my feverish curiosity. "You don't have to be shy. Like I said, it's a fuck-it kind of night for me."

He smirked. "You sure about what you're saying?"

No. But from this point forward, I'm going to act like I am.

"Yes."

"Then I guess I'm just wondering how a girl who looks like you has trouble getting someone to pin her down," he eyed me, "and fuck her as hard as she wants. Pretty sure any straight man would be happy to sacrifice a headboard or two for that."

Oh Jesus.

It took everything in me to refrain from actually fanning myself. I had no idea how to respond to that. All I knew was that I had to get it together. I had only so much of an elevator ride left with this mystery man of few words, and I wasn't going to leave it on him stunning me silent. It would be the greatest waste of serendipity known to man.

So tucking my hair behind my ear, I cleared my throat.

"What do... what do you mean someone who looks like me?" I finally asked.

"Don't be coy. You know what I mean."

I laughed. "I want to say I do, but I feel like I need to confirm, because this all feels very surreal right now."

Crap. Was I supposed to admit this? Wasn't I trying to play it cool? Whatever. Considering this guy's level of hot, the fact that I was still breathing was nothing short of a miracle.

"Fine. I meant that you're not just some average cute girl. You're... " He gave me that sexy laugh again as he watched the color rush to my cheeks. "Hot. Really fucking hot. The kind that makes men feel urgent."

"Urgent how?"

He looked at me like I was being insolent. "Like they need to jerk or fuck the image of you out of their head. Does that paint a clear picture for you?"

I swallowed. "Fairly."

"Any more questions?" he teased.

"Possibly," I teased back.

"Like?"

I crossed my arms. "Would you consider yourself among those men?"

He didn't hesitate.

"Considering I mentally fucked you in four different positions before you so much as laid eyes on me, I'd be inclined to say the answer is yes."

Oh my God. I was quiet for a second.

"And which position did you like best?"

Double oh my God! Holy shit, Sara. Nice one.

"I liked the one where I had you bent over the sink so I could watch everything bounce in the mirror." A leisurely smile curled his mouth. "But you straddling me to ride my cock was a very close second."

And... no words.

Speechless was actually an understatement for what I was as I stood there, the elevator finally opening at the bar I was supposed to get out at. I almost burst into flames when two women walked in, saw us, and promptly walked back out with giggles to each other. They already knew what I had yet to fully process till the doors closed and the elevator continued up to the penthouse.

"I think you missed your floor," he said. God, six words had never sounded so suggestive.

At least not until mine.

"I guess I'll go to yours."

A BLUR.

A hot, breathless blur – it was the only way I could describe the trip from the elevator to the door.

On no other night in the world would I be fine with my half-naked breasts being exposed in the middle of a hotel, but tonight, I was consumed – by the moment, the madness, by *him*. I didn't even know his name, but I didn't care. My pussy was throbbing without mercy for him, so at this particular moment, the only thing I cared about was getting this man naked and feeling his every hot, hard inch inside me.

"So sweet."

His murmur in my mouth was a stark contrast to his touch as he shoved me against the door, pinning my arms to my sides. My body strained impatiently for him but he was taking his time with me, forcing my fingers to flex and curl as he licked a thick, wet line along the curve of my neck. He didn't use the tip of his tongue – he used the flat of it, sending bolts of pleasure to every nerve ending in my body.

Holy shit. His mouth curved as it felt every tremble of my reaction. He knew he was torturing me, and it made him go even slower, swirling his tongue on my skin as he pushed his pulsing erection against my belly. It was at once hot as hell and completely fucking unbearable.

"Enough."

I shoved him hard, my stomach twisting with fear and excitement as he stood before me, eyes blazing.

"Don't tease me. I need you inside me already – please," I panted, swallowing hard as his eyes fell to my heaving chest.

It made me suddenly aware again that I was standing in just my black lace bra and black jeans, in the open hall of one of the most expensive hotels in Manhattan. It made me feel as if the cups containing me were shrinking in size, squeezing my breasts uncomfortably tight with every short breath I took in.

"Take it off first."

I exhaled. "What?"

"I want to watch you play with your tits. Then we'll go in."

I must have been crazy because I didn't think twice about obliging. In fact, I didn't even remember pushing the satin straps off my shoulders. I only came to as I arched my back off the door, reaching behind myself and undoing the clasp till my bra fell to the floor. I kicked it up at him. He caught it with his eyes still pinned to my breasts.

"Play with your nipples."

I enjoyed the low groan that rumbled from his chest as I did – almost as much as I enjoyed the clear as day outline of his cock against his pants. He was a steel fucking rod, and every inch what I needed tonight.

"*God*, just take me inside already," I begged.

This time he obliged.

Entwined inside the room, I moaned from the anticipation alone. It was my first time in a hotel penthouse, but I didn't care. I took no notice of any décor or furniture till he bent me over the back of the couch that faced the mirror, giving me a view of him removing his tie and his jacket before peeling first my jeans down my legs, then my panties.

"Christ. It just gets better and better," he murmured, that perfect frown pinching his brow as he tilted his head and ran his hand down the curve of my ass. He assessed it with a little jiggle. Then cupping the roundest part of its curve, he drew his palm back and spanked me so hard I hissed.

"*Fuck.*"

I gripped the couch, squeezing my eyes shut as he caressed my stinging skin. But once he'd fully rubbed the pain away, he spanked me again. I swallowed as my toes dug into the rug.

"More."

"What was that?" His voice was hoarse.

"I want more."

He didn't wait. I gasped sharply as I got my wish, and my whimper grew to a moan as for the next few seconds, he administered blow after blow, spanking me so hard I could feel myself jiggle all over.

"Mmmm... *God!*" The ragged sound left my mouth in a crescendo, drawing a growl from his lips as he grabbed a handful of my hair.

"Christ, you're getting me so fucking hard," he snarled. "Look at how fucking sexy you are."

I looked up in the mirror and let out a small breath.

Shit, Sara. I didn't recognize this reflection. My hair was damp, my cheeks were flushed and there was satisfaction in my panting, open-mouthed smile. *What have you done to me?* I wanted to ask as I stared at him through the mirror, drinking him in. He was a mix of hand-some and brutal as he tilted his head just so, sliding a long finger into my pussy.

Fuck, oh fuck, that feels good.

It felt even better as he leaned forward, deepening his push inside me as his free hand cupped my breast.

"Squeeze them hard," I whispered.

"My pleasure."

I had to be shameless. I had to ask for what I wanted, because come morning, this would be over. I'd never see this man again, and I couldn't have a single regret. So I let it all out with him.

"More," I breathed, moaning uncontrollably as he kneaded both my breasts with one hand, the other still playing with my pussy. He had two fingers pumping rapidly inside me now, and I couldn't believe how wet I sounded. I couldn't believe how incredibly good I felt.

With a throaty cry, I pitched forward. His strong arms caught me as I went limp, and there was a beat of silence before I heard his grav-elly whisper.

"Did you just come all over my hand, beautiful?"

"Yes," I replied, panting in shock as he rubbed my own juices all over my breast, his hand slick and slippery on my skin. *Holy shit.* I rolled my head back on his shoulder, closing my eyes as I felt him rub his erection against my ass. "I should be wet enough that you'll fit easily now," I murmured.

He paused.

"What did you say?" He laughed as I turned around to gaze into his intense stare. For a moment, he took me in, his eyes trailing from my wet breasts to my parted lips. "And here I thought I couldn't get any harder," he muttered, grabbing his heavy buckle and giving three swift jerks to undo his belt.

My pulse rose in anticipation.

It spiked the moment his cock sprang free, prompting my mouth to fall open. I knew he was grinning as he watched me stare. His hand cupped my waist as I slid my palm under his shaft, my toes curling as I tried to wrap my fingers around his thickness. It felt surprisingly silky on my skin. I loved the warmth, the heaviness, and I reveled in the sound of his groan as I started to stroke.

Just you wait, I bit my lip.

I'd never particularly cared for giving head, but I wanted his cock in my mouth. I wanted to taste him – to be the one in control for a moment before I let him fuck me as he pleased on whatever surface he chose.

"What are you doing?"

I enjoyed the unbridled surprise in his voice as I knelt before him. Gripping his thick root, I brushed my lips against the smooth head of his cock, drawing back just in time to see his glistening pre-cum beading. From under my lashes, I peered up to see him breathing hard and unblinking, practically drunk off his view.

God, yes.

He was strong, undoubtedly someone of power in this city, but I had him at my mercy and waiting desperately for just the tip of my tongue.

"Do it," he rasped, his urgency palpable in his grip on my hair. "Suck on it. Fucking hell, please," he hissed. "Let me feel your beautiful mouth on my cock."

Satisfied, I drew my tongue over his pulsing tip, swirling it around and drawing out the sexiest groan from the pit of his throat.

I heard it just a second before the front door of the room exploded wide open.

"Oh my God!"

The shriek that pierced my ears came from my own mouth, and it was followed by his growl of, "*Motherfucker!*" at the door.

Omigod.

What the fuck, what the fuck, what the fuck, I thought as I launched toward my clothes strewn over all parts of the floor.

Through the absolute chaos of shouting, I gathered that our intruder was a friend of his, but I still wasn't sticking around. Half naked with my pussy drenched and my lips still tingling from the taste of cock, the last thing I wanted was an audience. I was hot and humiliated, and within seconds, I was out the fucking door.

3

JULIAN

I pretended to watch the game as I sat at the back of my suite behind home plate. As far as I could tell, no one knew I was seething. I gave a nod and a clap at the top of the fifth, when we got out of a bases loaded, no-out jam. I posed for a few pictures and had a full conversation with my President of Baseball Operations. But I wasn't actually paying attention to any of these things.

My focus was entirely on the idiot brothers kicked back in their seats, shoes off and flirting with girls half their age like we weren't in the midst of a meeting they requested.

Breathe the fuck in. Breathe the fuck out.

Think numbers.

Billionaire's meditation.

That could be the name of this game. I forced myself to play it whenever I dealt with clients or partners who wasted my time. Instead of calling off all negotiations and telling everyone to fuck themselves, I told myself to breathe and calculated how much of my fortune was amassed by maintaining relationships with people I despised.

The answer was a lot.

And this evening, the answer was getting me through my meeting with Turner and Carter Roth. The California-bred trust fund babies had been semi-professional surfers as recently as three years ago. They had no detectable traces of common sense, discretion or business savvy, but since the passing of their father three months ago, they'd inherited seven billion dollars each and full control of Roth Entertainment Group, the world's leading sports and entertainment presenter. They were behind everything from the world's biggest boxing matches to rock concerts and tours, and they had no idea how powerful they were.

Thankfully, I did.

The downside was that I had a small window of time to strike a deal with them, which made every meeting increasingly urgent. And unfortunately, while we'd had four in person thus far, they pretty much all ended up like this – derailed by the sight of any moderately attractive face paired with long enough legs.

"Hey, Hoult," Turner called over his shoulder. "I got a pretty girl who wants to say hi."

I had just been burning holes in the back of his stupid head, but the moment he twisted around in his seat, my glare transitioned into something placid and easy.

"Yeah?"

"Yeah – listen, it's her twentieth birthday today and it's also her *first time* at Empire Stadium," he said, wagging his brow and nodding at the leggy blonde to his left. She wore two braids under her Empires cap and a kid's sized jersey as a dress. "Don't you, uh... don't you think she should get a nice tour from the owner of the American League champs? A nice, *personal* tour?" Turner threw in a wink, as if he'd been so subtle just now that I might need an extra hint to catch his drift. I offered the bright-eyed girl an almost-smile before looking back to him.

"You know, I did just have a thought."

His eyebrows jumped high. "Yeah?"

"Yeah." I paused till I had his full attention. "I was thinking we should take a trip out to the Biarritz property. You could get an in-person look at our clientele and all the improvements we've made since the – "

"Ah, *fuck*, you're talking business." Turner winced and shook it off like I'd just tricked him into holding a pile of dog shit. "Jesus, man. I got excited for a second. I thought you were about to suggest we do some blow."

"This is a family ballpark," I said. "You fucking animal," I had to add with irritation. Then I made sure to laugh. As long as I laughed, apparently, I could say anything. It was just taken as classic ball busting.

"Alright, easy. This guy here," Turner chortled. "So, fine. No blow. But will you please be a gentleman and take..." He trailed off and eyed the blonde.

"Hayley," she supplied.

"Hayley. Will you please take Hayley for a tour around the ballpark while I talk to..." He squinted at the girl in the chair to his right.

"Cass."

"*Cass*," Turner groaned skyward. "How could I forget? Cass with the ass," he growled, smoothing a hand over her thighs. Then with his eyes back to me, he lowered his voice. "Give me twenty minutes tops. Then you, me and the kid will get back to work."

By the kid, he meant his brother, Carter, who had been in the bathroom with Hayley's friend for about ten minutes now. I blamed him for all of this. I had actually done a decent job of keeping Turner on topic about purchasing my resort till Carter went off with a girl. At that point, all hope was lost. As the older of the two, Turner was never to be outdone, and if the kid managed to close, then Turner had to as well.

Nodding at the blonde, I had her walk ahead of me out the suite. "Twenty minutes," I repeated to Turner.

"Maybe thirty."

"Fifteen now," I said, hearing his snort before I walked out.

"WHO'S THAT?" Emmett asked as I deposited the pigtailed blonde in his suite. It was a short walk from mine but a stark contrast. Despite the game, there was usually music blaring and the tables were littered with beer, wings and giant platters of sashimi. *For the low-carb girls,* Emmett would say, since he rarely attended a game without at least two or three model-looking things in tow.

Standing at the back of the suite, we overlooked both the game and the antics of his unique social circle. My younger brother's friends ranged from lawyers to athletes to unemployed rich kids but they all had one thing in common: an affinity for drinking every night of the week.

"Her name is Hayley," I answered Emmett's question, watching Hayley instantly mingle with his friends. "I don't actually know her."

"Didn't think so. Let me guess – you're babysitting her for one of the Roths."

"Bingo."

Emmett snorted, twisting his baseball cap to the back and taking a swig of his beer. "I'd say forget them at this point but fuck, do those assholes have everything you need. And all that power just fell into their laps. They don't even know what to do with it."

"I'd prefer you not remind me."

"Alright, let's change the subject." His pause was deliberately short. "Oh, wait, there's no other subject with you besides work. Right?" I didn't say anything because there was no point in correcting him. That, and I could sense a certain topic coming up that I had no interest in discussing. "Except..."

"Don't."

"There *is* a topic we still haven't gotten the chance to clear up yet."

"Drop it, Emmett."

"Come on, dude. I need an explanation. Who was she? How'd you meet her? I've never seen you get so upset over a girl before."

I dragged my palm over my jaw and grumbled under my breath. "I wasn't upset over a girl. I was upset that you burst into the room while I was clearly in the middle of something with her."

I didn't want to think about it, but Christ, that night last week had been surreal. I'd been with my fair share of beautiful women, but the brunette I met Thursday night at the hotel had my dick half-hard even before I heard her talk about wanting to be pinned down and fucked senseless. Everything from her perfect tits to her nervous laugh made my dick jump. She was the sexual fantasy I never knew I had, and to say I was pissed I didn't get to finish my night with her was a gross, incredibly offensive understatement.

Great.

Now I was thinking about her.

"I can tell you're thinking about her."

"Fuck off."

"What?"

I looked at my brother. "I almost admire your nerve to single-handedly fuck up my night then taunt me about it."

"Are you mad at me or are you mad you're not over it yet?"

"Both."

"Christ, J." Emmett's mouth was stuffed with pizza as he laughed. "It's not the craziest thing in the world if you think about a girl for more than one night."

I don't know. Five days later and I still hadn't jerked off to any thought but her.

"Take it easy, brother. This just means you're human for once. Besides, it's New York. It's a small city. You'll run into her again."

"It's the fourth largest city in the world, but I appreciate your ability to always look on the bright side." I handed him my beer. "I should get back to my suite."

"Yeah, why not hurry up and wait. You're gonna get back there just in time to hear the Roths face-fucking twenty-year-old girls in the bathroom."

I grimaced. "Thank you for your colorful phrasing. And for putting that image in my head."

"Anytime. Now sit your ass down and watch this game with me. You own this damned team, you might as well try to care about them like you actually did when we were kids."

I shot him the look I generally did when I was getting thoroughly tired of his shit. Still, I took a seat and caught the last few outs before the seventh inning stretch, and as the customary rendition of "God Bless America" rang out, my mind drifted off.

I tugged on my lip.

God bless those fucking curves.

Thanks to Emmett, I was back to that dangerous rabbit hole of thinking about my mystery brunette from my night at the hotel. *God bless those curves and the way those full tits jiggled when I spanked that perfect ass over the couch.* Reliving the memory of her pink tongue on the tip of my dick was enough to get me both rock hard and pissed off, because I hadn't even gotten her name.

All I'd gotten were her panties.

They were silky, black, and I could have left them in the hotel room after checking out, but at this very moment, they sat on my dresser at home, next to the silver plate I put my watch on at the end of the day. As far as I was concerned, they were mine now. They were my only reminder of the nameless knockout who'd gotten me so hard so fast that I was ready to chase her out when she left and fuck her on the street if I had to.

Of course, shortly after I yanked my pants back on, Emmett's never-ending stream of friends came in, and just like that, she was lost forever.

But it was for the best.

That was at least what I told myself as I stared blankly at the field, watching the grounds crew prepare the dirt for the bottom of the seventh.

I had enough names to deal with. Turner Roth, Carter Roth, Hayley with the Braids, Cass with the Ass. Once I put a name to a face, I didn't forget it. I'd built my business from the ground up and along the way, I'd discovered there was no predicting when information could come in handy, no matter how insignificant it seemed.

"Jennifer." I stopped the waitress in the suite on her way out. She halted eagerly.

"Yes, Mr. Hoult?"

"I have to get back to the office, but I'd like you to do me a favor if you can."

"Yes, sir. Absolutely."

"I need you to go to my suite a few doors down. Turner Roth is the blonde-haired guy around six feet tall. He's wearing a blue shirt and he's with a girl in a yellow dress named Cass. I apologize in advance for whatever you might see them doing, but when they're done, will you give him this?" I handed her the business card I'd just scrawled a message on the back of.

She laughed breathily. "Of course, sir."

"Thank you, Jennifer."

"You're very welcome, Mr. Hoult." She hung around quietly for a second, like she always did. Then she was off, and I was up from my seat, sliding my phone from my pocket.

I had let go of any illusions that I'd be able to recapture Turner's attention tonight, so I decided to make the best of the situation by doing some maintenance. With a call, I reserved Turner the same penthouse I'd half-enjoyed last week at the Victorian Hotel, and I made sure to request a note beside the Cristal on ice, which would address both him and Cass – a simple gesture that would undoubt- edly make her feel special, since making her feel special was at least half the battle in sealing the deal.

Yes, I was winging for the assholes.

Because like sex, business was about making the client feel special, taken care of – like something between a friend and a rock star. So if I couldn't have a productive meeting with the Roths, then I was going to at least garner favor with them on a personal level by guaranteeing what they clearly cared about most – getting laid. Which was despicable, sure.

But too often, despicable happened to be great business.

4

SARA

This past week had not gone as planned – not by a long shot, and it showed on my face when Lia swung open the door of our favorite coffee shop and spotted me in the corner.

"Oh, bubs," she instantly pouted.

I was sulking at our usual table, wearing a long red maxi-dress and epitomizing the phrase "all dressed up and nowhere to go."

"I'm guessing dinner didn't go so well."

I made a face. "It was... bad. And awkward. And a little sexist at times."

"*What?* What did he say?"

"Lots of stuff about how I should stop freaking out about being unemployed, that it's okay for pretty girls to not have jobs. Then something about how women are actually a burden to companies, and maternity leave is unfair to men."

"Wow," Lia breathed. "That's super charming for a first date."

"Isn't it?" I said dryly.

Out of desperation, I'd tried a date tonight. The match I found on Tinder was a Cornell grad with what looked like a nice smile and a nicer body. I hoped he could be a distraction from the fact that I'd sent out hundreds of resumes in the past week and gotten no replies.

Six days wasn't a ton of time to be out of a job but still, I was getting restless, antsy, and worst of all, I was getting pretty frequently distracted from my job hunt by memories of that beautiful fucking man I was oh-so-close to sleeping with at the hotel last week.

It sounded dramatic, but I was pretty sure he'd ruined me.

I couldn't get dressed without looking at my own naked body and remembering the way he touched me, the way he licked my neck and kissed my breasts. In the shower, I ran my hands over the parts of me that he'd sucked and squeezed and spanked without mercy, and just *thinking* about that got me hotter than any sex I'd ever had.

It was torture. Pure torture.

The amount of times I had to pause my day and climb into my bed with my vibrator was actually embarrassing, so Josh from Tinder was my hope for relief.

But then he turned out to be a maternity leave-hating dickbag.

"It's okay, girl. Onto the next, right?" Lia tried to brush it off.

"I would say that, but I think Elevator Babe might've ruined my taste in men forever. The bar's been set *way* too high now."

"He was really that good-looking?" Lia whispered giddily.

I groaned into my hands. "He was literally the best-looking person I've ever laid eyes on in my life. In fact, I'm pretty sure he's the best-looking person anyone has ever laid eyes on in their life. In history and this entire world."

"Excuse me. I may be biased, but I think the best-looking person in the world is my boyfriend, Lukas, *but before you roll your eyes at me,*" Lia said hastily as I rolled my eyes at her, "I do know of someone in Lukas's social circle who you'd find attractive. In fact, I've told you about him before, but you were never interested in listening and he's also kind of a huge dick, so I figured it might be for the best," Lia laughed to herself. "But *anyway,* if it's not a dating thing and all you're looking for is a really hot guy to finish the job that Elevator Babe started then *Julian,*" she paused for effect after saying his name, "could be the one."

"Right. I think you've mentioned him before."

"I definitely have. Would you be interested in meeting him?"

"I guess."

Lia rolled her eyes at my indifference. "Oh my God, look, I know he might not end up as hot as your mysterious Elevator God, but I promise he's ten billion worlds better than Tinder Josh. In fact, I can say, despite being absurdly in love with Lukas, that Julian is objectively gorgeous. Like, really, really, almost annoyingly handsome – and mega rich, if you're into that. But anyway, I'm gonna Google him and prove it to you right now so I can go ahead and say I told you so."

"Lia." I gently set her phone back down on the table. "It's fine, girl, I trust you. Tell you what, the next time you text me that you're all hanging out, I'll actually join. I've always wanted to, but I actually have the time now. In fact, I have *way* too much time now," I muttered, plopping my pointy chin into my hand and glaring with frustration out the window.

"Ah, ah. No wallowing, Sara. I forbid it," Lia said firmly. Taking my hand, she gave it an encouraging squeeze. "Hey, look at me. Do you wanna do something fun tonight? You wanna see if there's a good chick flick at Alamo Drafthouse? We can get drunk off margaritas and laugh at how people never say 'bye' on the phone in movies."

"That's an idea."

"*Or*." Lia held up a finger while texting with the other hand on her phone. "We could drink unlimited Veuve Cliquot for free at some billionaire fundraiser on the West Side."

I had to take a second to process.

"Those are two very different options."

"I know. But Lukas is at the fundraiser right now, and he says it's not black tie, so we can totally go. *Also...*" She trailed off to text some more, silent for several extremely focused and fast-typing seconds. Out of nowhere, she gasped and pumped her fist. "*Yes!* Julian's there. We're going!"

"Oh God," I groaned teasingly as I let her drag me up off my chair.

"Don't 'oh God' me, you'll be thanking me soon," Lia snapped, slapping a few bills on the table before marching me out the door. "You and Julian, girl. It's happening. I mean he's kind of the worst, but he's probably at least decent in bed."

"Nice. You sold him," I snorted as we got on the sidewalk and hailed a cab.

It wasn't a black tie affair but I still felt underdressed, mostly because everyone around me just *exuded* wealth. Gliding elegantly past me in every direction were people in Cartier, Prada, Chanel – people boasting the kind of sparkle and polish I couldn't mimic with my head-to-toe H&M. And if the wardrobe discrepancy didn't tell me that I was among the one percent, the silver Maserati sitting in the back of the room most certainly did.

"But why?" I squinted at Lia.

"Silent auction?" Lia shrugged. Sipping her champagne, she leaned back on the bar and scanned the room. "There's Lukas talking to some people," she murmured. Her voice was casual but when I peeked over at her, she was wearing the dopiest grin from just looking at her boyfriend. I suppressed my giggle. "I don't see Julian anywhere near him though. I wonder where that jerk is."

"Again, you're really selling him."

"Oh, hush. I could sing nothing but praise and you still wouldn't care. You're just so... *hung up* on this elevator guy."

Ugh. It was true.

I'd gone ahead and gotten myself completely infatuated with a man I'd spent a grand total of fifteen minutes with. I was supposed to forget that night once it was done, but in my defense, it was never actually *finished*. I was at the peak of my arousal, more turned on than I'd ever been in my life when some asshole barreled into the room, ruined our night and left my libido hanging indefinitely, it seemed.

The worst part was that I couldn't feed even my smallest craving for him. Without his name, I couldn't even Google him and obsess over a single picture of him on Facebook or LinkedIn. I had no name, no leads and sadly, no interest in any other guy thus far. Looking around the room, there were plenty of attractive, impeccably well-dressed and presumably *very* wealthy men, but not a single one was doing a thing for me. It was bleak.

"Oh, oh!" Lia gasped. "I see Julian!"

I prioritized my last sip of champagne before glancing up and lazily craning my neck to look toward where she nodded. "Which one is he? The blonde guy in the blue?"

"Ugh, no, that guy is blocking him right now."

"Mm." I lost interest and opened up Instagram. Lia smacked me.

"Hey! Act like you care! Blue Suit's about to move so you can see Julian," she said eagerly. "There, there! The one in the dark grey! Quick, quick, look!"

"Okay, okay!" I stuffed my phone back into my purse and looked up.

Then I felt the blood promptly drain from my face.

The music and chatter dissolved from my ears as my eyes zoned in on the walking sex and perfection I'd recognize from a mile away. I couldn't believe it. It was *him* – my nameless hook-up from that filthy, unforgettable night at the hotel. He was standing under the highest point of the domed glass ceiling, surrounded by half a dozen colleagues, friends, and admirers, all of them looking so very rich, important, and dressed to kill.

Their eyes were all on him.

And he was staring directly at me.

5

JULIAN

I took a bigger than usual swig of Scotch, letting the liquid burn its way down my throat. I'd just lost Carter's attention to some girl, but his wasn't as important to me, anyway. When it came to business, he yielded to his brother, whose focus I still had.

Till this second, apparently.

"That motherfucker!" he laughed, pointing across the room at Carter. According to Turner, his brother had just claimed the "only real talent" at the party, and now it seemed he was doing his best to impress her by bidding on the stupid Maserati.

"Hey." Turner elbowed me. "Let's go over there and outbid him in front of her. It'll be epic."

I glanced at the car. "No."

"Oh, right, you're not impressed. You've got plenty of those babies."

I did. I kept my collection of cars and motorcycles in a four-story garage I owned on Eleventh Avenue, and for a moment I entertained the idea of going there, grabbing my bike, and riding the three hours to my home in East Hampton – just so I wouldn't be tempted to waste another minute trying to woo these assholes. But the fantasy was fleeting.

"Hey – why don't we take one of your rides for a spin? Maybe cruise around town and find some real talent since there's clearly none in this room," Turner said, his eyes following a petite brunette. "Boring," he remarked.

"Turner." I masked my disgust. "I should remind you that I'm trying to sell the Biarritz resort as soon as possible and you're by no means the only person interested in buying," I said, referring to the flagship property in my small chain of luxury hotels.

It was enjoying record profits this year, but I was still eager to get it off my hands. I didn't want to look at it anymore. Aside from the obvious reason I wanted it gone, I was also in the process of freeing up capital for a privately financed renovation of Empire Stadium. Doing that in partnership with Roth Entertainment would be ideal. It would put me at an advantage for booking concerts and tours, capitalizing on both road games and the offseason to make the stadium profitable year round. I could get fucking hard thinking about how much money could be made from our collaborative efforts.

Of course, those efforts required Turner's focused attention, which I knew I wasn't getting when he grabbed my shoulder and grinned.

"Hey. Anyone ever tell you to just relax, Hoult? We're at a party. Enjoy yourself." He gave me a shake. "Tell you what, man." This was the part where he suggested we hit the club to drink and fuck all night before getting to business on Monday. "Why don't we see what's going on at 1OAK tonight? We'll grab Carter, take a spin in one of your cars, and we'll have a grand finale of balls to the wall partying before buckling down on Monday and really getting to – " He cut off. "*Fuck.*"

I looked at him, almost certain that wasn't the actual end of his sentence. "What?" I asked with irritation.

"Who's that fuckin' beauty?" he asked, his face lit up like a Vegas slot machine. Ridiculous. I had to hide my resentment as I turned toward the bar to see what he was seeing.

The long, black hair struck me first. Then it was the knockout fucking figure wrapped in a long, red dress. *Gotta give it to him this time*, I thought wryly as my gaze moved the rest of the way up to the girl's face.

When my eyes locked on hers, my heart jumped into my throat.

I stepped back.

"The hell is she doing here?" I hadn't meant for the question to escape my mouth, but it came out in a shocked mutter that more than caught Turner's attention.

"What? You know her? Who is she?"

She was the woman I was never supposed to see again, yet here we were. She was a thousand times sexier than I remembered, and I was at a complete loss for words.

"Jesus, Hoult. Hello? Don't keep me hanging. I'm dying here."

I tore my gaze off her to look at Turner's stare fixed with a comical urgency on me. I noted with amusement that for the first time tonight, he had come alive.

"She's my assistant," I said.

The words rolled off my tongue before I really thought about what I was saying. I cleared my throat when I finally processed what I'd just done.

"Your *assistant*? Why haven't you brought her around? Are you fucking crazy?" Turner laughed joyously like he'd just hit the jackpot.

I glanced up at her again. She'd spotted me with those big eyes, and I wanted nothing more than to make a beeline for her, rip that dress off her tits and bend that perfect body right over that bar.

But I had a lumbering idiot to tend to.

"What?" I frowned at Turner.

"Jesus – I asked why you've never brought her around before. If she's your assistant, where the hell has she been?"

I thought on my feet.

"She was away the past few weeks," I said, my heart beating faster as I came up with my story. "She was overseeing the renovation and management change at the Biarritz resort. Her flight just got in tonight, so I wasn't expecting to see her here."

Not bad. I had to give it to myself as Turner nodded, accepting my lie.

"No shit," he muttered, both of us staring at her now. "Poor girl just wants to party."

I suppressed my smirk as she blushed and squirmed in her seat. I knew the look.

Her pussy was wet.

Christ. I clenched my jaw, wishing badly that I could go back to tasting every inch of her at my leisure. From as far as I stood, I could see her perfect nipples were hard, straining against that thin, red dress. *Fuck me.* I knew exactly what they looked like under there. I remembered exactly how fucking sweet they were on my tongue, and my mouth watered with the need to suck them again.

But outwardly, I wore no hint of expression as Turner grinned at me.

"Hoult, I owe you an apology," he declared, patting my back. "I thought you were too straight-laced to hire smoking hot girls like her. Fuck did my dad call them again?" He snapped his fingers when he thought of it. "*Office-wreckers.*"

"I hire based on capability, and I have a strict rule against interoffice dating."

"You're crazy." Turner licked his lips. "I mean Christ, do you see those tits? Look at those tits."

Trust me, asshole. I'm looking.

"I have eyes. I know she's attractive. She's just far too valuable of an employee to risk anything with," I bullshitted.

"Uh-huh," he responded distractedly. "So you, uh... you said she's your expert on the Biarritz resort? What's the name of the place again?"

"Hotel Piera." My mind raced, but I took a casual drink to hide it. "If you're interested in hearing her reports, I'd be happy to have you at the office on Tuesday. That's her first official day back."

"Yeah?" Turner looked at her again. "Set it up, Hoult. Tuesday's good. Noon work for you?"

"Noon's perfect," I said smoothly as I returned my eyes to the woman I'd just made my non-consenting pawn. *Shit.* I thought fast as I stared at her. She was wearing that sultry fuck-me look of hers that made me want to forget everything and just bury myself inside her, but I needed to focus and excuse myself from Turner fast.

I had a plan I was improvising on the fly as I walked toward her.

And it involved a hundred percent of her willingness to lie for me.

SARA

I BARELY HAD time to breathe let alone understand.

"Don't look surprised. Just come with me."

Those had been his only words before he took my hand and brought me down a grand hallway toward a marble staircase. I hastily gathered my skirt in my hand as we ascended, our shoes a noisy chorus of *click-clacks* that echoed up every step.

My thoughts were scrambled.

"What's going on?" I asked, breathless once we were mostly alone on the second floor. Two vested servers wheeled a cart of dirty plates from an empty ballroom down the hall, but save for a few curious looks, they paid us no mind. "Hey." I grabbed Julian's forearm to bring his attention from them back to me, but I dropped it like a hot potato when I felt that rigid knot of muscle. *Answers.* I needed to prioritize getting answers over getting distracted by my unbelievable lust for him. "*Hey.* Can you please tell me what's happening?"

His eyes slid back to me. "My colleague downstairs has his eye on you," he said, his jaw slightly clenching when he eyed my dress. I looked down at myself, realizing that in our rush, the strap of my dress had fallen well off my shoulder. I didn't fix it. "And I need to brief you on a lie I involved you in before he tries to introduce himself."

"What the hell are you talking about, Julian?"

He paused hard at the sound of his name from my lips. I could tell he wanted to ask how I knew it, but it was clear that whatever he was just talking about took priority.

"You have Turner Roth's attention. I want his. For that reason, I'd like to hire you for a very short and specific job. To be safe, we can make it a three-month contract, and I'll pay however much your last employer offered for a full year."

"*What?*" Seriously, what? "Wait. I don't understand – what kind of job is this?"

"You'd be posing as my assistant, and by Tuesday, I'd need you to have memorized a full report on a twenty-million-dollar renovation to a resort in Biarritz, France that I'm looking to sell to Turner and Carter Roth." He eyed the fallen strap of my dress. "I'll also be needing you to present this information to them in a rather specific way."

"How is that?"

"I need you seduce them."

I stared. "*Excuse* me?"

"By seduce, I don't at all mean sleep with them."

"Thank God for that, but then what *do* you mean? Because I think I need a very thorough explanation," I said. Despite my frustration, I stared unblinkingly at the way he ran his hand across his jaw.

"I have a limited amount of time to strike an important deal with the Roths," he explained, standing close as I leaned back on a wall. "They just inherited the biggest sports and entertainment presenter in America, despite the fact that they're by no means actual or savvy businessmen. In fact, their particular egos make it so that they feel little reason to pay attention to anything unless it involves instant gratification, generally in the form of impressing a beautiful woman. Of course, from what I've gathered, they lose that interest the moment they actually have sex with the woman, so your job is to be professional while also dressing provocatively and flirting enough to maintain their interest. All I need is for them to listen long enough to connect me with their business advisors, with whom I'll actually have productive meetings. So realistically, the hardest part of your job could be done within just a few meetings."

I stared. I couldn't quite believe what I was hearing. But presuming I'd just understood correctly, I was curious, and... thrilled, even?

I wet my lips.

"Okay, so... correct me if I'm wrong, but you're saying you want me to string these guys along with my sexual allure, and force them to pay attention to your pitch in the process?"

"Yes. But you'll never spend any time alone with them. You'll only ever be accompanying me during meetings and business trips, and when we're not doing anything involving the Roths, which will probably be most days of your week, you're free to use the resources at my office to send resumes, or work on your own projects."

Damn it. I was already halfway sold before knowing I could use the time to continue my job hunt.

"What are you thinking?" Julian asked.

"That this is crazy," I said, if only to remind myself that it was. The near stranger I'd almost fucked in an elevator last week, whom I'd spent the past six days obsessing over, was proposing to hire me as sexual bait for a couple of sleazy billionaires. The money made me want to say yes, but I knew I owed myself a moment to consider the cons of the situation. There were probably tons.

I just couldn't think of any.

"Tell me about the job you quit," Julian said, breaking my weak train of thought. "Where was it?"

"June Magazine."

He laughed. "You're kidding."

I looked at him curiously. "I'm not. Why?"

"No reason," he replied, the closest I'd ever seen him to smug. "But if I told you that I could guarantee getting you either your job back or a better one after our contract is finished, would you agree to work for me?"

I blinked.

Okay, *this* was one of the cons – the fact that this man was making such lofty promises while remaining a complete fucking mystery to me. I had no reason to trust him. I knew nothing about him except that I made rash decisions around him, and that he disabled my logic with just a look in my eyes. My heartbeat was never steady around him, and it always inclined me to do something reckless, impulsive.

So in what world was it a good idea for me to work for him? And in such a strange, sexual role?

My best bet by far here was to decline, invite him back to my apartment, and sleep with him for the first and last time. After that, I'd cut myself off before getting addicted. That was the smart thing to do. The *right* thing to do.

Of course, I'd established a pattern of doing very much the wrong thing around Julian.

"Okay," I blurted before I could stop myself.

Even Julian looked partially surprised by the speed of my response, which had me instantly questioning my decision. But when he extended his hand and asked, "We have a deal?" I gazed at that slight but stunning curl of his lips and forgot to backtrack or at least ask a couple questions like I told myself I would.

"Yes." I let out the breath I was holding. "We have a deal." I swallowed the knot in my throat. "And in case you were at all interested, my name is Sara."

His voice softened unexpectedly.

"Sara," Julian repeated as he shook my hand. My pulse picked up as his gaze grew heavy, taking its time to look me up and down. "It was nice to meet you last week, Sara," he smiled, sending a shiver up my spine. "I look forward to working with you."

"Likewise," I said, pretending to be casual despite the fact that I was still processing what I'd just done, and telling myself the same thing on repeat in my head.

You are fucked, Sara.

You are so incredibly fucked.

6

SARA

I was going to be late for my first day at the office if I didn't stop Googling, but I was just too. Damned. Floored.

I thought the surprises were over after not only seeing my mystery man again yesterday, but also realizing that he was *Lukas and Lia's* Julian. All that was very much shocking enough without the bombshell that dropped during my cab ride home while searching the full name on the bone white business card that Julian gave me.

Julian Hoult.

He was *Julian Hoult*. As in Hoult Communications, which owned Hoult Publishing, which of course owned about half the magazines of my career dreams. The company was so revered in the magazine world that my former employer had consistently tried and failed for years to get bought out by Hoult. The fact that I now worked so closely with the man they fell to their knees for was exhilarating. It already felt like sweet, sweet revenge on its own. Of course, it would be even better if they knew, but whatever. I was no longer thinking about them anymore. I was thinking about the exciting new chapter in my life that had fallen into my lap.

And, of course, I was still Googling.

"I maintain that I told you about him before," Lia said for the fifth time this morning, clinking away at her dishes now. We'd been lazily on speakerphone with each other since 6:30AM, drifting in and out of our half-assed argument to brush our teeth, make coffee and get ready.

"Disagree." I sat hunched over my laptop at the end of my dining table, wearing just a bra and a half-zipped pencil skirt. I really needed to get my shit together, but Internet stalking was like Pringles. Once you pop, the fun don't stop. "I swear, you didn't tell me shit, woman."

"Oh no," Lia muttered distractedly to herself. "Did I just chip my favorite mug?" I heard some tinkering before she breathed out in relief. "Oh, thank God, I didn't. You know what I did do though? Tell you about Julian. A *long* time ago. On three or four separate occasions."

Yeah, she was probably right. I had just been so absorbed in work back then.

"Well, if you did, you didn't harass me hard enough to listen. *Or* offer the juicy details, like how he owns *Hoult* Freaking *Publishing*," I said as I scrolled through Getty Images of Julian in crisp suits, looking devastatingly handsome at various glitzy events. *Chill*, I told myself as I compared two pictures, trying to distinguish if he was posing with the same pretty girl in both. The answer was no, but I wasn't pleased with myself for getting that worked up for a second.

"Whatever. Stop Googling pictures of him. I can hear you furiously clicking."

"*Hoult Publishing*, Lia," I derailed. "I'll never forgive you for this."

"Yeah, yeah." I heard her cracking eggs on the other end as she giggled. "To be fair, I have no idea what Hoult Publishing is. When I first met Julian, everyone was talking about how he just bought a baseball team, so I thought that was what he did."

"Yeah, that's *also* fucking crazy. The fact that he owns the Empires? They're killing it this season."

"Whatever. Is baseball brown ball or white ball? And are you leaving for work yet?"

"Almost. I just need to finish getting dressed."

"Isn't the point of your dirty little job to *not* be dressed?" Lia teased.

"Only on days that I'm meeting with the Perv Brothers, and even then, I do have to keep it tasteful. I can't just waltz into the conference room wearing a thong and fishnets."

Lia scoffed. "Of course not. You'd need sequined nipple tassels too."

"I would never wear sequins to work, Lia. You know I would keep it classy – pinstriped nipple tassels, only. Maybe khaki ones on Fridays," I grinned as she audibly choked on her coffee. "In all seriousness though, I do need to maintain some air of professionalism... which probably also requires being on time," I groaned, finally dragging my ass away from my laptop and to my closet. I grabbed the blue button-up I'd ironed last night and my thin red belt with the fine gold clasp. Lia read my mind.

"Time check is eight-fifteen."

"Shit, really?" My fingers flew over my buttons as I glanced over at the clock on the nightstand. "God, I refuse to be late. On the first day or any."

"Breathe, girl. You won't be late if you leave right now. Just check for panty lines on the way out," Lia instructed just as I twisted my body while passing the bathroom mirror.

"All good."

"Buttons straight?"

Grabbing my purse, I glanced down my front to confirm the buttons, but instead I laughed aloud at the sight of my cleavage.

"Oh God. This bra is killer," I said as I shoved ear buds into my phone to take Lia off speaker and bring her with me out the door.

"Tell me you wore The One."

"I did." It was by far the best push-up in my small collection, but The One was rarely ever worn. Its lifting powers were too intense for a regular day basis, so it was saved for special occasions – and, apparently, first days of work.

"He's gonna get one look of the girls in that thing and go nuts. I hope you're prepared for some hot, sweaty, bent-over-the-desk office sex. You realize that's happening, right?"

"As much as I wouldn't mind it, I'm not sure," I smirked as I flew down the hall of my building and out the door.

"What? Why aren't you sure?" Lia asked incredulously. "That man is definitely dying to get a moment alone with you already. First it was that barge-in at the hotel, then it was hiding you from that guy yesterday," she said, referring to Julian hastily sending me home in a cab so I could avoid Turner Roth and any questions about working for Julian that I wouldn't know how to answer. "Trust me, girl. That man is waiting to pounce."

"We'll see. Judging from yesterday, Julian Hoult is a very different beast when he's in work mode. He's in a different world completely. He's intense, and he's focused, and actually, it's insanely fucking hot and I'm really not sure how I'm going to handle it. But anyway, I'm almost at the train so I'm gonna lose service. I'll call you at the end of the day."

"No, you'll text me live updates as your day goes on, except for when you're actively having sex with Julian."

"Ha. I'll talk to you later."

"Later, girl," Lia said. "Enjoy your first day as a professional sex kitten."

~

CRAP.

I hadn't expected this to be the first part of the day to throw me off. Of course, I should have guessed that I'd run into some sort of trouble in an elevator. That was just becoming the pattern this week.

Just smile and be confident, I told myself despite the fact that I'd received the onceover from every last person who'd filed into the elevator. It was men and women alike, and it was nothing offensively leering or critical – it was just, apparently, a huge yet surprisingly cliquey building, and they all quietly knew that I didn't belong.

The fact only grew clearer as the elevator started moving. Despite all heading to different floors, everyone began chatting casually. They smiled and laughed as they talked about their weekends – about finally trying that *omakase* on Twelfth Street, or escaping to a friend's house in the Hamptons. Everyone was of a certain status here. Everyone maintained a certain lifestyle, and everyone knew each other.

Except for me.

I looked away after catching someone's eye and hearing him drop his voice to a mutter. "Who's that?" he asked his colleague, who responded with something I couldn't hear. Whatever it was, it prompted them both to laugh.

Good Lord.

Who knew the suits at Hoult Tower could be so catty? And who knew that after all these years, the new girl feeling would still strike fear in my heart? It brought me right back to all the memories I'd convinced myself were mostly gone. God, I'd clearly been premature in patting myself on the back for getting over all those.

Apparently, all it took was being an outsider again for everything to come back.

Dammit, Sara, you're twenty-seven, I berated myself. That seemed about the right age to outgrow bad memories. Right? I didn't have the answer to that question, and I didn't actually want to think about it now, so I just tucked myself into the corner and closed my eyes, doing my best to drive the useless thoughts out of my head. *Good,* I thought as the elevator stopped again. It gave me more time to meditate.

At least I thought it did. But then I felt the hush fall over the small space. I felt a strange little shift in the air, and I could practically hear everyone's posture creaking straight.

Then came the first, "Good morning, Mr. Hoult."

I opened my eyes to find Julian's electric stare already pinned on mine from the door. My pulse jumped, but with a flick, he returned his gaze to the man who'd greeted him. They exchanged a line of polite conversation before Julian moved through the small huddle of suits. I watched the way everyone swiftly changed around him. They stood at attention, presented themselves better. It was kind of fascinating.

"Good morning, sir."

"Morning, Mr. Hoult."

He acknowledged each greeting with an efficient nod before finding his way to the back corner. My cheeks were on fire but I did my best to maintain professionalism as I looked him in the eye and smiled.

"Mr. Hoult," I said.

"Ms. Hanna."

I could feel the attention of the others as he greeted me by name. Just like that, an invisible spotlight was cast upon me. Thankfully, despite a knowing and almost wicked smile, Julian spoke with the utmost professionalism.

"How are you this morning?" he asked me.

"Very well, thank you," I responded, allowing myself a peek at him. *Yes, please.* Dark blue suit and tie. Cufflinks worth more than my savings. He was effortless beauty as usual, but I was getting better at breathing steady around it. "I did start a little nervous, but I'm better now," I confessed as the elevator opened again to let in a few more.

The huddle shifted wordlessly to make room, and I bit my lip when I found myself pressed against the back wall, Julian standing directly over me. He indulged in a second-long glance of my absurdly pushed-up breasts, but he swiftly averted his eye when I asked, "How are you?"

His eyes locked on mine. "Better now as well. Thank you."

I blushed. The suits were all quiet as mice now, sneaking the occasional glance at Julian and me through the mirrors. *Yeah, if you think this is scandalous, you should have seen the last elevator we were in,* I thought as the doors opened again, this time welcoming an older, incredibly boisterous man complaining about something or another. Whoever he was, the many eye rolls I spotted told me that the suits was used to his daily antics. With a short laugh, Julian leaned into me.

"Get ready," he whispered.

Before I could ask what he meant, I felt a sharp jostle, the huddle swelling dramatically to make room for the sheer size and volume of our new guest. I felt a second of Julian's chest pressed hard against mine, and my mouth stayed locked in a little O when he pulled back to find my palm laid flat on his solid abs.

His brows lifted at the same languid pace that I curled my fingers against his ridges.

Oops.

I had to.

"Ms. Hanna." Julian feigned a frown as I looked up with a shameful little thrill in my eyes. "Little forward of you," he murmured with a smirk.

"Sorry," I whispered up at him, a bit surprised with myself as well.

"Don't be sorry, just don't make that face right now."

"What face?"

"The one you made right before you put my cock in your mouth."

My jaw dropped and my eyes promptly darted around to make sure no one had heard, but it was clear that Big Guy had their focus collectively occupied.

"Now you're just teasing me," Julian said. Snapping my mouth shut, I looked back up at him, wearing a smirk as I contained my urge to smack him hard on the chest.

"Risky of you," I remarked quietly.

"You bring it out of me, but I agree," Julian murmured. "Let's behave."

With that, we both faced forward just in time to see Big Guy out. By the time eyes returned to us, we were the ones standing perfectly still in the back, and quiet as mice. But I could still feel the mischief in the air between us, and it was so hard not to smile as we stood side-by-side, hands folded in front of ourselves like the good little children we were not.

Yes. Go on. Get out.

Mischief touched my placid smile as the elevator emptied floor by floor. Julian and I remained still in the back, but his lips were twisting slowly, gorgeously up in a grin, and I could almost hear the energy crackle between us as the doors opened to let the final two out.

We were alone barely a second when he spoke.

"I should fuck you right in this elevator."

The rasp in his voice spiked my pulse, and I sucked in a sharp breath when he walked me up against the wall.

"You can't."

"Why not?"

"We don't have enough time," I hissed, my fingers hooked in his belt.

"Is the lack of time your only qualm about getting fucked in here?" he asked, smoothing my hand down to mold over his cock. My thighs pumped as he hardened against my palm.

"Yes," I whispered breathlessly. "That's the only reason."

Julian peered over his shoulder at the indicator. We had five floors to go.

"Then let's do what we have time for," he said as he sank down to his knee, giving me no time to think before he pushed my skirt up my thighs and pulled my thong aside to expose my pussy.

"Julian!" I gasped as he spread my lips apart just enough to lick my clit. "Oh my God." My eyes watered from the instant sensation – from the bolt of pleasure to my core as he flicked his tongue over me then sucked. My knees buckled as he pushed two fingers inside me, licking and tunneling furiously for another two seconds before snatching the bliss away and returning swiftly to his feet.

My breath was still caught in my throat as I felt him pull my skirt back down over my legs. I was only just starting to catch my breath as Julian straightened his tie and looked me in the eyes.

"Ready?" he asked.

And just then, the doors opened to the offices of Hoult Communications.

7

JULIAN

I had to be impressed with her.

From what I could tell, and from what I was told, Sara did well on her first day – no easy feat for a newcomer. Being new in my office was daunting. My staff spoke rapidly with little patience to explain their long-established ways, but Sara had found a way to ease herself into the mix with grace and determination. She was bold but respectful – unafraid to ask questions, but well aware of when and how to approach. It was a skill I wished upon more of my staff, and I had to admire her for it.

Especially considering what happened this morning in the elevator.

For someone who started her day with maybe five whole seconds of her boss's tongue between her legs, she was conducting herself well. Save for the coffee she half-spilled the one time she caught me staring, her day had gone on without a blemish.

"She's pretty much memorized on general information – facts about the building, architecture, Basque Country itself. She's going to take information home to keep studying, but the past hour, she's been looking at the quarterlies. Just so she can start getting acquainted with sales," Colin said, sitting across from my desk and shuffling in a blur through his files. He was one of my actual assistants – the person who had actually spent the past two weeks overseeing the new changes at my Biarritz resort. Sara would essentially be playing the role of Colin in front of the Roth brothers, and thus far, it seemed she was absorbing his information with ease.

"So she's right on schedule."

"Ahead, if anything. Like you said, the Roths are unlikely to ask about numbers tomorrow."

"Yes, and she knows the short-term goal here is to get the Roths to agree on a trip out to Biarritz?"

"Yes," Colin said. "She's confident she can influence them. She's very eager."

That she was.

Eager was in fact the word I'd use to describe Sara today. Since stepping foot into the office, she'd been eager to learn, introduce herself, and act as if nothing had happened in the elevator. Her cheeks were still rosy and flushed for her first ten or so minutes in the office, but soon enough, she was eagerly avoiding my eye to let Colin show her the ropes.

I admired her innate respect for a job.

Lukas had mentioned something about Sara having "similar workaholic tendencies" as myself, and I could see that from watching her instantly mold into the office setting. She wanted to work, to be busy. It was her natural state, and I liked that about her much more than I wanted to. I didn't need anything more to fuel my fixation. I'd watched her from my office all day, and I didn't have the time to be this curious about her. I hadn't done enough today to fantasize so much about sitting her naked on my lap, playing with her tits while I worked and then fucking her hard over my desk.

Right now, it felt like there was nothing I wanted more than to do exactly that.

Of course I couldn't allow it.

Fucking painful as it was, I had my rule. My only rule. It was there for a reason, and there couldn't be an exception. They were a slippery slope, and I didn't get to where I was at the pace that I did by giving myself leeway on every self-imposed restriction.

Not even for someone like Sara.

More than anything, I was a man of my word, and the best way to force myself to follow through on something was to make it a promise to somebody else – which I planned on doing right now.

Before I didn't.

"So if we're all set, I can send her home?" Colin asked, getting up and gathering his folders. I glanced at the clock. A quarter past five.

"Yes. But have her stop in here on her way out."

"You got it."

"Thank you," I said as I gripped the knot of my tie. I leaned back as I loosened it, bracing myself for Sara to come knocking within a few minutes. But when she did, I was still forced to clench my jaw. *Fuck.* Held up in a ponytail before, her long dark hair hung loose now, flipped to one side and gathered over her shoulder. I pictured the moment she arched her back and let it down. I pictured her breasts in the air as she ran her fingers through it, and I envied Colin for probably having witnessed it all.

"Come in. Have a seat." I rounded the desk to lean against its front. "How was your first day?"

"Good. I enjoyed myself," Sara smiled as she folded her hands in her lap. Now that it was the end of the day, I could see her getting flirty again. I did my best to ignore it.

"Colin said you did a great job. Do you feel comfortable with the material you went over with him?"

"Absolutely. That resort is..." She exhaled with genuine awe. "*So* beautiful, Julian. I can hardly believe you want to sell it when you had it built from the ground up."

My stare flickered over the earnest look on her face. I was irritated that she thought that an appropriate thing to say, but maybe I was being irrational. Maybe I was looking for a reason to be less than pleased with her. Adjusting my cufflinks, I moved past the comment about the resort.

"Do you have any questions thus far?"

"About the resort? Or my day in general?"

"Either."

She chewed her lip, smoothing her hands over the little skirt I'd fantasized about all day.

"Well, I *was* wondering... obviously, Colin knows a few details about my contract since he's been training me on the resort information. But what does the rest of your office know about my role in this company? Do they know... what I was hired for?"

"Absolutely not. As far as the office is concerned, you're training to be a third assistant. They won't at any point learn about the specifics of your contract. It's sensitive information."

"Okay, thank God," she breathed. "I just wouldn't want my role here to be misconstrued, considering how it's kind of... risqué in nature. I obviously trust you with the information, but not anyone else."

"Understood entirely. No one in this office or building will know about your contract. I have no intention of putting you in a position where you could be viewed differently here."

"I appreciate it," Sara said with relief. A mischievous smile twitched on her lips. "I take it then that what happens in the elevator before work is an exception."

"Actually, I called you in here to touch upon that."

"Oh?" She arched an eyebrow. "What exactly would you like to touch upon?"

Her phrasing lured my eyes down to her tight little body. *What would I like to touch upon?* I had a lot of answers for that question, none of them usable.

Just fucking say it, Hoult.

"I wanted to talk to you about a rule I've enforced at this company for as long as it's been around. It applies to everyone, myself included, and it's been crucial for us in terms of running business in a seamless, strictly professional way," I said. I took in the slowly changing look on her face.

Gradually, her faint smile fell. Her warmth and any hint of playfulness faded into something guarded, stiff. I hated being responsible for that, but I forced myself to go on.

"In short, I have a zero tolerance rule on interoffice dating. Romances, sexual relations of any kind – they're all off the table, and I felt the need to tell you that despite your unique contract, and despite what happened between us before work this morning, I can't allow any exceptions to that rule."

Sara raised her eyebrows high.

"So, what happened this morning didn't count?" she asked slowly. "Simply because I hadn't officially started the job yet?"

"I didn't come in this morning with the intention of taking advantage of some loophole. I hadn't actually thought about it. My intention was to be professional with you from the start. Of course, I didn't exactly control myself as I should have this morning, and I take full responsibility for that," I said. "But moving forward, I hope we can start anew and give your contract with this company the full respect it deserves."

I waited for some form of confusion or protest when I finished. I'd prepared myself for it, but there was only a moment of pause before Sara blinked and nodded.

"Okay."

My eyebrows lifted. I studied her, unsure if I should feel relieved or wary.

"I appreciate your understanding," I said, my gaze still trained with uncertainty on her as she rose from her seat. She caught my expression and broke into a smile.

"Of course. You might not know this, but if anyone were to understand work rules, it's me," she said.

"Then that's a relief to hear. And thank you again for understanding," I said, unable to take my eyes off of her. "I do appreciate it."

"Well, I appreciate the opportunity just to work here," she said breezily. "It's crazy how much I've picked up from your staff in one day. I'm pretty sure I'll learn quite a few things in just a few months here."

"I hope that you do."

Her dark eyes glimmered as she nodded. "Is that all you wanted to discuss with me, Mr. Hoult?"

Mr. Hoult. My instinct was to invite her to call me Julian, but I refrained.

"Yes," I said. "That's all. You're free to leave for the day."

"Great. Thank you again for everything," she said on her way out. "And have a good night. I'll see you tomorrow."

"You too," I returned, memorizing the smile she flashed me over her shoulder before letting that tight ass hypnotize me on the way out.

Fuck me. This was going to be rough.

8

SARA

I was an asshole for ignoring my mom's calls since quitting the magazine. But ignoring her last night, after utilizing the stunning poker face I'd never have without her, was especially shitty.

"I'm so sorry, Sara. I feel like it's my fault," Lia sighed as she slid a tray of chocolate-coated truffle molds into her industrial freezer. It was barely 8AM and we were in the kitchen of her shop. She'd been in the Hamptons with Lukas last night, so she was unavailable to properly receive my ranting and raving over the latest bombshell on my week.

As much as I hated to admit it, I was pissed.

I was actually extremely and thoroughly upset about what Julian dropped on me last night at the end of my first day of work.

But you accepted this job for the perks, the connections, the incredible money to make up for being unemployed. It's not like you took this job to be close to Julian. It's not like you wanted to work with him because you wanted to be with him. I told myself that.

And I believed it, too. But after a long walk home from Hoult Tower, since I apparently needed time to process the no-sex clause, I'd come to a much more honest assessment of myself – and the truth was that while I had plenty of good reasons to accept the job offer, I had said "yes" out of pure sexual attraction.

I'd let my damned libido make a major life decision and now, as I so clearly deserved, I was paying the price.

"It's my fault, Lia, trust me. You didn't tell me to take this job offer."

"Yeah, but I did try to set you up with Julian."

"And it might've worked if I didn't decide to become his subordinate. Now he's probably already ceased all sexual attraction for me like the work-addicted robot he is."

"Psh, right. Lukas said he's never seen Julian look at a girl with the intensity that he looked at you."

"Yeah, because I'm an element of his job now," I snorted. "He salivates over me because he can't wait to utilize me for the purposes of this stupid contract with the Perv Bros. I'm as good as a stapler to him now. Or an extra-sturdy paper clip."

"Oh, shut it. You know that despite that stupid rule of his, he definitely still has sexual thoughts about you. I mean he admitted as much in the elevator yesterday, right?"

God. Yes, he did. And it had taken everything in me to carry on as usual after that – to stroll into his stunning, double-height office and professionally greet his assistant, Colin, despite the fact that my face was burning hot and my panties were soaking wet.

In my own defense, how else was I supposed to react?

I had just spent an entire elevator ride watching everyone in the building stand at attention for Julian Hoult. He was revered and respected, a presence that even the most intimidating of people yielded to.

And he'd just taken a knee in the elevator to run his tongue all over my clit.

"Earth to Sara."

I was vaguely aware of Lia waving in my peripherals but I didn't break from my haze till she waved a fresh lavender truffle in my face. I blinked and smirked at her.

"Thanks. I needed to snap out of that."

"Yeah, that was uncomfortable for me. You looked like you were seconds from the big O."

"Shut up. And cut me some slack. I'm dealing with an absurdly hot boss who's done everything but fuck me, and now that we work in the same office, I get nothing. I also have no idea how to un-turn myself on when I so much as think of him."

"Let me help. Your mom's calling. Again." Lia held out my phone. I shook my head till she put it back down.

"I can't right now. I suck at lying to her and I'm pretty sure she's calling because she has a sixth sense when it comes to me. She definitely knows I did a bad thing this week."

"*A* bad thing?" Lia giggled. "Which of your many bad things are you referring to? You're like a different person this week."

"Hey, don't you talk to me about abrupt transformations – you went from celibate for three years to having sex with Lukas in a public bathroom."

"Sara!" Lia laughed so hard she snorted something legitimately startling that had us cracking up harder. "Oh God. You need to get out of here or I'm never going to finish this batch," she wheezed. "And don't you have your super important meeting with the Perv Bros today?"

"Yes. But I can be a little late. I have to pick up lunch for the meeting from some restaurant in SoHo."

"And you're wearing that?" Lia asked, nodding at my outfit.

"Totally," I said as we both turned around to peek at ourselves in the mirror. We were twins in butter-smudged aprons, our messy topknots stuffed into yellow hairnets to protect the chocolates. If there was anything sexy in the room, it was the chocolate. Next would be the stainless steel fridge. "I brought a change of clothes, obviously."

"Okay, phew. Then get your cute butt going," Lia giggled, nudging me toward the door. "And girl, you better kill it 'cause I'm pissed at Julian on your behalf and I want you to torture him with how hard you bring it for this meeting."

"Trust me, I'm well prepared, and I have every intention of making it hurt for him today."

"Atta girl. Is that what that thing is about?" Lia grinned, nodding toward the garment bag I'd hung in her office.

"Mm-hm," I smirked as I shed my hairnet and apron.

The one bright side of having worked for a magazine was having had access to clothes I'd never dare to buy, and today's dress most certainly qualified as one of those "I could *never*" get-ups that I was finally working up the nerve to wear. With it, I was prepared to rock platform heels a full two inches higher than I'd ever walked in, and matte lipstick so lusciously berry-hued that it was almost audible in the way it screamed sex.

On most days, the prospect of wasting my one tube of MAC lipstick, or maybe falling flat on my face was enough to deter me from dressing like this. But today, I had all the motivation to be fearless. In every way – the way I looked, the way I spoke, and the way I commanded a room. I was meeting with the infamous Turner and Carter Roth, but on top of that, I had a gorgeous prick of a boss who talked dirty to me one second and shunned me the next. Irritating to say the least, but nothing I couldn't get over by simply hitting it out of the park today and leaving him as stunned as he left me yesterday.

With a kiss on Lia's cheek, I grabbed my bags and said bye, shaking out my hair and heading breezily for the door.

Julian Hoult, today's swagger is dedicated to you.

9

JULIAN

She was late.

Or at least my definition of late, which was anything but seated five minutes early. Drumming my fingers on the conference table, I glanced at the lacquered dial on my dad's old Rolex. Fine. It was a whole quarter till noon. She wasn't late, I was just anxious to see her get in. The Roths were miraculously early for a change and they were already kicked back, tossing a baseball from my desk to and fro while asking about "the assistant."

"Sara. She looks like a Sara," Turner decided after asking for her name.

"What does a Sara look like?" Carter asked.

"Brunette. Long legs. Great tits."

"Gentlemen." I flashed a look of apology to my office manager of six years, Tori. She was no-nonsense even before getting pregnant. At eight weeks now, she was incapable of entertaining this kind of bullshit. Her lips were pursed as she set the bottles of water down before us, and she said nothing before she exited the room.

"Jesus Christ. She seems fun," Turner snorted. *Because women exist to be fun for you.* "My question is who thought it was a good idea to knock her up?"

"I want to buy that guy a beer," Carter laughed.

"Fuck a beer. Double Scotch is what he needs," Turner said. "See, that's the thing about hiring women. You gotta hire them pretty to make it worth it."

I rapped once on the desk to get their attention. "Don't talk about my employees like that."

"Oh... *Je*-sus. Mr. No Fun right here," Turner laughed, flashing Carter a look that said *yikes*.

Eyeing them, I considered calling it quits again, like I did at least once during each of our meetings. But this time, the thought didn't promptly disappear because I had Sara on my mind. I was quickly regretting putting her in this situation. Considering I could barely stomach the Roths' idiot misogyny, I had trouble imagining she could. She was the one they'd be staring at, hitting on, touching as much as they could possibly get away with. I could already see all the unnecessary contact – little pinches on her arm, the quick hands on her waist here and there. My lip curled when I pictured Turner eventually escalating it with a hand up her skirt or his hotel key slid in her palm.

I reached for my phone.

ME: Possible change of plans. Call me before you get in.

I sent the text to her before I could think twice about it. I was going to give her an out.

In just the past few seconds, I'd made up my mind on it.

Of course the moment the word *"Delivered"* appeared under my message, the door to the conference room swung open, and my mouth snapped shut as Sara walked into the room. She was dangling a paper bag on each slender wrist and wearing a dress too white and tight to coexist with panties. My frenzied eyes had drunk her in twice before I even realized that like the Roths, I was suddenly on my feet, and feeling a tinge of anger for the fact that Turner received her first dazzling smile.

"Thank you so much!" she laughed as Turner rushed to grab the bags from her.

"You're very welcome. Sara, right? I can't believe Julian's got you carrying heavy bags like this," he clucked. It was then that Sara's glimmering eyes found me.

"Oh, he knows I can take it," she grinned, the sound of her voice going straight to my cock. She let her gaze linger for just another second before engaging in whatever Turner was talking about now. My pulse rose steadily as I watched his eyes devour her. It wasn't long before she had both brothers standing too close to her, giving her barely any room to breathe with their overzealous introductions. Jesus Christ, if I hated watching just this then I was fucked.

Reaching my limit, I cleared my throat.

"Gentlemen, why don't we sit?" I said.

I gave the verbal suggestion, but Sara carried it out as she walked over to her chair. Three pairs of eyes watched in silence as her hips swayed from side to side, drawing us into a trance. Her silhouette was particularly striking as she leaned over the table to slide into her seat, smoothing her hands down the dip and curve of her sides.

I had to smirk. As if there was a single wrinkle on that dress. It was practically sewn onto her mouthwatering figure. But I got it. It was all for show. The exact one I'd asked her to put on.

Then again maybe she had this in the bag.

"So," Sara started brightly. "I'm excited to finally meet you gentlemen. Julian told me while I was out in Biarritz that there were a lot of people interested in the property and it made me *so* happy. And, well, a little sad at the same time," she added with a sheepish laugh.

Turner grinned wide. "Happy and sad? Why's that?"

"Oh, well," Sara bit her smile as she eyed me. "I think Julian hates when I say this, but that resort is to *die* for. It's so elegant, so beautifully designed. Every detail is deliberately thought out to ensure the most relaxing time ever – I barely felt like I was working."

"Wow," Turner murmured as I told myself not to be annoyed. The resort was a sore spot, but Sara didn't know. On top of that, she was acting, and she had her audience captivated. "That true, Hoult?" Turner finally tore his eyes off of her to grin at me.

"I do hate when she says that. It's not like I won't miss the place once it's gone. I'm just moving away from hospitality, and the resort doesn't suit my direction anymore."

"But it more than suits yours, right, gentlemen?" Sara asked, looking at Carter then Turner. "I understand you guys were pro surfers – which, by the way, is really amazing."

Turner sat upright. "I was pro. Carter was semi-pro."

"I was pro," Carter argued.

"You were both pro then," Sara settled it warmly, shutting them up. "And I understand you're in the market for the resort because…"

She leaned over to grab a file I'd watched her push away when she first sat down. Now I realized she'd done it just to give herself an excuse to angle forward and show off just enough cleavage to leave all three of us wanting more.

"You're looking to bring a… luxury surfing competition to Biarritz?" Sara said, reading off some notes. "Wow." She paused for effect. "That's so interesting."

Christ. She was blowing smoke up their asses but she made it look goddamned good. Every little twist and turn of her body, every flick of her hair elicited a reaction. Without doing much at all, she exuded sex appeal, and at this point, I couldn't stop watching. I was riveted. I had to cover a grin to hide my amusement when she snuck a look at me before giving Turner her undivided attention, nodding along and offering the occasional "*wow*" and "*absolutely*" as he pitched her his vision for a Basque Country surfing competition.

I was already impressed as it was.

But she didn't stop there.

"And Carter – I'm so lost. Could you help me with the logistics of bringing a brand new surfing event to this town?" Sara asked after spending six straight minutes on Turner. "How long would that even take?"

Carter jumped at the chance to be useful. Of course, Turner was never to be outdone, so both brothers wound up explaining eagerly, assuring her that with their sports and entertainment resources, they could get a fully sponsored pro event up and running within two years.

"Wow," Sara breathed, shuffling her papers. "So you'll be needing this property sooner than I thought."

I raised my eyebrows. When she glanced at me, I shot a look that said, *I see what you're doing.* She hit me with the quickest little smirk as Turner laughed.

"Damn, I guess so. We gotta get shit moving," he said to Carter, keeping his eyes on Sara.

He was watching her simply study some notes, idly running her fingertips along her collarbone. His stare remained as she then cocked her head, smiled and asked Carter when he'd started surfing. She chatted with such casual brightness that neither Roth noticed when she changed the subject back to business, suggesting a trip out to Biarritz.

"You guys can teach me how to surf like I've always wanted," she said. "And, of course, we can have you check out the property first-hand so you can really gauge your interest."

"Oh, I'll teach you to surf. I'll have you rippin' waves like The Duke."

"I have no idea who that is, but I look forward to getting a full-on surf education from you, Turner," Sara giggled.

"You will, you will. We'll have to set a date soon."

And just like that, she had them.

All I had to do was sit back and watch the scene unfold, Sara directing every second with such effortless charm that the Roths had no clue they were falling right into neatly laid traps. Fuck. How had I even doubted her? She was nailing it better than I could have ever imagined, and I was so turned on by that fact that I could hardly sit still. I'd seen this woman ass naked bent over a couch for me last week, yet I was certain I'd never been more attracted to her than I was now. Every sound she made – every curious turn of the head and little burst of a smile lifted a weight in my chest I didn't know I had.

If her act was working on even my cold, dead heart, then the Roths stood no chance.

Opening my group text with Emmett and Lukas, I fired a quick summary of the meeting they'd insisted on.

> **ME:** *She just got them to agree to the Biarritz trip without even trying.*
> **EMMETT:** *Damn. You should consider growing a pair of tits*
> **ME:** *She has more in her arsenal than just that.*
> **EMMETT:** *Ahh look he's defending her*
> **LUKAS:** *Adorable*

Regretting my text, I clicked my phone off and slid it down the table.

When the meeting was all over, I saw the Roths to the elevator, Sara following closely behind. The neat little clicks of her heels were an unbelievable tease for my cock. All I wanted was to turn around and get a long look at those fucking sexy legs, but it was my turn to actually do my part for this meeting.

"Gentlemen. We'll touch base soon," I said, using Turner's own vague line on them. This time, he was the one who got specific.

"Yeah, yeah, well, why don't we shoot for sometime next week? I'm booked through the weekend, but how about we link up again Monday?" Turner asked, making sure to flick his eyes past my shoulder at Sara. I assumed she nodded because he smiled.

"Monday it is," I decided, watching Turner struggle to leave without getting Sara's attention a couple more times. When they were finally gone, I turned to find her narrowed eyes on me.

"You didn't think I could do it," she said before I could even congratulate her on the job well done. I cocked an eyebrow.

"Excuse me?"

"You texted me before the meeting started. 'Possible change of plans?'" she quoted me. The smirk on my lips was tight as I found myself caught red-handed. I gripped my tie and adjusted as we started walking.

"I wasn't doubting your ability so much as trying to give you an out. The Roths were being particularly intolerable before you arrived, and it gave me certain ideas of how they'd behave around you."

"Certain ideas? Like?"

I drew in a neat breath between my teeth. "Like using certain language and putting their hands all over you in ways I didn't care to see."

"I thought you'd hired me for that specific reason, sir."

I flinched at the word *sir*.

"I did. Today, I entertained second-thoughts," I replied brusquely.

"I didn't pin you for someone who had those," Sara lilted, pissing me off and turning me on in the same breath.

"Well, I imagine there's a first time for everything, Sara."

"Fine. But if it happened because you feel in some way protective or doubtful of me, you can relax," she said, walking ahead of me up the stairs. My jaw clenched as my eyes instinctively fell to her round ass. "As far as I can tell, you have full confidence in Colin and Tori and every other employee of yours in this office. So if I'm just another one of them, sir, you can feel free to let me do my job."

"There's a unique nature to your contract," I ground out as she stopped midway up to face me. She looked a bit smug when she caught my eyes where they shouldn't have been.

"Yes, there's a unique nature to my contract, but if all the same rules apply to me, then what I simply ask is that you respect me in the same way you do everyone else. Anything short of that is completely hypocritical," she said. Then as if she hadn't just laid into me, she lifted her voice and smiled. "Anyway, may I go on my lunch break now, sir?"

"Why are you doing that?" I asked.

She tilted her head. "Doing what?"

"The way you're calling me 'sir.' It's odd."

"I'm just trying to be as professional as you want me to be."

My laugh was brusque as I confirmed my suspicion that she was essentially taunting me with the word.

"I believe the term you're looking for is passive aggressive."

Sara bristled. "What would you prefer I call you?"

"Julian."

"Alright, Julian. Is it alright if I go on my lunch break now?" she asked, back to flashing me that deliberately over-polite smile that made me want to punish her in a million ways I couldn't think about right now. Suppressing my fantasies, I mirrored her corporate smile.

"You may go to lunch."

"Thank you, Julian."

"You're welcome, Sara," I said, keeping my poker face straight as I watched her ass twitch away.

Fucking fuck.

I was supposed to enjoy this – having a new employee who was eager to fulfill her every duty and simply do her job. Considering my need for efficiency, I should be grateful to have someone as ready, willing and able as Sara on my team.

The only thing was that she was playing my game a little too well.

And the fact of the matter was that I already hated it.

10

SARA

There was progress in the elevator by Thursday morning, and it came with the riders I'd nicknamed Gucci and Bald Guy – Gucci for her bag, and Bald Guy for, well, obvious reasons.

Alright, I congratulated myself after both got in and gave me that silent but cordial greeting. *Two nods.* I'd collected two whole nods *and* a few lunch buddies during my first week at the very clique-y Hoult Tower. The developments were small, but it was still something in terms of knocking the wall down.

But upon getting into the office, I found that a new one was officially up.

Like yesterday, I got no hello from Julian as he passed me with Colin and a few others. He was dressed to kill in a three-piece suit that stopped my heart for as many beats, and yes, he was busy, but he *did* take the time to flick those blue eyes over to me and slide them down the front of my wrap dress. He remained thoroughly stoic in the process, and while the others managed a nod or a "morning" as they passed, Julian opted out of either.

It could mean nothing, I tried telling myself.

But then there were the two occasions during which my entrance to a particular room resulted in his exit within the minute, with barely a glance in my direction. Again, no *solid* confirmation of bad blood, especially since we still spoke cordially about the Roths, but still.

The strict lack of non-work eye contact or conversation was enough to have me consider that we were in some kind of office Cold War – some bid to out-professional one another, and to be honest, it was a well-matched battle. We were both proud, tenacious and stubbornly single-minded. We could very well do this dance forever.

That idea didn't interest Lia.

"I don't think you're bringing it hard enough," she decided as we sat in Hoult Tower's tenth floor *pantry* – the fancy word for their cafeteria. "This could be a double date right now, but it's not."

As if to offset Julian and my Cold War in the office, the weather all week had been sweltering, and by Friday, we'd finally reached a hundred-plus degrees out – nasty anywhere, but particularly Manhattan. You could pretty much stick your tongue out and lick the humidity, so thanks to that, the cafeteria had been unusually crowded of late. Even the higher-ups were forgoing their two-minute walks to the usual steakhouse to eat lunch in the building.

Unlike my fellow caf regulars, I didn't mind the crowd. The luxe room was far too big and beautiful for the meager amount of people it usually attracted. Like the offices of Hoult Communications, it was a sleek, blindingly white double-height space with a second floor and matching double-height windows to let the sun pour in. Filled with people, it felt much less like a sterile, futuristic museum.

And, of course, the crowd was also better for people watching, which I got to enjoy with Lia this afternoon since she was in the building to visit Lukas.

"Sorry, love." I forked around my salad before digging in. "Pretty sure the boss and I are at a standstill."

"I should have known you two were too similar," Lia crinkled her nose. "You and Julian having sex would probably be nonstop rolling over to fight for the top. You would need wrestling mats and an entire gym."

I choked on a crouton. "Please keep in mind the man works in this building."

"He owns the building. What do I care?"

"Yeah, also, please don't remind me that he owns the building."

"Why not?" Lia grinned, studying the frustration on my face. "Because his power turns you on?"

"Yes, very much so, actually. And right now, I'm trying to manage my arousal for the sake of maintaining *utmost* professionalism."

"Right. How's that going, by the way?"

"Swimmingly. Hence the standstill."

"So you've officially mastered the casual-despite-my-wet-panties look?"

"You'll be proud to know that I have."

Lia popped one of my croutons in her mouth. "Well, that's good because here comes my boyfriend and your boss looking like an Armani billboard."

For the second time, I nearly asphyxiated. Coughing sharply, I found myself with just enough time to shoot Lia daggers before Lukas approached our table with Julian trailing two steps behind. His eyes were already fixed tight on me, and unless I imagined it, he didn't look pleased.

"*Hey*, Julian," Lia greeted him brightly. He was humorless as he slid his hands in his pockets and looked at her like he knew she was talking shit a second ago.

"Hello." From her, his eyes turned to me. "Sara."

"Mr. Hoult."

"Oh, God," Lia grimaced. "Do you really make her call you that?" she asked Julian, who looked decidedly elsewhere, as if looking for an escape. Seeing none, he answered Lia blankly.

"I don't, actually." He lifted his gaze to me. "I remember telling you as much, Sara."

"My apologies. I must have forgotten."

"Oh no. Couple's quarrel?" Lia cringed. I shot her a look. "What?" She played dumb. "I can tell you guys what Lukas and I do to fix things after we fight."

"*Lia*," I warned in unison with Lukas. Hardly a rare occurrence anymore, considering the balls she'd grown of late.

"Seriously. You all know I ignored this advice for too long myself, but sometimes you just gotta bang it out and – "

"I'm getting a coffee," I announced, making a beeline for the bar while texting furiously along the way.

> **ME:** *Holy shit woman cool it. He's still my boss. Remember that whole professionalism thing?*
> **LIA:** *I do.*
> **LIA:** *Makes me wonder why he's mentally removing your skirt as you walk away.*

I turned around to catch Julian staring at me. There was no flicker of apology in his eyes, which I found oddly daunting, so I averted my gaze and focused on approaching the coffee bar. I started to order, but I could tell by the way the young barista paused and looked past me that Julian was approaching.

"I should have considered Lia before hiring you."

My pulse picked up. I didn't need to turn around to gauge his proximity. Hit with his masculine scent, my entire body tensed up.

"What about her?"

"She's here enough as it is for Lukas," Julian said before finishing my coffee order with the barista and adding a double espresso for himself. "But aside from that, I'd prefer you two refrain from discussing whatever it was that you clearly were just now."

I stepped back to stare in disbelief at him.

"I would think this was obvious, but forbidding certain topics of conversation with my friends is way outside the realm of what you're allowed to do as my boss."

"I'm aware of that," he said dryly. "What I'm asking is for you to not discuss anything sexual that happened between us while you're on work premises. I'm sure you've noticed, but this large building is a rather small community. People talk, and I have no interest in giving them anything to discuss."

"Fair enough. I apologize on Lia's behalf," I said tartly. "She's not usually like this."

"I know her as well, Sara, and she's always like this."

"You've only known her for as long as she's been dating Lukas," I argued. "And it's only because of him that she's gotten this carefree and outspoken, *which*, in her defense, is not a bad thing. I guess it's just what happens when you're in a happy and fulfilling relationship."

"You guess?" Julian repeated.

My reply was clipped. "Yes. I can only guess."

"That's right." Julian leaned back on his heels, offering a cordial smile to the barista as she set our drinks on the counter. "Fulfilling was the opposite of the last relationship you had," he smirked as he grabbed our coffees and handed me mine. "See you back at the office, Ms. Hanna."

My mouth dropped open as I watched him go, realizing at a delay what he was even referring to – the depressingly underwhelming sex life I'd once had with Vanilla Jeff, my former friend with benefits.

What... in the actual fuck?

Standing there, I fumed. Well, that was definitely not playing fair. The rules of our office Cold War were one, be professional and two, be professional. Mentioning the sex life he'd overheard me talk about on the night he fingered me to orgasm did not constitute as professional. At all.

I pursed my lips into a line as I watched him go, but in all honesty, it was no problem to me. I'd been itching to even slightly cross the line with him, so if Julian wanted to play dirty, then fine.

I was more than happy to.

11

SARA

"Sure you don't want to come with us?" Colin asked, slinging the strap of his briefcase onto his shoulder. "Is it because of the pineapple shorts?" His smile was deliberately awkward. "Oh God, it's because of the pineapple shorts."

"It's *not* because of the pineapple shorts," I laughed, though I did need a second look at his pineapple printed shorts.

Thanks to the heat wave, a memo had been sent out earlier in the week regarding post-work changes of clothes. The general rule for Hoult Tower was that work appropriate clothing was required so long as you were in the building, even if you were off the clock. That meant no changing at the end of the day and walking out in shorts and T-shirts. So long as you were within its walls, you were to properly represent Hoult Tower.

Except this week.

I hadn't taken advantage of the amendment yet, but today, I had a change of heart – and an actual change of clothes with me, thanks to the bag Lia dropped off at reception.

LIA: I know you said to bring something "reasonably" sexy

but I decided that wasn't fun. Off to the Hamptons with
Lukas now so you can't kill me ok love you bye

Oh Jesus.

I braced myself as I went over to reception to pick up my change of clothes. I peeked into the bag on my way to the bathroom and had to say, "*Jesus*, Lia," for what she'd purchased me to wear. I'd asked for "reasonably sexy summer clothes, but nothing too crazy." She gave me ripped denim shorts that would make Daisy Duke blush. One pair was white, the other light blue. Thankfully, the tops she chose weren't studded bustiers like I half expected they'd be, so with a few texts to my fellow cafeteria regulars, I started changing.

When I emerged from the bathroom, Colin caught me.

"Whoa," he said, adjusting his black frames.

I laughed. *Well, that's a good sign.* As far as professionalism went, Colin was the one person who bested even Julian. I was positive that following the rules was his number one turn-on, so for him to check me out was pretty big.

"You look... very wow," he said, blushing as he eyed my little blue shorts and flowy white top. But with a nervous glance up the stairs, he cleared his throat. "Oh Christ, he's gonna fire me now," he laughed under his breath before flashing a tight-lipped smile and hurrying off.

I chewed the corner of my mouth, well aware that I was going to turn around to find Julian at the top of the steps. Still, when I did, my heart thumped. His authority was unquestionable from this angle, and his voice practically echoed in the empty office.

"Sara. A word."

There it is. I'd expected some kind of reaction, so with a nod, I started up the stairs. But he stopped me halfway up.

"I need you to change out of that first."

I paused. "Excuse me?"

"That's not workplace appropriate. Put on what you were wearing before," Julian said before disappearing into his office.

Completely stunned, I stared up the steps, physically unable to blink.

Are you fucking serious?

I had expected a reaction, but definitely not this. This took the fun out of it pretty much immediately.

Already furious, I trudged back into the women's room to violently shimmy out of my shorts and yank off my shirt, my heart-beat rising as I buttoned myself back into my top and zipped myself back into my skirt. Out of pure defiance, I opted out of the belt I'd had on. It was my pathetic little form of rebellion before marching up the steps and into Julian's office.

He was just getting seated behind his desk as I walked in.

"Was that really necessary?" I demanded upfront.

He glanced up at me while adjusting his tie. "You can't dress like that here," he said casually before turning his eyes to his computer screen. My jaw tightened.

"Everyone changed after work today. Not just me."

"Everyone changed into something casual, like a summer dress, or a polo and shorts." Julian slid his gaze to me and let it dip. "Denim panties weren't what I had in mind when I sent that memo."

"Well, I apologize," I said as evenly as I could through clenched teeth. "But I do feel the need to point out that several other women in this office left in dresses that were the same length as my shorts, with no sleeves, and you didn't call them in to reprimand them."

"You're right. I didn't," he said.

There was no follow-up.

Asshole. Standing before Julian's desk, I fumed, thoroughly ticked off by how relaxed he was as he sat back, his jacket draped over the back of his chair and his sleeves pushed up to his elbows. I ripped my eyes off the deep lines of his forearms to arch an expectant eyebrow at him.

"So, I don't get an explanation for that inconsistency?"

Julian took his time to switch his gaze from his screen to me.

"No," he finally said.

Disbelief hissed from my lips.

"That hardly seems fair, and again, I can't help but suspect you're treating me differently than the rest of the office," I said hotly. "Actually, you *are* treating me differently than the rest of the office. The fact of the matter is, I know why you're singling me out. We both do. And for you to use that as a reason to make my life difficult today is completely unfair given your problem is something *you* alone created."

Shit.

I was breathless. I didn't know how it happened, but I'd just let it all out. I'd given my office-appropriate version of "if you want to fuck me, then fuck me" and suddenly, it was Julian's turn to raise his eyebrows.

"And for what reason do you think I'm singling you out?" he asked.

"Can I say it or do I need to use your beloved corporate-speak?"

"Just say it."

"Because you want to fuck me, Julian," I ground out. "You want to fuck me, you won't let yourself fuck me, so you're taking it *out* on me – since that makes so much sense, right?" I gave him a second to answer and got nothing. "Right. Well, if you have nothing left to say, then I'm going to go. I have to find some Starbucks to change in now, and I'm pretty sure I'll be late to meet the guys for happy hour, so bye."

"Who are you meeting?"

It was less a question than a demand and it made my entire body tingle with fury. I turned back on my heel to face him.

"Guys from Kinsley-Weiss," I answered, referring to the notorious boys club on the thirty-third floor. I took a sick pleasure in the way Julian's brow pulled together.

"Just you and them?"

"Just me and them."

"I thought you were going to drinks with Colin."

I crossed my arms over my chest. "I decided against it. He works in my office, so it's probably safer to have drinks with men I don't run the risk of losing my job with should I choose to go home with them."

Julian's shoulders went rigid. He still looked poised, controlled, but I could see the glint of fire behind his blue eyes.

"So your plan is to sleep with someone tonight."

"That's none of your business, and I'm leaving," I muttered, but my breath caught fast in my throat because Julian stood in front of me within seconds. I started again toward the door, but he stepped neatly sideways to block me.

"It's every bit my business when you're going with people I know, and in particular don't trust."

I gave a bitter laugh.

"You strike me as someone who doesn't trust, period, and we've already established the parameters of your authority over me, Julian. Yes, you can tell me what I can and cannot wear, but no, you don't get to decide where I go after work or who I want to fuck, especially when I'm the one waiting for you," I seethed. "You're the one with the rule, so either make a move, asshole, or get out of my way."

I could have sworn I saw hatred boiling in his eyes. I practically heard it in his voice when, with a glance at his desk, he finally spoke.

"Take a seat, Sara," he said.

"Julian, I *told* you –"

"Unbutton your shirt before you sit down."

I shut my mouth. A chill rippled over my skin as I watched Julian remove his hand from the door, his shoulders slightly relaxing.

"What exactly are you asking of me right now?" I clarified.

"I'm asking you to take a seat in front of my desk, Sara. And I want you to take your shirt off for me."

Got it.

Turning stiffly, I saw him calmly return to his chair, watching me closely as I faced him once again. I was heated a second ago, but now I was hot. Searing. I swallowed away the tightness in my throat as I slowly made my way toward the desk, taking a seat in front of Julian as he'd asked me to.

"Unbutton," he said with a glance down my front. I wet my lips as I shakily started but he stopped me. "Slowly."

I glared. "Are you going to fuck me?"

"I don't enjoy contradicting myself. If you're making me break my rule, I'm going to take my time with you."

I gulped.

Fair enough.

Breathing steady, I slowly unbuttoned my shirt, my eyes moving from the peek of my lacy bra to Julian's wolfish gaze as he took me in from behind his desk. I kept my pace unhurried for him, despite the fact that it tormented me. It forced me to feel every ripple of sensation in slow motion, from the throbbing between my own legs to the shiver that crawled over the tops of my breasts as the ice-cold air hit my skin.

Leaning back, Julian simply watched me as I untucked my fully unbuttoned top from my skirt.

"Slow," he reminded me as I let the shirt fall off my shoulders and down my arms. I shot him a look as if to say, *don't push it*. He smirked. "Am I exhausting your patience right now, Ms. Hanna?"

"You've been." Arching my back, I folded my hands in my lap, sitting perfectly straight before him in just my black bra and tan pencil skirt. "You're torturing me, actually, but I realize that's the point."

"You do pick things up quickly," he murmured, eyes still on me as he undid his belt. "You know what I want to see next."

He laughed as I rolled my eyes away from him, looking decidedly out the window at the view of the Empire State as I reached behind myself and unclasped my bra. My breasts felt swollen, painfully heavy as the lace cups fell out from underneath them. I heard the sharp breath Julian drew in, and when I returned my eyes to him, I bit down hard on my lip. He looked every bit the practiced and polished authority he always did in that chair.

The only difference now was that he had his hard cock out, his hand wrapped around it, stroking languidly from root to tip.

My sex clenched from the sight alone. My hands instinctively moved toward the zipper behind my skirt, but Julian stopped me.

"Keep it on," he said. "Stand up for me."

I smirked.

"Let me guess," I said, inching my fingers down my sides and curling them to gather up my skirt. I felt the rush of wetness in my pussy as I stood there pulling my skirt up for Julian, his gaze pinned so tight on me I felt magnetic. He didn't so much as blink let alone look away as I sat back down in my panties, my skirt hiked up and my hand idling between my thighs.

"Do it," he said. "Touch yourself."

I did, closing my eyes as I pushed the lace aside to circle my fingers over my clit. That first wave of heat surged up my body and settled in my cheeks. My pulse was in my ears, but I could still hear when Julian's chair creaked forward and his footsteps neared.

Writhing under my own fingers, I kept my eyes shut. I wasn't ready for the sight of him yet. I wanted to process this first – the fact that I was sitting topless and touching myself in Julian Hoult's shiny office at the top of the tower.

But I had little time before I felt him reach down from above me, his fingertips on the underside of my breast. I shivered when his hand fully cupped me and slowly squeezed.

With a gasp, I opened my eyes.

Holy shit.

Julian stood at my side. Without peering to my right, all I could see was his forearm, his expensive watch and his hand playing with my breast as I stared out the windows at Midtown Manhattan.

It was surreal.

Everything was still in place. His desk was neat, a gleaming surface that held only his laptop, his planner, one folder and one pen. His shelf was a towering display of books, awards and baseballs enshrined in glass cases.

Everything was as it was supposed to be.

Except for us.

"Julian." I clasped my hand over his, holding it still over my breast as I turned to look up at him.

His every muscle was tight as he watched my other hand tease my clit. His eyes were hooded, and he was still stroking himself. My view combined with his touch was unbelievable. It had to be the definition of erotic: my boss looking sharp in his brilliant white shirt and expensive tie, jerking himself off as he massaged my naked breasts in his office.

"Stand for me," he rasped.

I was on my feet barely a second before he was kissing me, both hands cupped around my face as I took over pumping his cock. I moaned against his mouth as he claimed mine, each wet stroke of his tongue reminding me that he was in control. I was frenzied, desperate to feel more and to feel it faster, but he kept me in check with just the deliberate movements of his tongue – sharp one second, leisurely the next.

Like he said, he was going to take his time with me.

"Three days." Julian muttered as he brought me to the end of the leather couch. "You got me to break in three days."

He pinched my nipple between his fingers and pulled away from my lips, prompting my mouth to fall desperately open in his absence. I moaned as he tugged on me lightly. Then harder.

"Look at me," he said. I forced my eyes open despite the perfect mix of torment and pleasure he had blitzing through my body. "You do know you're playing with fire, right?" he asked as his free hand pulled my panties down. I answered just as they fell in a ring of lace around my feet.

"Yes."

Julian soaked in my answer for a second before turning me gently around and lifting my leg to place my knee on the armrest. I leaned forward to grab onto the back of the couch, sharply arching my back when I felt his fingers dip into my pussy.

"Good." His low rumble and the ease with which he glided in told me just how incredibly wet I was. Already panting hard, I stared at my white knuckles, my ears perking to the sound of crinkling foil behind me. I glanced slightly over my shoulder to see a condom stretching shiny and thin over the flared tip of his cock. It struggled down every last inch of his thick shaft, causing the hot anticipation to churn in my belly as he drew closer. His eyes locked on mine, Julian shook his head. "You should see how fucking sexy you look right now."

"Why don't you just make me feel it?"

"I'll be fucking you harder for that."

"Do it," I murmured, putting a smile on his lips. It spread wider as he ran the head of his dick along the length of my sex, taking pleasure in my brows pulled tight and my mouth hanging open. Just as I found the breath to beg for it already, he plunged inside me.

From there, slow was no longer in our vocabulary.

Gripping my hips, he pumped so deep and so hard inside me that my tits bounced just under my chin. My nails dug into leather as he leaned over and kissed my shoulders, my neck. Circling one arm tight around my waist, he freed his other to catch my jaw and turn my face to his.

"Is this what you wanted?" he demanded in a low whisper. "Or do you want me to pin you down and fuck you on the floor?"

He chuckled at my inability to answer him.

"Where do you want me to fuck you tomorrow, Sara?" he asked, prodding my emotions in the midst of his cock slamming inside me. *How fucking worked up was he trying to get me?*

"I don't care, Julian." The words hurtled from my lips. "I just want you to fuck me and make me come."

"I will. You've opened the floodgates, Sara, so I have every intention of fucking you whenever and however I want in this office." His ruthless words lit my every nerve ending on fire. "And I promise I'll make that pussy come." He thrust hard from behind. "Again." Another. "And again." I moaned. "And again," he growled as he kept himself pressed balls-deep inside me, grinding himself against a sweet spot that made me almost scream. "I may just have to carry you home when I'm done," he murmured, licking the underside of my jaw as he battered inside me.

Fuck.

I couldn't stop moaning. I tried to control my volume, but it was in vain, and Julian loved every second of it, feigning surprise as he teased me in a low mutter.

"You're such a good girl in my office. Who knew I could get you to be so loud?"

"Screw you," I grinned just before letting out a yelp as he lifted me swiftly and laid me on my back on the couch. I gasped as he wrapped my legs around his back and entered me again, but at a pace now that I found brutally slow. Inch by inch, our eyes locked on one another, his steel length parted me.

And suddenly, I was overwhelmed.

I reveled in his weight on top of my body. Face to face with Julian, his cock felt deliriously good. Every stroke felt longer, deeper – less frantic, more deliberate. The air seized from my lungs as he studied me from my eyes to my nose to my lips, rocking inside me at a torturously languorous pace. My fingers dipped in every slow flex of his muscles as I grabbed his ass, and my heels dug into his sculpted back as I brought him all the way inside me.

Our eyes stayed locked as the pleasure grew.

And as it grew, the air shifted.

Sweat misted on my forehead. I swore it took every ounce of my strength just to return Julian's electrifying gaze. His power, his intellect was already above all, but inside me, it multiplied. It made me feel as if he was claiming something of mine, discovering something about me that even I never knew. Without speaking a word, he asked me a question then found the answer himself.

It was insanely fucking daunting. I could barely take it anymore.

"Look at me," Julian growled when I turned away. His pace quickened inside me, his intensity mounting. "Look at me, Sara. You're going to let me watch you come."

I ignored him, so he caught my jaw and kissed me forcefully, the shock of his tongue sending my body plunging into an orgasm.

Oh God.

It felt too big for my body. I must've made a sound, because Julian muttered, "I've got you," before pinning me down and absorbing every wild second of my pleasure, his strength swallowing every twitch and buck of my body till he was hissing *"fuck"* under his breath. His body caged around me. Then with a vicious jerk, he let out a groan, the sound so deep and guttural it sent jolting aftershocks ripping through me.

He didn't immediately get up off me. His lips were against my neck as we caught our breath, and only when he pulled away did I realize that our hands had been above my head, clasped together the whole time.

The void I felt when he withdrew from me hurt.

My nails dug into the couch, and I stared at the cum-filled tip of the condom as he slowly got up, his eyes still on me. He studied my nakedness from head to toe, refusing to break his gaze even as I drew my legs to my chest and got up.

"Sara."

His voice was back to steady as I rushed to get dressed. I tossed him a hurried smile, though I knew I wasn't fooling him. Something was bothering me. He knew that.

But I myself didn't know what it was.

All I knew was that while I had wanted to be fucked, Julian had done something a little more than fuck me just now. And despite the hot, full-body pleasure I was still very much reeling from, I was suddenly feeling a bit lost, with not a single clue how to feel.

12

JULIAN

It was Sunday, and I had to clear my head before I left to meet them.

My hope was that this would help.

Leaning back in my chair, I tilted my head down. My neck was rigid as my gaze traveled over my flinching pecs, my palm running over my clenching abs as I felt myself getting closer.

Like the one at Hoult Tower, the office in my TriBeCa loft was located at the highest point of the building, in a sky-lit room with walls of windows facing both south and west. My chair was turned toward them as I sat with my legs wide, and my thighs flexing as I jacked my cock at a furious pace.

I was still thinking about her.

I couldn't stop.

Fucking generally helped in these situations, but apparently, this one was an outlier, and I probably should have guessed it would be.

I'd fantasized about Sara at length for almost two weeks after we met. The explicit images started the second I laid eyes on her, and they continued onto her first day of work. After what we did in the elevator, I'd closed the door of my office and jerked off like an animal in a three thousand dollar suit.

In short, I'd spent a lot of time thinking about how incredibly good it would feel to fuck her.

But combined, none of those fantasies came close to how good it actually was.

Her pussy was so tight but eager, a perfect fit for my cock. I could have taken her again on Friday – all night, if she had let me. But she wound up doing what no woman had ever done to me after sex, and that was volunteer to leave. I had gotten another taste of her mouth and the sweet little spot under her jaw before she rushed out with her lips swollen, her bra on my floor, and the buttons barely done on her shirt.

Yet another image for me to get hard over.

"*Fuck.*"

I rolled my head back, my every muscle flexed tight till the second I pumped thick jets of cum from my tip, catching them in her panties. Breathing hard, I held the deep frown in my brow as I tipped my head forward again to stare down at my handiwork. Ropes of thick white on her fine, black silk.

God, I wanted to cum on her. Inside her.

I wanted to rub myself into her skin and watch it shine under light.

Now that I'd had her, the fantasies had only multiplied, and for fuck's sake, I couldn't afford that – especially not today. For that reason, I was almost thankful when about ten minutes later, as I was standing in my closet, Emmett called.

"What?" I answered.

"Think it's cool if I bring a girl again this week?"

"No. I think it's cruel, actually."

"To who? The girl?" Emmett asked. In the background, I could hear him making his first protein shake of the day. "Or Mom?"

"Mom. You're teasing her with the idea of marriage despite the fact that we all know you're going to take another fifteen to twenty years for that."

Emmett set his blender off, and I winced as I removed a light blue shirt from its hanger.

"You guys give me no credit," he said once the grating sound was finished. "I date a lot in order to effectively assess my preferences, as well as her true potential. I'm sure you can understand that, especially since I phrased it in Julian-speak."

"Very nice."

"I don't appreciate the sarcasm, but at least I can take comfort in the fact that I'll still get married before you."

"Unlikely," I hit back, but I paused in the midst of buttoning my shirt, realizing that my instinct to fight Emmett came out before I recognized that he was baiting me. "If you ask about her again, I'm going to kill you the second I see you," I said between my teeth.

"Would that be worth it though? Jail time means no fucking Sara."

"Don't talk about fucking her."

"I'm talking about *you* fucking her, asshole."

I growled when I realized I'd missed a button. "Don't talk about her in general is what I mean," I muttered, glancing at the time. "And in case you still smell like last night's tequila, I suggest you shower now and get going so you're not thirty minutes late like you were last week."

"Fine. Hey, anyone ever tell you how much fun you're not?"

I whipped a tie out of my drawer and rolled my eyes.

"I'm hanging up, Emmett. See you at the stadium."

"Who's that?"

I looked down at my phone. I'd vaguely registered the sound of its ring, but there was too much on my mind to fully process it till my mother nudged me and asked the question. It was Turner calling. I looked away.

"You're not going to pick it up?" Mom asked.

Her sixtieth birthday was last week, but she still looked every bit the regal, bright-eyed girl my father called princess since the day he met her. I turned from the game to face her with a quizzical look.

"Since when have you been eager for me to take work calls on Sundays?"

"I'm not," she said, moving her hair with her as she shrugged. She still wore it down and curled just above her shoulder like she did when Emmett and I were kids. The only difference now was that it was tinted silver-grey instead of blonde. But whatever color she wore, she looked classically beautiful. The only time Lia endeared herself to me was when she said Mom reminded her of Grace Kelly.

I had always thought the same, though I would admit her voice was a stark contrast to the wispiness of old Hollywood.

When she spoke, my mother's voice was blunt, borderline harsh. And I wouldn't have it any other way.

"I just figured it might be someone important calling. And yes, I know, 'it's always someone important calling,' but considering you've let two whole calls go to voicemail since we've been here, I thought maybe something, or *someone* had taken your mind off of work for once."

"Emmett introduces you to a new girlfriend every week. Why not pin your hopes of grandchildren on him instead?" I teased.

"Because of that reason exactly. He's not going to settle down with anyone anytime soon."

"You don't know that!" Emmett called over his shoulder at us. He was down front in our suite behind home plate, one arm hugging Ozzy to his chest and the other draped over Grandma's diminutive shoulders. Last year, she wouldn't go near Emmett's dog. Now, she had the thing eating peanuts out of her hand. "*Gram*, no more," Emmett groaned, turning back around.

Mom laughed at them both, but I could see that look casting over her, and her smile fading slowly as her lake blue eyes floated toward the outfield.

Not now, Mom. Please.

I wasn't prepared for another trip down memory lane, but it had happened during last Sunday's game as well, so I probably should've known it was coming.

Following my mother's gaze, I looked out toward the back of the stadium.

We used to sit out there a good twenty, twenty-five years ago – back when the Hoults "rolled deep" as Emmett said. Our family took up a big chunk of right field every Sunday, when we packed our things and made a day of going to the stadium. It was our grandparents, my family, two pairs of aunts and uncles, and their children. Over the years, we became friends with the other season ticket holders in the bleachers, as well as their own kids, and it practically felt as if we owned the outfield.

Unlike Grandma, Mom never cared for baseball. She said she went to the games every Sunday to play with the kids. It worked out well. No one's love for baseball matched Grandma's, and no one's love for kids matched my mom's. Everyone was happy.

Back then at least.

With a glance at me, Mom gauged that I'd followed her eye line and thus, her train of thought.

"You were so good with them," she said. "You always helped me keep the little ones behaved."

"Despite being a kid myself. I was ten when you had me babysitting everyone."

"But you had fun, remember? You loved making up games to keep them distracted. I can't even count the number of tantrums you saved us," she laughed to herself. It wound down to a sigh. "You're like your father. Very stern, very serious. But you light up around children."

"Mom," I warned.

"Okay, alright." She held her hands up, her voice quickly losing its dreamy quality. "I'm sorry. I was just going through the old photo albums last night, and I found so many baby pictures," she explained. "I actually have a nice one of Lucie. I don't know if you might want that."

I turned to face my mother, unsure if it was a serious question. "No. I don't want that."

"Okay. Sorry." She was genuinely apologetic this time. I could feel her watching me for the next few seconds that I kept my eyes decidedly on the game. Reaching for my hand, Mom squeezed it. "Listen, Julian," she started seriously. I feared the speech she was preparing to launch into. But with a smile, she said, "Ozzy's my grandchild."

I broke into a grin. My eyes slid over to Ozzy.

"Yes. Your drooling, orange grandchild," I said, amused as usual by the Staffordshire bull terrier staring back at me over Emmett's shoulder. It was always wearing the same stupid perma-grin as my brother, and the two were both simple, easygoing – generally motivated by food, so they really did bear a father-son resemblance.

"Anyway, I meant to tell you I made a reservation at Greta's for Father's Day next week, since that's Dad's favorite. All six of your cousins will be in attendance this year. Significant others, too."

"That sounds good," I lied, catching the tennis ball Emmett lobbed at me without warning. I tossed it somewhere safe for Ozzy to fetch. "There's a slight chance I'll be away on business, but I doubt it'll fall on Father's Day."

"Oh." Her voice was deliberately flat. "Are you finally selling the thing?"

The *thing*. That was what she called that multi-million dollar resort in Biarritz. My teeth clenched at first, but I relaxed.

"Yes. As soon as possible, and hopefully to Turner and Carter Roth. You've met them."

"Oh yes, I remember those two."

"Yeah, they're... idiots. But idiots that can do a lot of good for this stadium. Their resources can help us make this stadium what we all dreamed of," I said just as Ozzy jumped on me with the tennis ball half-annihilated in his mouth. Mom barely flinched as she wrestled the slobbery thing out from his jaws and tossed it at Emmett.

"You've been working so hard," she said, watching Ozzy dart around. "They would both be so proud of you, Julian. I sincerely hope you know that."

It was as much of a compliment as it was a request that I relax at some point, and let everything go. I wasn't sure if that was going to happen, nor did I want to entertain the discussion. Thankfully, Mom let me off the hook to lecture Emmett.

"Emmett, maybe you should get him a brother to play with."

"Ma, you gotta be kidding me. Ozzy's three. I can't handle another one now."

"I read somewhere it's not good to keep a dog without giving it a friend."

"*Mom*." Emmett groaned to the skies. "Stop with the grandkid thing," he said. "Ask Julian about a girl named Sara."

Mom sat upright to stare at me.

"*Who?*"

Little shit. I directed my death look at Emmett before promptly excusing myself and striding out of the suite before I could be questioned.

> **ME:** *I'm going to have you banned from the stadium.*

I sent the text to Emmett as my footsteps echoed down the empty hall. He fired back fast.

> **EMMETT:** *Gram would kill you. I'm her favorite.*
> **EMMETT:** *You going to see the girl?*
> **ME:** *No. What makes you think that*

He ignored my last text, which annoyed me, because it left the conversation about Sara unfinished, and I was having a shit enough time as it was trying to think of something, anything besides her.

The fact that we had our next meeting with the Roths tomorrow was eating at me now too, because while I loved watching her put on a show for them, I also hated it. I hated watching their tongues hang out of their mouths as they dragged their greedy eyes all over her body, and I hated anticipating the ways they would try to touch her, get closer to her.

But I'd put myself in this position.

I'd asked for all of this, and I tried reminding myself of that as I stood in the empty hall. Of course, the attempt was in vain, because when my phone buzzed in my pocket, I picked up with a tart, "What?"

"Jesus Christ. Hello to you too, Hoult."

I recognized Turner's voice and exhaled.

"Sorry. I thought you were my brother."

"Emmett? Love that guy."

"You would," I laughed, almost genuinely.

"Yeah, I don't even know how you two are related," Turner snorted, some girl's voice in the background. "Anyway, listen, I know we said we were gonna meet tomorrow..."

"You're not going to cancel on me."

"Easy, Hoult. I wasn't going to cancel, I was gonna say I know we set it for noon at your office tomorrow, but some... thing just came up for me," he said, sounding half-assed. "I'm in Miami right now, and I'm actually going to be flying back to New York at around five tomorrow, so what do you say we all meet up around six?"

I couldn't help suspecting that Turner was only in Miami to party, and that he preferred a late meeting tomorrow because it took us out of the conference room, and more than likely, somewhere with more distractions.

"Where do you want to meet?" I asked.

"I really liked that hotel you set me up with a couple weeks back. When I fucked that thing with the ass?"

"Cass."

"Jesus, you really don't forget shit. Yeah, her. They have a few rooftop bars there. A few pools. Figured we could have our meeting on a nice part of the roof with a good view – get ourselves some sun to set the mood to talk Biarritz. Right?"

"It's going to be ninety degrees out, Turner."

He laughed for longer than I cared to hear. "Oh, I know. Did you hear me say pools? Besides, you can just wear a T-shirt and shorts – you know I don't give a fuck. Keep it casual for once," he said, quickly muttering to the girl with him before coming back to me. "Matter fact, I have a surprise for Sara, so you should both bring swimsuits, actually. Or something you don't mind getting wet."

It was my turn to laugh. "That's not happening at all."

"Don't say that to me. Also, I sent a little gift basket to your office. Should get there by tomorrow morning."

"What is it?" I asked.

"Anthrax – the fuck do you think it is? It's surfing gear from my line. Shit that sold out in stores the week it hit, so you're welcome," Turner said. I held the phone away from my ear as he suddenly groaned. I didn't know what the fuck he was doing with that girl, but I didn't want to know.

"Jesus Christ, Turner. I'll talk to you tomorrow. Six o'clock at the top of The Victorian," I said as he chuckled, still half-groaning during his goodbye.

"See you there, buddy."

13

SARA

I didn't know what to expect when I walked into the office Monday morning. I'd spent the weekend in a mental limbo.

Friday evening had been a complete mind-fuck for me, and a weekend later, I wasn't completely sure why. All I really knew was that I'd had sex with Julian in his office, it was way better than I imagined, and possibly way better than I wanted.

What that meant, however, I wasn't sure. The further removed I was from the day the less I understood my reaction to whatever Julian and I shared. At the time, it felt as if I had to leave, or else I wouldn't be able to breathe. But over the weekend, I repeatedly wished that I had stayed.

Especially since Julian was ready to go again by the time I slipped out the door. He kept stopping me as I got dressed, running his smooth lips along my mouth, my neck. I'd spent both Saturday and Sunday thinking about how he went from half-mast to rock-hard again the moment I'd kissed him back. It made me feel so good, so insanely *sexy*.

But then he didn't contact me once over the weekend. And naturally, I told myself he was with a girl.

A *woman*, rather. I imagined him with a woman, actually – some willowy, impeccably styled socialite who worked in a gallery in Chelsea. I imagined him taking her to a Michelin-starred restaurant by Central Park where they would talk about an art exhibit, or the last time they went to Ibiza, and how it's lost its *je ne sais quois* since their last visit ten years ago – just a bunch of sophisticated, borderline douchey topics I'd never have any business participating in.

Oh yeah.

I was hardcore psyching myself out. And it sucked.

I'd never done it before, but I'd seen various girlfriends through the process. I told them that while they were being irrational, it was okay. Expected, even. Hormones went a little crazy after good sex with an attractive man, but everything would eventually settle down and fall into place.

You just have to ride it out, I said.

Now, I wished I could personally call every one of my friends I'd given that generic speech to and apologize profusely, because as I tried it on myself, I realized it didn't do jack shit.

"Hey."

At the sound of Julian's voice, I jumped. Once I faced him at the kitchen counter in the office, I found him already frowning at me.

"You alright?" he asked.

"Yes," I answered too quickly.

"You look like you just saw a ghost."

"I'm fine," I smiled a little more convincingly now, though still gripping my coffee tight. It was another hot day and Julian was without a jacket, wearing a black tie with a pale grey shirt that was fitted well to his delectably V-shaped torso. I curled my bottom lip against my tongue.

I hadn't seen him fully naked yet.

That thought crossed my mind just as he leaned in to grab something behind me. My eyelids were heavy for the second that I breathed his intoxicating scent. *Soap and skin*. It was all natural, but bottled and sold, it would make millions.

"You spilled on yourself," Julian said, using the napkin he'd grabbed to wipe away the coffee streaming down my arm.

I blinked down at myself.

"Oh. I didn't realize," I murmured, blushing when I caught Colin's curious eye as he passed. *Shit.* I wasn't sure what we looked like just now, and I wished I knew exactly why I felt so thrown off – like I'd completely forgotten how to act around Julian.

God, Sara. A part of me had really thought I could just "bang it out" with this man and carry on. The rest of me was laughing at that part now, especially as Julian gave that sexy nod to indicate *"my office."*

My heartbeat quickened as I followed him out of the kitchen and headed for the stairs.

"So, I know you're probably prepared to meet with the Roths in a few hours, but I should let you know they postponed our meeting till six tonight."

The news was surprising enough that I somewhat snapped out of my fog.

"Really?" I made a face. But when we looked at each other, we both laughed. "Actually, yeah. That sounds about right."

"It does, doesn't it? Though I should've told you to save your initial surprise for the location he chose."

"Oh no. Where did he choose?" I asked, watching Julian kind of shake his head to himself, rubbing his jaw as he grinned. *Can you cool it? With the sexiness? Seriously.* I was already getting nervous and hot, and that was before he spoke his next few words.

"He wants us at the hotel."

"The hotel?" I repeated.

"The Victorian." Julian eyed me wickedly as we reached the top of the steps. "I believe you're familiar with it."

My heart skipped a beat.

"Yes." My eyes fluttered when I looked up and let his gorgeous smile really hit me. "I am."

Our eyes were on each other as we entered his office, but once I got in, my attention was drawn quickly to the big, ugly box sitting on his desk. It was bright yellow, a glaring eyesore among Julian's otherwise sophisticated décor.

"Unfortunately," he started as we stood side by side in front of his desk, just staring at the ugly box. "We won't be meeting in the comfort of a room tonight so much as some private part of the roof, despite this weather."

I raised my eyebrows. "We're going to be burning."

"I know. I'm not entirely sure what Turner has up his sleeve for tonight, but as you can see, he sent us a lot of surfing gear that we really have no use for."

I burst out laughing.

"What is he on?"

"I wish I knew. But he did say the surprise he had in store for us tonight required swimsuits." If a voice could roll its eyes, Julian's just did. "And while I have no intentions for either of us to play into the swimsuit request, I would recommend you either go home and find a change of clothes or take this to buy something lightweight for tonight."

I looked down to find Julian handing me a heavy, black credit card.

"Company expense. You can either buy something or grab it from home," he said, rounding his desk and taking a seat in his chair. "Whichever option you choose, feel free to take the day off till six, since you'll be working from then till presumably eight or nine o' clock tonight."

"Oh."

I stared at the card. On one hand, it was nice to have the company pay for my personal wardrobe additions. On the other hand, I didn't want to be out of the office. I had been hoping to stay and feel out the energy between Julian and myself, because if I had any more time alone with my thoughts, I might actually implode.

"Should I... leave right now?" I asked.

"Yes, I'd prefer that." Julian sat back to study what I imagined was visible disappointment on my face. "I was a little eager to make use of the time that opened up after the Roths rescheduled, so I have back-to-back meetings starting in fifteen minutes," he said. Off my silence, he smiled. "In case I'm not being clear enough, I don't regard fifteen minutes as enough time to do anything for pleasure."

The grin that curved my lips was a slow one.

"Thank you for the clarification."

"You're very welcome."

"But in that case, I should remind you of what you subjected me to on my first day working here."

Julian sat forward, eyebrow cocked – his silent invitation for me to go on. I smirked.

"Bluntly put, Mr. Hoult, you licked my pussy in the elevator for about six seconds before you had to stop. In your opinion, that was what we had time for, so," I glanced at the clock, "I can't help but imagine that fourteen minutes is more than enough time for what I have in mind."

His cufflink gleamed as he brought his hand under his chin.

"And what is it that you have in mind?"

"I want to finish what I started the night we met."

"Please clarify."

"I want your cock in my mouth, Julian," I said as a wicked look flashed in his eyes. "And this time, I want to make you come."

He was quiet for two seconds then drew in a deep breath and groaned.

"You're killing me," he muttered, but before I knew it, I could hear his belt jangling under the desk.

His eyes stayed pinned on mine as I made my way over to him, his jaw growing tighter with every precise click of my heels. It was as if the sound entranced him because it took awhile before he caught himself and hastily murmured, "Close the door."

I glanced back at the open door then down at his desk. It was huge, and it went fully down to the floor, so I decidedly ignored his request.

"You've got to be fucking kidding me." Julian's voice was hoarse when I reached him. After another quick peek outside, I lowered myself to my knees, undoing the button on his black slacks and pulling down the zipper. I looked up to see his stare flickering between the door and me, his expression a cross between high alert and higher anticipation.

His breath shortened when I reached into his grey boxers to free his hot erection, and he muffled his groan against his fist when I gave the first lick of his shaft. Flattening my tongue against his smooth underside, I drew it up slowly till I could wrap my lips around the head, sucking vigorously till my hair fell into my eyes.

"What are you doing?" Julian pleaded when I pulled back suddenly.

I answered by grabbing the pen off his desk and arching my back. His eyes glazed over as I slowly wound my long hair into a knot at the top of my head. I took my time, enjoying my view of Julian Hoult waiting eagerly for me. But his patience wore thin quickly.

"Fucking hell," he hissed, angling forward to grip my jaw and kiss me as his free hand squeezed my breast.

Fastening my topknot with the pen, my grinning lips returned Julian's kiss, but the moment footsteps sounded outside, he pulled swiftly back. With my hair out of the way, I peered up to see Julian nodding a hello at someone. He'd barely finished before I had his cock back in my mouth.

"*Fuck.*" His hand grabbed the top of the armrest as I bobbed up and down on him, my every stroke slicker and smoother than the last. "Christ, Sara," Julian hissed, gripping my topknot as I let my tongue acquaint itself with every ridge and vein on his impressive shaft.

For several minutes, I got to spoil it uninterrupted, sucking so eagerly I wondered if the smacking sounds were echoing out into the hall. I decided on no. As busy as my lips were, I could still hear the low and gravelly filth Julian muttered to me as I got him rock-hard in my mouth. He held me closer to him, his grip on my topknot tightening with my every wet pull.

I knew when he released my hair that someone had just passed his doorway. I paused, waiting for the moment to pass.

But this time, it didn't.

"Hey, Julian. McKinley's here a little early for the meeting."

I stopped, eyes wide when I recognized Colin's voice at the door. My heart pounded as I slid my eyes up to Julian.

Holy shit. In no time, he'd executed his impossibly smooth transition into pure stoicism. His throbbing dick still rested on my bottom lip as I watched him, mouth hung open with awe. A bit of a teasing awe, really. I wanted him to glance down at me, but he didn't.

So naturally, I started sucking again.

The awkward grunt I got out of him made it entirely worth it.

"If you could get him water or coffee for now, that'd be great," Julian said, punishing me with a quick tug on my hair. "I'll meet him in the conference room shortly."

"Great. He says Eli couldn't make it because – "

"That's fine," Julian cut him off, his voice tight as I touched his cock to the back of my throat. I saw his knuckles go white as he gripped the armrest. "That's fine. Just... go," he exhaled hard. "I'll be there soon."

A devilish thrill coursed through my veins as I heard Colin walk away. But the smile fell fast from my lips when Julian abruptly pulled out of my mouth and zipped back up.

I fell briefly onto my hands and knees as he got up from his seat and went for the door. My heart beat fast as I anticipated him walking out in fury. But from the floor behind his desk, I didn't hear his footsteps pace down the hall.

Instead, I heard him close the door and lock it.

My pulse was racing by the time he reappeared to stand above me, his eyes cold and hard as he unzipped again and pulled out his cock.

"Get up," he said.

My pussy throbbed in response to the command.

"Give me your panties."

Julian watched me reach under my skirt, his fiery stare calming the slightest bit when my thong fell to my ankles. I let my mouth graze his cock on the way down to retrieve them, grinning at how he flexed his jaw over the brief contact. At that point, I still had him at my mercy.

But once my thong was in his palm, he had me swiftly spun around and bent over his desk.

I squeaked in surprise when he pulled my arms behind my back, knotting my own panties around my wrists before cupping the fullest part of my ass and spanking it hard.

"Was that amusing for you?" he asked, neglecting to rub away the pain before spanking me again. When I yelped, a low rumble escaped his chest. "You enjoyed tormenting me, didn't you?"

A sharp thrill raced to my clit.

"Yes."

"I could feel you smiling against my cock while I was talking to Colin. I'm glad you had so much fun with that," Julian said, his voice tinged with mischief.

Uh oh. I knew from just the sound that the tables had turned – as if being tied and spanked over his desk weren't a good enough hint.

"But now that you've had your fun – " Julian audibly stroked his cock behind me with the wetness I left on his shaft. " – I'm going to have mine."

He smoothed his hand over my ass again, building my senses up to brace for another tingling blow.

But what I felt instead was the warm flat of his tongue on my pussy.

My mouth fell open as my knees buckled hard against the desk. I moaned as Julian securely gripped my legs, holding them slightly bent and together as he switched between licking and furiously lapping at me. He groaned low, with pleasure, as if I were the best thing he'd ever tasted.

"Holy shit."

My eyes shut tight as Julian devoured me, squeezing my knees together and *lifting my heels off the floor* while still licking my pussy. *Oh my God.* I writhed on the desk, gasping at my sheer instability – at the fact that I could still feel such ecstasy while having no control of my balance whatsoever. My legs trembled in Julian's grip, my hands still tied behind my back and my feet now well off the ground. All I knew for sure was that my cheek and breasts were pressed against his desk, and his tongue was sliding so deep in my pussy I could hardly fathom his skill.

If there was a definition for *at his mercy*, this was it.

And while I was sure that Julian wouldn't let me come, he made me his priority for the last five minutes that he had before his meeting, his tongue bathing my pussy till I saw stars behind my eyes.

My orgasm was a second from tearing through me when he stopped and rose to his feet.

"*Julian!*" I cried loud enough for at least someone to hear outside, but he only gave a dark laugh.

Freeing my wrists, he spun me around and hoisted me up onto the edge of his desk, right in front of his chair. Taking a seat, he spread my legs wide, draping them over his shoulders before leaning in and licking the full length of my sex.

"Oh my *God*."

That was all it took to launch my senses right back to where he'd left me. Jerking his own cock, Julian furiously sucked on my clit till I was grasping his hair and gasping his name. When my furious orgasm hit, I barely muffled my lips in time. I was delirious. My back arched taut as a surge of wetness rushed onto Julian's tongue, and my cheeks burned as I tried pushing his head away. But he refused to budge. His wicked mouth was greedy, sopping me up like I was his own personal supply of honey.

"Oh my God, Julian..."

"Fuck, I'm going to come."

His words were harsh, tight, and they filled me with an unfamiliar sense of urgency. Before I knew it, I was back on my knees in front of him, my mouth wrapping around his cock and giving two wet pulls before his liquid heat flooded my tongue.

"Fuck, Sara," Julian groaned, staring down at me. He watched me bring him to a true finish, cleaning him off with my mouth and then tucking his still-hard cock back into his boxers. "Jesus fucking Christ, you're so sexy," he growled, releasing his handful of my hair. "Get the fuck up here."

He pulled me up onto his lap and for the last sixty seconds we had, he kissed gently along my neck while stroking my thighs. And just like the last time, it felt a little too dangerously good.

14

JULIAN

I t was my turn to be late for once.

I kept the Roths waiting on the roof as I sat in the back of my car, parked directly in front of the hotel's side entrance. My stare was trained out the window, giving only occasional glances at Turner's asinine texts.

> **TURNER:** 6:02 *Hoult. Are you shittin me??*
> **TURNER:** *For your tardiness you will be drinking copious amounts of tequila with me tonight.*
> **TURNER:** *Same goes for that little assistant of yours*
> **TURNER:** *Might have to do body shots with her*

The last one came in just as I spotted that long dark hair down the block.

I tensed as I sat forward. I hadn't seen Sara since she'd milked every drop of cum from my cock this morning, and I was practically fucking dizzy looking at her now. She was wrapped in a light brown dress that didn't show so much as a hint of cleavage, but it was form-fitting with a hem that skimmed several inches above mid-thigh. It made me want to lick those fucking legs from ankle to pussy.

Christ.

I wasn't entirely sure how I was already missing the taste of her skin on my lips. I'd gotten more than my fair share of satisfaction this morning, but seeing her now, I was back to square fucking one.

"Hey." Her greeting was breathy, half-surprised when she saw me. "I thought you'd be upstairs already. It's past six."

"Yes. Turner has kept me painfully aware of the time," I said, walking slightly behind her as we entered the hotel. "He's early again."

"Shocking, actually. And you're late."

"I preferred to wait for you to go in."

"Mm. Didn't think I could handle being alone with those two?"

"No, I didn't want those two to see the way I looked at you tonight. I needed some time to react alone first."

"Oh."

That certainly shut her smart mouth. My lips twitched with amusement as we entered the hotel through the lesser-known side entrance, our eyes finding each other as we waited for the elevator we'd met in.

"So have you fully reacted yet?" Sara teased. I smirked as, on cue, the elevator arrived.

"Almost," I replied as we stepped in.

The moment the doors closed, my hands were on her.

She moaned as I palmed her pussy under her skirt, sucking her lip into my mouth.

I tortured myself as I groped up her body and felt no bra under her dress.

Every little breath of hers went straight to my balls. Every little whimper sent my blood fucking rushing.

But just as quickly as we'd started we stopped, standing apart as a couple entered on the tenth floor. They rode with us up to the roof, stepping off before us and giving me a chance to rub my hand over Sara's ass before we were promptly greeted and taken to meet the Roths.

SARA

THERE WASN'T SO MUCH as an umbrella to provide shade for us at our table, and every time I fanned myself, Turner stopped what he was saying to watch me.

"I've got a surprise for you. Don't you worry," he grinned every time.

I had no idea what he meant. In fact, Carter looked as confused as Julian and I did. But I didn't ask questions. A part of me hoped that whatever the surprise was, Turner would forget after enough margaritas.

He was on his fourth, Carter on his third.

Julian and I were on our second – technically. Turner insisted, but while he and I spoke after he ordered, I spotted Julian's quick exchange with the waitress from my peripherals. And with that, we were served virgin drinks anytime Turner ordered.

"I'm sorry," Julian had whispered to me. "I'm not drinking tequila with these guys. We'll get actual drinks when this is over."

I did my best not to grin over the invitation for a private night out. Carter had already caught a flirtatious look I'd given Julian at the start of the meeting. After, he'd kept his stare pinned on me till I looked at him, as if forcing me to acknowledge what he'd just seen.

"Obviously, we're going to need more than a few rooms when we go out there," Turner said, still on the topic of what kind of suites Julian would offer him for the trip out to the resort in Biarritz. "It's not gonna be just me and Carter out there. I've got my business advisors, financial consultants, lawyers." He lifted his eyebrows at Julian as if waiting for him to be impressed, or daunted maybe. Of course, he was neither.

He looked calm, collected, far too dashing in classic Persol shades and a white linen shirt with the sleeves rolled up. He looked to me like he should be driving some shiny wooden speedboat in Lake Como, not dealing with Turner Roth's insufferable drunkenness.

"I look forward to meeting your advisors," Julian said evenly.

"You should. They're smart men. I'm bringing the whole fuckin' team, and they sure as shit ain't gonna share rooms."

"It's high season, but once you agree on an actual date, I'll be sure to call the resort to arrange for the proper amount of suites," Julian said.

"Yeah... I'm bringing a bunch of old fucks who sleep at like, ten, so their rooms actually matter," Turner snorted, draping an arm over the glass railing of the balcony. We were twenty floors above ground, but with a flick, he tossed his garnish over the side of the roof. "The four of us though... I hope you know we're going to have some late nights in Biarritz."

"And why is that?" Julian asked.

"Well, I haven't been out there in years, and you two are the experts. You gotta show me where the gems are. I gotta feel like I wanna take my business to that town, you know what I mean?"

"That just sounds like an excuse for you to get shitfaced instead of work," Julian said.

My jaw fell open. A brief silence followed, and I looked up from my drink to see Julian and Turner smiling at each other despite the palpable tension at the table.

"What can I say? You know me by now, Hoult. I work hard, and I play hard."

Julian's laugh was genuine, and I knew it was because he found only the latter half of Turner's claim to be true. He played hard, and he played hard. Even I knew that at this point.

"Well, regardless, I'll at least have your advisors on board at that point. That'll guarantee me at least a couple sober minds to talk to."

"Yeah, maybe you can all talk shop and sleep at ten while I take Sara out for drinks. How about that?" Turner asked, his glassy eyes unblinking at Julian.

"How about we get back on topic?" Julian suggested, his mouth still curved slightly up despite his voice sounding as brittle as ice. Even Carter flashed me a *what just happened* look over the exchange.

I had no idea, and Julian wasn't giving me any directions, so feeling slightly awkward, I excused myself.

In the bathroom, I used a paper towel to dab at the beads of sweat forming on my hairline. I was dying to put my hair up, but I'd left my only racer back bra with Julian, and I had no intention of giving the Roths *that* much of a show. Besides, the biggest battle was almost over. Turner and Carter had agreed on the trip to the Biarritz resort, and once we got out there, their advisors would more than likely tell them the purchase was a no-brainer, and this would all be over. We'd probably complete the trip within the next few weeks, and then negotiations would take place for some time after.

Well before the end of the summer, this would all be done.

Holding my hair off the back of my neck, I stared at myself in the mirror.

I didn't want to admit to myself that I already feared this being over. But that was a difficult truth to suppress considering anytime I so much as looked in the mirror lately, I saw the body Julian couldn't keep his hands off of. I imagined the heat of his broad chest behind me, his lips on my neck and his palms smoothing down my hips.

He was the one responsible for whatever reawakening I'd had since quitting my job, and now I was screwed. Now, I couldn't imagine wanting anyone else. I'd seen plenty of good-looking men since meeting Julian - at the gala, at Hoult Tower. They were all polished, handsome and put together. Technically, Turner and Carter were handsome. But Julian's allure had completely spoiled me to the point that I found myself almost annoyed by how little my favorite actors and TV stars did for me at this point.

He really had ruined my taste and ability to have a normal attraction for others. So what was I supposed to do with myself when he moved on from me? Become asexual? The thought made me feel grim.

But I couldn't afford to be grim.

I had to be strictly bright and engaging for the Roths, so with a splash of water to my face, I snapped myself out of it, or at least tried.

Of course when I returned to the table, I found Julian looking just as dark and somber as I had a second ago.

"What's going on?" I asked, feeling wary when I noticed Turner's big, shit-eating grin.

"Oh, I was just telling Julian that before we set a date for the trip, we gotta make sure of one thing."

I cocked my head. "What's that?"

Turner wiggled his eyebrows.

"We gotta make sure you know how to surf."

15

SARA

Lights beamed up from the bottom of the indoor pool on the twelfth floor. There was a blue tint to the long stretch of a room, and the tranquil reflection of water glittered on the stone walls, making them look as if they were slow dancing. Luxuriously white chaise lounges lined the edges of the pool, flickering candles centered on the low tables beside them.

It was all for us.

But as beautiful as it was, Julian and I were stiff and silent as Turner, drunk and swaying, led us into the space.

Floating ominously in the middle of the water was a surfboard – bright white with my name painted in pink cursive over the top. He'd spelled it "Sarah" with an *h*, but I said nothing. I wasn't pleased about what he wanted me to do, and neither at all was Julian, but I couldn't let it show.

Not with Turner holding the entire trip over our heads.

"Couldn't possibly commit to a date for the trip till I knew Sara had the basics down," he said, seeming to enjoy whatever disbelief had struck both Julian and my face. "Besides, you can't possibly say no when I went to such great lengths to make this a nice night. Right?"

He didn't actually wait or care for an answer. From roasting us like pigs on the roof to providing swimsuits, since he knew we wouldn't bring our own, it was clear Turner had long planned to get me in the pool and to get Julian to play the game his way for once. The moment he stepped away to say hi to the girls Carter brought in, Julian turned his back on him to face me.

"He's trying to see how much he can get me to do for free before committing to the trip," he said. Both his expression and his voice were neutral, but his eyes were livid. The pool water glimmered in his intense stare. "And, obviously, he wants to see you in a swimsuit."

"I figured as much," I said under my breath as I held the bag of bikinis Turner gave me. It felt as if I was his puppet tonight, but for fear of getting Julian more worked up than he was, I played it down. "It's not a big deal, Julian. We'll take a swim, we'll pretend to party for him, and then we'll set a date for the trip. If humoring Turner gets us to Biarritz and connects you with his advisors, it's worth it. At least then you won't have to deal with trying to talk to him or Carter about business they clearly don't know how to discuss."

Julian eyed me. For the first time since meeting the Roths tonight, I detected a real smile on his lips.

"What?" I whispered, the hard *t* sound bouncing off the walls of the quiet room. Julian dropped his voice.

"That was oddly arousing."

"What was?"

"You taking control. I can only imagine how good you look on top."

I smiled despite my blushing. "We can find out tonight. That is, if you're interested."

"I think you know at this point that I'm interested, Sara," Julian murmured, his eyes scintillating. "Whether I want to be or not."

My smile wavered. "You had to add that last part?"

"Why shouldn't I?"

"I don't know. Because it hurt," I said truthfully.

"You know what it's like to have rules," Julian said, unapologetic. "You should know how it feels to break them."

"It's felt nothing but good for me so far," I murmured as I saw Turner coming back. "But I take it you regret what's happened between us."

He had exactly two seconds to respond, but he didn't use them. And soon enough, Turner came back to ask what we were doing. From there, we went in opposite directions to change in the locker rooms.

~

NOT A SINGLE DROP of water sounded in the stone and marble locker room.

It was completely still and quiet, and somehow even quieter as I stood alone by the empty glass and marble showers, staring numbly into the mirror.

I noted vaguely that I actually liked this simple black bikini, but despite my eyes on my reflection, I wasn't really looking at myself anymore. I had finished changing five, maybe ten minutes ago, but I didn't move. I was daring someone to come in here and get me. If not, maybe I'd stay here forever. I needed to reflect, anyway. To understand how I'd even gotten to this point.

Gathering my dark hair over my shoulder, I moved my eyes across my reflection, trying to recognize even a part of myself. No dice. My familiarity with myself had faded completely since the last time I'd been here less than three weeks ago.

Eighteen days, to be exact.

Eighteen days ago, in this hotel, I'd met Julian Hoult. That never sounded like much time to me before. Back when I had deadlines, assignments piled on top of assignments, eighteen days was nothing. But since the day I quit, that amount of time had somehow become an eternity.

It was enough to break me out of the box I'd spent years building around myself, and it was enough to hook me on a brand new addiction. Gone was my dependency on working day and night, on finding my worth in the thrill of *just* making it every time

– *just* meeting the deadline and somehow staying alive in the process

Replacing it now was my need for a man I tried to remind myself I didn't know.

I knew his name. I knew what he did for a living. I knew that he made me realize the full capacity of what my mind and body could feel.

But beyond that, I knew nothing. I didn't know where he lived, how he lived, how or if he spent his nights at home. Ninety-nine percent of the time, I didn't know what he thought, what he was capable of, and if one morning I'd walk into the office to find his wall up again.

I didn't know any of that, so why was I risking these feelings for him? Why was I wasting my hurt on the fact that he regretted sleeping with me?

I stared at myself.

I really wished I didn't ask myself these questions, because I knew every answer. It just took awhile to realize sometimes, since I'd just tricked myself for so long into believing I was a normal woman, not a girl hiding something ugly and embarrassing.

"You are so, *so* bad..."

I heard one of Carter's girls lilting outside. The other one laughed over something or another, her shrill pitch bouncing off the walls. The sound woke me up enough to remind me of the way their big eyes had followed Julian the moment they entered the room with their fruity cocktails, wearing those little bikinis. They stayed smartly draped all over Carter, but after one glance at my boss, their eyes kept coming back.

I imagined them crawling all over him now, straddling him on the chaise lounge as he sat back and watched pool water drip from the ends of their hair onto his chest. I imagined that faint grin I sometimes fantasized that he reserved just for me.

Fuck, Sara, I cursed myself as I finally started out of the locker room.

I wanted to confirm that those girls were or weren't all over him, which I hated about myself. I kept trying to care less. I kept pretending I was only here for the job.

And time after time, I failed.

"There she is."

It was Turner who announced me, his watery, red eyes lighting up with my entrance. But to my relief, the girl in the blue bikini whispered something in his ear to draw his attention back to her. Her blonder friend was sitting on Carter's lap, and it was probably her flag-printed bikini, but suddenly I was picturing the normal, all-American high school and college years that brought them here. In my mind, they'd never struggled to fit in. They were the picture of the kids in the movies who threw toga parties and played beer pong with red Solo cups. I was so attached to those images as a kid that thinking of them now, at twenty-seven, made me feel as if I were regressing.

Thank God for the energy that suddenly grabbed hold of me, pulling my eyes away from them, and from the mouth of the dark, vicious spiral. It was a life-saving distraction, and I knew from the strength of it that it was Julian.

Sliding my stare across the glow of the pool, my eyes met his just as he walked out of the men's locker room.

Shirtless.

The view struck me so hard it stung, and yet my feet brought me immediately closer. *Masochist.*

I could hardly breathe already, my eyes stealing the oxygen from my lungs to fully take Julian in. His body was ripped but lean, every cut on his chest and abs carved to boast perfect symmetry and definition. As if he didn't look irresistible enough, the water reflected off his skin, flickering like tiny crystals on his face and his body.

I was numb before. Now my fingers twitched to life at my sides.

I wanted to touch him. I felt like I needed to. It wasn't fair that my first look at him like this had to come in front of the Roths. I wanted free rein to do whatever I wanted to Julian, and his tight, intense stare on me told me that perhaps he felt the same.

As if suddenly aware of how much time we didn't have, our eyes began traveling fast over each other's body. I felt his gaze move down my front as my own skimmed the width of his shoulders, traveling down his rock-like triceps to his forearms, till I was following those beautifully slanted lines of his hipbones. I traced the outline of his cock straining against his black swimsuit, and when I returned my eyes to his, I knew I'd been caught in the act.

His head was tilted slightly up now, his gaze heavy but wearing a delectable smirk as it watched me.

It remained on me even as Turner came up behind me and led me into the pool. His girl in the blue bikini gladly skipped over to Julian, but I didn't flinch as I descended the tile steps into the water.

I had Julian's stare locked so tight on me she backed up for a second.

Without saying a word, our connection was magnetic enough for her to take pause. I knew we should dial it back, especially as Turner helped me onto the surfboard, but he seemed too drunk to notice, and Carter was too preoccupied to look.

"You look good in this swimsuit," Turner murmured as I lay on my stomach.

His eyes were on my breasts pressed up against the board. He brought my hands out from under my chin, wrapping his hand lightly around my arm as he brought it into the water. Julian's stare burned into me from the surface of the pool as Turner then murmured close to my ear.

"Riding isn't the hard part," he said, his blonde hair dark now that it was wet. "Paddling out then popping up – that's half the battle."

I attempted the paddling on my stomach. I gave an earnest try at popping up on the board. I did okay, but I wasn't really paying attention to myself.

Despite engaging with Turner, it felt like my attention had never truly left Julian since leaving the locker room. His had certainly not left me. In fact, his focus had only strengthened, refusing now to even acknowledge the girl. They had been talking before. He'd answered her questions politely.

Now, as he watched me dripping wet on the board, he either couldn't hear her anymore, or he no longer cared to.

I hardly processed Turner's hand touching the back of my thighs as he reached across my body. Gripping the edges of the board, he showed me how to sink its pointed tip into the water – to swim under the "waves" we pretended were there. I even a mustered a laugh for him after I tried my first one and got way too much water in my eyes.

Outwardly, I looked like I was enjoying Turner's lesson.

But in reality, I was so far from being there with him it was crazy.

I was still locked in sync with Julian. I didn't know how, considering I was in the water and he was dry on the ground, but we'd just spent the past ten minutes in silent conversation. I knew what he was saying. He'd said it to me before.

I've got you.

Turner had his hands on my shoulders, my arms, my back. But Julian had his eye on me, his instincts sharpened and primed for the second Turner crossed the line.

To my surprise, he didn't.

For the next twenty minutes, Turner switched between giving me tips and telling me stories about his worst wipeouts. I laughed and listened genuinely at his recount of the time he nearly passed out over a shark sighting in Hawaii. But as it turned out, it wasn't so much a shark as a dolphin who, according to him, "was trying to fuck with him."

"Dolphins are smart," I pointed out.

"And a little shitty sometimes," Turner said. "He was circling me like he knew that's what sharks do in the movies. Then right when I was gonna have a heart attack, he popped up with this big smile, like '*psych,* got you, bitch.'"

I cracked up. Straddling my board, I looked up at Julian, half-expecting to see him looking stiff or displeased.

He was neither.

His elbows rested on his knees, his fingers interlocked and his expression neutral till I caught his eye. Then he smiled. It was easy, content and it filled me with a calm till Turner spoke again.

"What are these?"

He tightly held my wrists with my palm facing up. I yanked my arm back before even looking at him.

"Whoa." We'd had a few good minutes, but that shit-eating grin returned to his lips as he looked up from my scars. "Sore spot, eh?"

"That's incredibly rude, Turner," I said, feeling as if I were speaking to a child. He reacted like one.

"What, are you embarrassed now?" he grinned. "Don't be. Nothing wrong with having a bit of a dark side. Lord knows I do."

My stomach turned, and the blood drained from my face as Turner dropped his voice to say something else, but just as he started, he was interrupted.

"Roth."

We both looked up at the same time to see Julian standing at the edge of the pool. Turner grinned like a kid who'd just gotten busted by his father.

"We're done here, correct?" Julian said, holding his hand out to me. I went to him fast.

"She did great. Can't fucking wait for Biarritz," Turner replied. I knew his eyes fell to my ass as I hoisted myself out of the pool, because Julian shot him a look that sent a chill down my spine.

"Perfect. Have your assistants email Colin or me in the morning."

"You got it. Hey, Sara."

I turned around to see Turner looking at me, his head starting to bob the way it did before a drunken night turned into a blackout.

"What's the 'F' stand for?" he asked.

I felt Julian pull me slightly closer. I knew he didn't understand the question, but somehow he knew it shook me. My hands were shaking, and whatever face I was making, Turner looked thoroughly satisfied.

"Goodnight, Turner," I finally. "Drink lots of water tonight."

He responded with a big laugh.

"Ain't my first rodeo, love."

∾

I SAT on the stone sink in the locker room, my back facing the mirror.

I was still able to hear the Roths and the girls outside, laughing and splashing in the pool. Either more girls had joined, or the same ones were getting drunker and louder. Their sounds weren't particularly pleasant, but I concentrated on them to distract myself from the pit of dread building in my stomach.

My heart was pounding, and I was paranoid that each breath I sucked in was getting shorter. But I knew what this was, so I tried talking myself down from it.

You're not dying.

You're okay.

Just breathe.

I needed this to fade fast, because I had no doubt Julian would somehow find his way in here soon. I didn't know how he would get in without attracting attention – I just knew he was perfectly capable of doing so.

More importantly, I knew he wanted to.

I felt it in our wordless conversation outside, and in the hesitation he had to let me go before I stalked off to the change in the locker room.

Not that I had started changing.

My hair was almost dry at this point, and my swimsuit as well. But I still sat there mentally walking the tight rope between normal and spiral. I hadn't chosen a side yet by the time Julian's low voice sounded before me.

"What did Turner say to you?"

I had heard his footsteps, so I knew his voice was coming. Still, it made my heart thump.

"Not much, actually." My whisper was shaky in a way that drew him immediately close.

"What's going on? Are you okay?"

I paced my breathing as I stared ahead at the buttons of his shirt. He was changed again, looking as if we'd never taken that pointless intermission. I closed my eyes as I let him tip my face up toward his. When I opened them, my body tensed.

He was looking at me differently than I'd ever seen.

Instead of looking knowing and at ease, like he could see under my clothes, even my skin, Julian's gaze was exposed as he watched me now. I'd seen it when he helped me out of the pool. I thought it was just the reflection of water then, but now I knew I saw some glint of emotion. I wasn't sure what kind, but it was there. It filled my lungs with air and snatched my breath away at the same time.

Not the best time for that sensation.

"I can't..." I closed my eyes again to phrase this properly. From what I learned, blurting *I can't breathe* around people not well-versed with my situation was anything from startling to fucking terrifying, so I looked for better words. "I need a minute." My words sounded like a small car driving over speed bumps. Pressing his lips into a line, Julian tipped my chin up again.

"You're having a panic attack."

"I know."

"If you've had them before, then you know everything is going to be fine. Just breathe," he murmured, eyeing my fingers on the edge of the counter. I was wiggling them to shake out the numbness, not that that ever helped. "Do you know what triggers these?"

"Lots of things. Haven't had one in a long time."

"What does it feel like right now?"

"Can't breathe. Heart's beating fast. Feels like I could die." I tried to laugh off the last part, but it was hard. "I know it sounds like I'm being a drama queen. When I say that. I just – "

"I'm informed on panic attacks. I know you're not being dramatic, " Julian said sternly as he reached behind me to turn on the faucet. "Stand up and turn around."

"What?" The look I gave him made him crack a smile.

"I'm not about to fuck you in the middle of your panic attack, Sara, so don't look at me like that. I want you to run your wrists under the cold water and see if that helps."

I shut up and did as I was told. I winced and closed my eyes. I could hardly tell if the water was ice cold or burning hot, but to my surprise, it had me breathing again within five minutes.

It also had Julian's gaze on my scars for about three seconds, but he said nothing, and the silence continued as I finally started moving, grabbing the dress I had worn before Turner insisted on the pool.

It felt far too quiet as I changed out of my bikini in front of Julian.

"You've seen everything already," I said softly as he stood in front of me, his stare directed pointedly elsewhere.

"I'm not interested in getting hard right now, Sara."

I didn't question it. I had other things to ask about – namely his trick. I'd gone through dozens of approaches over the years, but Julian's ice water trick had been by far the fastest in quelling my panic attack.

"Do you get them too?" I asked.

"What?"

"Panic attacks."

He looked at me. "No." His eyes traveled over my braless chest as I pulled my dress back on.

"Where'd you learn that trick?" I asked. I ran my hands through my hair but they slowed as I watched Julian's expression darken. He turned to me, assessing my fully dressed body before nodding toward the door.

"Let's get you home before Turner realizes we're still here," he said.

And that was that.

16

JULIAN

"How is everything so far, gentlemen?"

I didn't glance up from my phone to answer the waitress. Lukas and Emmett had it covered, and I was vaguely annoyed that she'd just asked the same question thrice in ten minutes. It wasn't an uncommon occurrence when the three of us went out for lunch, but that didn't make it any more tolerable for me.

I was also particularly on edge thanks to both the content of my texts, and the topic of conversation Lukas and Emmett had been on for far too long now. I could understand up to six minutes on the subject of home décor, but not a second more. It was a miracle that Lukas even had Emmett engaged in stories about furnishing his new home in the Hamptons with Lia. Then again, he was talking about throwing a party in it, so that offered at least some explanation.

"We should be done with everything around Lia's birthday," Lukas said. "So it can be a birthday-housewarming combo party."

"Christ, you sound like you drive a mini van and shit on the refs at your kids' Little League games."

"That's actually the goal at some point, minus the ref abuse," Lukas smirked. "By the way, you should bring Sara to the party," he added, looking pleased with the look I directed at him.

"You should stop letting your girlfriend influence the things we talk about."

"That suggestion was actually all mine, though I won't deny that Lia's been rooting for you two to become some sort of thing. Which is strange, honestly, because she loves Sara, but you," he paused, "not so much."

"I would say the feeling is mutual, but I'd prefer you not throw a tantrum in public."

"Good call. Any decent man would defend his woman," Lukas said. "I'm sure you've been well acquainted with the feeling lately. Something tells me you don't particularly enjoy watching the Roths slobber all over Sara."

"You're not incorrect."

I didn't enjoy it, and I definitely didn't enjoy whatever the fuck had happened Monday night at the pool. It was still plaguing me, and once again, I was second-guessing whether Turner Roth was in fact worth the trouble.

Abandoning this project would have been a fair idea to consider three weeks ago, when I'd yet to make progress with them. Now, with a date set for our trip to Biarritz, and the purchase finally looking serious, it was an absurd notion. If someone had told me three weeks ago that I'd consider ceasing negotiations for the sake of anyone besides my family or myself, I'd have told that person to fuck himself.

But thanks to Monday, I was having doubts.

I'd screwed up that night.

I had made sure to keep my every sense trained tightly on Sara to guarantee intervention before Turner so much as irked her. But I'd failed in that regard. I let her fall into some dark place at the end of the evening, and days later I was still working on the rage I felt over it.

Rubbing my jaw, I set my phone aside, realizing my texts had become ineloquent since I started thinking about Sara.

"Who are you texting, anyway?" Emmett asked as Lukas excused himself to take a call.

"No one."

"Well, no one sure has you worked up," Emmett said, eyeing my phone when it lit with a new message. I removed it from the table, but it was too late, he'd seen. "You have got to be shitting me," he said, his entire body going slack with disbelief. I glared.

"Mind your own business, Emmett."

"How the fuck is this not my business?" he asked, losing all humor in his voice. "I thought you were putting an official end to that chapter in your life."

"Trust me, I am. Do you not see me trying to sell that resort?"

Emmett held onto his jaw as he shook his head and sneered. "You know, it's fucking crazy. You're a hard-ass ninety-nine-point-nine percent of the time, and then the other one percent – "

"Your math is off."

"Shut up. Listen to me. I don't ever give you shit, Julian. I'm as easy as they come. You know that," Emmett said earnestly. "So when I say that you need to cut that crazy person off, I fucking mean it. You don't owe anyone anything. Aside from your family – your *real* family – you shouldn't have to break your back for anyone."

I was silent for a moment as I suppressed the urge to lay into my little brother.

I wanted to tell him that he didn't possess anything resembling a shred of responsibility in his life, so he wouldn't understand. Save for his dog, he was a man of leisure living off minority interest in the Victorian Hotel, and a couple nightclubs in the city. He'd made some good early investments off my advice, and since, he'd held no real job, had no serious relationships, and generally coasted from day to day.

I wanted to say all that.

But then I remembered the fucking disaster I left him with eleven years ago, and the fact that he didn't actually coast by. He was stuck being everyone's rock while I was gone, and I'd be a complete piece of shit to indulge myself by dropping those low blows on him.

"Move past it," I simply said.

"How much money are you sending this time?"

"I said move past it."

Emmett blew out a harsh breath of air, but after rubbing his entire face several times, he inhaled, exhaled, and he was done.

I always regarded that like a fucking magic trick every time. How he managed to move on from things so quickly was beyond me, but I envied him for it.

"Fine, well now you owe me a couple minutes talking about Sara."

"I can't at all grasp why you're so interested in this topic."

"Well, I haven't seen you actually invested in a girl in a long fucking time, and the sooner you settle down and have kids, the sooner Mom stops bugging me about it." Emmett shoved a handful of fries in his mouth. "You gonna take her on a real date anytime soon?"

"Absolutely not."

"Why the fuck not?"

"I see her every day at work. What more do I need?"

Emmett choked on his food then stared like maybe I'd made a joke.

"Wait. Is that a serious question?" he asked. I didn't respond, so he jabbed his finger at me when Lukas returned and slid back into his seat. "He just said he'll never ask Sara out, because he already sees her at work every day."

Lukas burst out laughing. "Jesus. Yeah, that sounds about right."

I looked away from the table, the overbearing waitress suddenly looking like a good conversation partner to me. Unsurprisingly, she caught my eye and immediately flounced over.

"Is everything okay here?" she asked me.

"Yes, I'll just take the check, please," I said, prompting simultaneous groans from Emmett and Lukas. The waitress laughed with them as they informed her that I was no fun, and to put a few bottles of champagne on the bill before handing it to me. When she disappeared in a flurry of giggles, I returned my eyes to them. "You know, you're both fairly intolerable on a regular basis, but when your forces combine, it can really clear a room."

"You love us," Emmett said, chucking at me a French fry that I caught and tossed back.

"Enjoy the rest of your lunch, gentlemen," I said to their stupid, grinning faces.

After settling up the check, I made a sharp line for the exit. I'd almost escaped when Emmett caught up with me at the door.

"Hey."

"What?"

He laughed at my terseness.

"Listen, do me a favor, alright? Don't... text ol' Crazy Person back till after Sunday. Give yourself a break from that shit, and just enjoy the good things going on right now, like the fact that you got a date set for this trip, the hard part is over, *and* you may or may not have a girl you're interested in. Focus on just the good. For the next five days. That's all I ask of you."

I smirked. "So live like you, you mean."

"Yes. Why the fuck else do you think I'm always so happy?" Emmett asked, holding his arms out wide. "If I like something, man, I let myself have it – without stressing myself out about the possible consequences."

"That's incredibly reckless, I'm sure you know."

"Of course. That's why I'm not you. I'm not a fuckin' workaholic billionaire," Emmett laughed. "But since you already are, you might as well give yourself a couple days to actually chill and indulge in the things you want. I'm not telling you to take a whole week of sick days and bail on work, I'm just telling you to relax for once. Don't force yourself to put out all the little fires. Just let them burn for a bit," he said. "Till Sunday – how about that? Then after our big fat Father's Day brunch, you can go back to being ol' No Fun Julian."

"You really sold it with the last line."

Emmett grinned. "Right?"

I had to laugh. "See you Sunday."

"Just think about it!" he called after me as I stepped onto the sidewalk.

17

SARA

"What kind of assignment is this? You've had a thousand deadlines, Sara. You would still always text back," Mom pointed out.

The fact that I couldn't hear her moving around the house doing a million different things while on the phone was unnerving. My mother never ever stayed still, not even while watching TV. If she was actually sitting down to give this conversation her undivided attention that meant she was still on high alert.

She knew I was lying about something.

And I was. I'd yet to tell her about quitting June Magazine. I still couldn't bring myself to do it.

"It's... a very complicated assignment, Mama," I said, suppressing my sigh at my desk.

"Tell Robin you can't work any more Sundays. Tell her that will put less pressure on you, and you'll have more energy," Mom said, referring to my boss at June. My *ex*-boss, rather, and the woman who had smiled coldly and told me I'd amount to nothing on the day I quit. The sound of her name made my teeth clench.

"I'll talk to her about it," I said just as I saw Julian coming up the stairs from his lunch break. He had the jacket of his three-piece suit off, giving me a better than usual view of that tapered torso. Glancing down at his Rolex, he then looked up at me, wearing a slight frown that asked why I hadn't left for lunch yet. He knew I was starving, but I'd been stuck on a long conference call with Colin and the people at the resort before, so I wasn't able to leave.

Then once I was, my mother called.

"Listen, Ma – Robin's coming by, so I gotta get off the phone," I said hurriedly under my breath, but I knew Julian heard me because I caught the quizzical tilt of his head before he disappeared into his office. "Yeah. Okay. I promise I'll call you tonight to talk longer. Okay, will do – bye-bye."

I hung up and sat frozen with my hand still on the receiver, listening to the footsteps of Julian coming back outside, hands in his pockets as he stood in front of my desk. I lifted my eyes off his shiny belt buckle, trailing them slowly up the buttons of his fitted grey vest till I was smiling back at the teasing look he had on for me.

"I'm almost certain my name isn't Robin."

"Yes. It's not. It's just, um…" I cleared my throat. "The thing is that – "

"It's okay, you don't have to explain if you don't want to," he said earnestly despite his look of sheer amusement. "I only came out here to see if you wanted to join me for lunch."

My eyes fluttered. "I thought you just had lunch?"

"I spent it in poor company. I'd like to do it over."

"Oh." I took my hand off the receiver and sat straight. "Is this so we can discuss the Biarritz itinerary?" I asked.

"No. Remember, we'll be doing that with Colin at three in the conference room. I reminded you this morning."

"You did, I just – " *Wanted to see if this was a business lunch or a... lunch-lunch.* "Never mind," I gave him a smile and grabbed my purse. "Let's go eat."

CREAMY LEATHER CHAIRS and walnut tabletops graced the enormous dining room of the restaurant Julian chose for our power lunch. Upon sitting, I was unsurprised to find that like the maître d', the servers knew Julian by name. A little more surprising, however, was the fact that he remembered all of theirs.

"Do you come here often?" I asked once we finished ordering.

"Not as often as other places. Why do you ask?"

"You know everyone's names."

"I try to remember names once they've been given. It's only ever been helpful to me, especially when it comes to running a business."

I lifted my brows. "That makes sense. Is that the trick to owning the empire that you do at your age?"

"One of several," he smiled. "It also took a fair amount of sleepless nights and busting my ass. Nothing you don't know about though."

I grinned at the way he sat back and let his eyes settle on me. I wasn't sure what I had done or what I was doing to deserve the way he looked at me, but I didn't question it.

"Yes, of course, all your ass-busting led to where you are now, whereas mine was apparently all in vain," I said with a wince. "I don't know why I put so much time into that company when they treated me like shit."

Actually, I did know why, and I prayed to God Julian wouldn't press me for details on why I stayed. He didn't.

"I take it you don't want me to get you your job back there when our contract is finished."

"No, actually. I don't," I laughed, realizing that only just now.

"Are there any other magazines under Hoult Publishing that you'd like to work for?" he asked.

"Several," I answered so fast and vigorously it made him laugh. I blushed a bit. "Actually, one magazine in particular is the reason I even switched majors to journalism in college."

"Really?" He leaned forward with interest. "Which?"

"Una Magazine," I replied. "I think your company acquired it two or three years ago."

"Four."

I blinked. God, he never stopped being on top of it.

"Right. It's named after The Una, which was one of the first women's periodicals back in the day."

"The eighteen hundreds, correct?"

"Eighteen fifty-three," I said slowly, cocking my head at him. "You keep knowing more than I think you would."

"Thank you, I'm sure."

I laughed. "It's a compliment. But anyway, that's pretty much my dream magazine. It had a very significant impact on me during my most formative years, and if I could work for them and help change even one other girl's life then I'd be incredibly grateful."

Julian nodded as he studied me. We were briefly silent as a vested bus boy came by to refill our waters. When he was gone, Julian sat back.

"I'll be sure to find you a position there when we're done with the Roths."

I choked on nothing. "Really?"

"Did I not promise you that when you first agreed to work for me?"

"You did, I just…"

"Didn't believe me."

"I'm pretty sure I believed you, but I really didn't know you at all at the time, and I wasn't entirely sure anything coming out of your mouth was true."

The ends of his lips remained curved as his brows pulled together. "That angers me."

I bit my nervous grin. "It's not meant as a slight toward you, Julian. I just didn't know you at all back then. I still don't know that much about you now."

"What do you want to know?"

His intensity was briefly daunting as I searched myself for the answer. But I had too many.

"What don't I want to know is probably a more appropriate question," I replied with little shame, returning the crooked smile to his lips.

"Start small."

I inwardly rejoiced at the two-word invitation, but smoothing my napkin over my lap, I kept my poise.

"Okay." I leaned back to let two servers gracefully set down our first course. "You mentioned you have a brother. Tell me about him."

"Emmett? He's the one who barged in on us the night we met."

"You've mentioned that before," I teased. "And with deep irritation, might I add."

"He lives to irritate me deeply, so that would make sense," Julian said, quiet for a moment as he watched me take a bite of my Nantucket bluefin. "He's five years younger than me, and were it not for the fact that we share many of the same features, no one would believe we were related."

"Now I'm curious to see a picture," I said, smirking at the look Julian gave me. He held it even as he reached into his pocket for his phone.

"I don't have many pictures," he warned when he started scrolling. "This is about the best you're going to get," he said, handing his phone across the table. I took it carefully, cradling it in both hands as I looked down at the photo.

"Wow. Look at that smile," I said, beaming myself at the unbridled joy on both Julian and Emmett's faces. They did in fact have the same eyes and lips, even the same smile, but otherwise, they didn't look very similar. "You look so happy. When was this?"

"Last year, when the Empires won the American League pennant. First time since the eighties, and the first time in my era of ownership, so that was nice."

I glanced up to catch him smiling wide down at his phone in my hand. I looked back down fast so he'd feel free to keep grinning.

"And who's this?" I held the screen up and pointed at the white-haired woman he and his brother posed with. She couldn't be more than five feet tall, but she was holding and drinking from her own bottle of champagne. Julian's eyes crinkled adorably as he laughed.

Lord, I thought to myself, noting that I hadn't seen that particular laugh before.

"That's my grandma. Rosemarie Hoult," he answered with a glimmer of pride in both his voice and his eye. "She immigrated from Germany when she was eighteen, and the first thing she did when she arrived was go to a baseball game. She said it felt appropriately American."

"Sounds about right," I said, already charmed. "I'm going to assume it was an Empires game."

"Absolutely. She was hell-bent on learning every detail of the game, and her sisters were very much disinterested, so she went alone, and eventually, my grandfather spotted her. He was an usher, and the day she sat in his section – according to him – he decided he had to marry her."

"Oh God, that's too cute."

"It is." Julian crinkled his nose. *Another new one!* I thought with delight, mentally collecting all his new expressions this afternoon. "Needless to say, we grew up an Empires family."

"And now you own the team." I shook my head. "If that's not the happiest story I've ever heard, then I don't know what is."

His expression faltered slightly. "Yes, well, there's certainly a lot that happened in between, but ultimately, it's a happy story," he said, a bit less enthused than he was a second ago.

My expression fell as I watched all shreds of joy or excitement leave Julian's face. *Damn it, what did I say?* I lamented Julian's smile when it faded fully back to his neutral look. I touched my neck, wondering if I was pushing it to ask if something specific had happened in between to make this anything but the perfect American dream story. I touched my neck unsurely.

"Was there... something that – "

"Tell me about your family," Julian interrupted. The stern look on his face was my confirmation that he didn't want to delve further into the topic of the Hoults. He took a drink of water. "You told your mother my name was Robin." I was relieved by the teasing look in his eye. "If you'd like to explain that now, I'm all ears."

I grimaced as I took my own slow drink of water to stall.

"Robin was my last boss. I said her name because my mom...

doesn't know I quit June Magazine yet." I stared into my water as I wrung my hands in my lap. "She sees that place as my miracle job – prestigious, decent pay, full health benefits. So, I've been acting as if I still work there."

"Why can't you tell her you now work for Hoult Communications? I imagine that would sound even more prestigious."

"Well, because my contract with Hoult Communications ends within a few months, sir," I said, enjoying the way Julian so hated that word from my mouth. He lifted his gaze from my lips to my eyes and gave a smirk.

"I'm glad you're so pleased with yourself."

"Getting reactions out of you is fun."

"I hope you and Emmett never meet," he said before going back to our original topic. "Can you not tell your mom that after this contract is over, you'll be with Hoult Publishing?"

I let out a sigh. "Again, this is no slight to you, but I would rather not tell her anything like that until a contract has been signed, and everything is solid. She is absolutely paranoid and untrusting when it comes to me, and she leaves no stone unturned when questioning even minor changes in my life."

I could tell Julian was confused because while he frowned only slightly, he was quiet for several seconds. I knew he had to be wondering whether my mother was just paranoid by nature, or if I'd given her some reason to be this way. I braced myself for a question about it, but instead, he changed the subject.

"Una Magazine is based near Columbus Circle. Is that close to where you live?"

"No, but I can take the D train from Broadway-Lafayette. I live on Mulberry Street. I'm a downtown girl."

"I prefer downtown myself."

"Oh? Where do you live?"

"TriBeCa."

I rolled my eyes with a smile. "Of course. I'm sure you own *entire buildings* in TriBeCa."

"No. Just one. But I have others nearby in SoHo and DUMBO."

"I was just teasing you," I snorted. "But thank you for reminding me of the full extent of your wealth. Meanwhile, I'm just hoping I can afford to buy a five hundred-square-foot studio in this city before I turn thirty-five."

"Well, I hear Una Magazine compensates well, so you're in luck."

"Oh yeah?" I cocked an eyebrow. "What else do you hear about Una, since you know so very much?"

He answered without a hint of my playfulness.

"I know it's a women's magazine that deals specifically with mental health and trauma."

I coughed as my water promptly went down the wrong pipe.

Crap.

How the hell did I not realize what I'd revealed about myself before? The magazine I pined to work for was famous for being one of the first publications to talk frankly about women's struggles with things like depression and abuse. While it offered the usual content like fashion, social and world news, it was most famous for its monthly pieces that shone unabashed light on everything from post-partum depression to trauma from sexual abuse. It was an incredible magazine.

But it had just exposed me to Julian Hoult.

"Um." I thanked God for the waiters returning to exchange our plates for the second course. It gave me time to think of a response. Whether or not I used that time was a different story.

"Why did that particular magazine influence you so much?" Julian asked, giving me little time to recover.

Jesus Christ. Go for the jugular, why don't you? I held up my finger as I chewed on my food. He took a drink of water as he waited for my answer.

"Reasons," I finally said, enjoying his unamused look.

"I'm not sure that constitutes as an answer."

"Why isn't your purchase of the Empires a happy story?" I countered.

He sat back. "Touché. How's your paillard?"

"Very good." I cut a bite. "And your steak?"

"Excellent."

We exchanged little smiles to acknowledge our little standoff just now, and then without missing a beat, our conversation carried on smoothly.

From lunch, Julian left directly for a meeting in the Financial District, but he made sure to call me a car. When it arrived, he started off the sidewalk to help me with the door, but swiftly rounding the vehicle was the driver to hold it open for me.

Leaving Julian and me standing on the sidewalk, standing close and just looking at each other.

We wore the same little smiles we had after our little standoff before, but unlike that one, this one ended with a minor hitch.

"Okay, I guess I'll see you..." I trailed off as I watched him take a step closer to me. His hands hooked in his pockets, he tilted his head down at me, eyeing the way I nervously wet my lips. Then he gazed so directly into my eyes I felt heat in my face and pressure buckling my knees. "Okay, later. Bye."

I rushed into the car after my inexplicably awkward exit, and I wanted to yell, "*Shut up!*" out the window when I spotted Julian chuckling to himself on the sidewalk.

Jesus, Sara.

Sexually, the man had done everything to me thus far, but apparently, I couldn't hold it together for a non-corporate goodbye after lunch. Even the driver laughed as I shook my head in my hands and kicked my feet in the backseat, trying to get rid of the embarrassed tinglies all over my skin.

It took a good two minutes to overcome, but it started up again when a text buzzed in my phone.

> *JULIAN: Yes, I was going in for a kiss. You should let me next time. See you at 3.*

18

JULIAN

I was greeted by the low hum of efficiency when I got back to the office. I nodded in return of every murmured hello as I made my way up the stairs, going straight for the conference room to begin my meeting with Sara and Colin. I expected to see them both seated with their itineraries printed and ready to go.

Instead, I found Sara sitting alone.

I paused in the doorway, pleased with how headphones had her oblivious to my presence.

I took advantage of the moment, watching her as I shrugged my jacket off and adjusted my cufflinks. She was in deep concentration, still reading her itinerary as she pulled her hair up high in a ponytail. I smiled as two dark locks fluttered down to loosely frame her face.

I couldn't help enjoying how big those eyes got when they spotted me.

"Oh my God, Julian." She ripped her ear buds out and clasped a hand over her heart. "You scared me."

"I'm sorry."

"You don't sound it," she teased as I took my seat next to her. Her cheeks flushed as she looked at me looking at her. "What?"

"You didn't respond to my text," I said, taking full pleasure in the way she immediately started squirming.

"What was I supposed to say?" She was playfully defensive as she returned her eyes to the itinerary.

"You could have let me kiss you," I laughed. "I've done it before. In fact, I've put my mouth on just about every part of your body."

"Don't get me turned on right now. Colin should be here in ten," she said, sitting forward on her chair and marking something with her red pen.

"He should be here now. Why is he late?"

"Whoever he was meeting at the stadium wasn't there when he arrived, so he had to wait. He asked me to tell you, and he said he didn't call because he didn't want to disrupt your meeting."

"Fair enough. Are those extras you printed?" I asked, eyeing the pile of papers across the table.

"Yes. Want one?"

"Please."

I leaned back as Sara stood and reached across the wide surface of the table. I knew she'd peered back mid-reach – there was no way she couldn't feel the heat of my eyes on her backside – but I didn't look away.

"Are you peeking up my skirt, Mr. Hoult?"

"Yes," I replied as my phone rang. "Colin," I answered as I pulled Sara in front of me, running my hand slowly up and down her hips. "Yes, she told me McKinley wasn't there when you got to the stadium. It's fine," I said as I palmed the soft material stretched over Sara's curves.

Tilting my head, I lifted her skirt up to present myself with the view of that perfect ass of hers giving hell to a pair of skimpy lace panties. *Jesus fucking Christ.* They stretched thin over her round cheeks, begging to be ripped the fuck off.

"If he says he'll be there soon, just wait it out for him, Colin. You're already there," I continued on the phone, looking up to catch the dirty glimmer in Sara's eye. She had two hands on the table, her back arched and a smirk tossed over her shoulder. It spread into a wicked smile as I said, "I'll review the itinerary with Sara for now. We'll catch you up once you get back."

"Wow. You are such an understanding boss," Sara said wryly when I hung up.

"What can I say." Sliding my phone onto the desk, I eyed the door of the conference room. It was closed, not locked, but fuck it. I wasn't getting up at this point. "Do me a favor. Read me the time of our flight next week?"

"May I sit, or would you like me to stay like this?"

"Stay like this," I said as I flipped her skirt completely up to free my hands. "Now what time is our flight?" I eyed the schedule from behind her as I pulled her panties down her ass and her legs.

"Six-fifteen private charter from Teterboro," Sara replied, lifting her legs out of her panties without my instruction.

"Good girl," I murmured, pushing her panties into my pocket. "And what time do we arrive in Biarritz?"

Sara breathed hard as I spread her ass cheeks to see how wet her pussy was for me.

"We arrive..." I heard her paper crinkle in her hands. "Oh God, what are you doing?"

"I'm admiring how wet you are."

"I mean are you going to do more than that? Because I can't take the teasing."

"You can," I assured her teasingly. "And you will. Now tell me what time our flight arrives."

"Eight at night in Biarritz," Sara murmured fast, writhing against the table as I massaged her ass with one hand, using the other to undo my belt. The metal sound of my buckle was enough to make her moan.

"Not so loud," I grinned as I freed my dick from the tent it pitched, releasing my handful of Sara to reach into my pocket. I heard her whisper "*thank God*" after turning to confirm my teeth tearing open a condom. "Now tell me how much time we have in Biarritz before the Roths arrive."

"You and I will be arriving the night before the Roths, so I can get acquainted with the property. Colin will be arriving the next morning, the same time that Turner, Carter and their advisors touch down. Oh God, Julian..."

Fuck, I was enjoying this too much. I wanted to hear every sexy, tortured little sound Sara could make for me.

"Julian..." She pressed her thighs together as she waited impatiently for my instruction. I loved every fucking second of it. "Please. Tell me what now."

"Unbutton your shirt. Only enough to pull your bra down," I said as I brought my seat directly behind her, watching her arms hastily move to free her tits. When she was finished with my request, she braced herself with her hands back on the table.

"What now?"

I smoothed my hand over the rubber stretched tight over me. "I want you to sit on my cock."

Her thighs flexed at my command, and our eyes locked as she looked over her shoulder. I gripped the base of my dick as she positioned herself over the head. With my free hand, I cupped her ass, guiding her till she was exactly where she needed to be.

"Easy," I murmured, watching her slick pussy stretch perfectly for me as she lowered onto my shaft. "*Fuck.*"

The word ground out in two syllables. She was so damned tight. Tighter than I remembered. I groaned, tipping my head back for all of two seconds before I returned my attention to my incredible view. She was on her elbows now, her ponytail swaying in front of me as she inched further down toward my base.

"God, it doesn't stop," she moaned, tightening my balls. "Am I close?"

"Few inches left."

"Holy shit, I just felt you get so much harder," she whispered.

"Keep talking dirty like that."

"I'm not trying to."

"That's why I like it," I muttered, letting out a grunt once she sat all the way down on me, her body rigid as it struggled to take my size. "Breathe."

I circled my arms around her waist, clenching my jaw as I focused on not blowing my fucking load right away. It was impossible. She felt like heaven wrapped wet and tight around my cock, and every time I got a hold of myself, she made some breathy noise to put me right back in danger.

"God, you feel so fucking big," she practically whimpered. Jesus fuck, she was going to make me explode.

"Take it slow." I leaned into her back and kissed her shoulders. "Breathe for me."

"Breathing," she exhaled softly.

"Good girl. Sit all the way. Give me all your weight."

Sara whimpered but did as she was told, letting her body melt against me. She leaned all the way back on my chest, rolling her head onto my shoulder and making the sexiest little sounds as she started to move her hips around me.

"Oh... that feels nice," she started to giggle, putting a grin on my lips. "Oh God, that feels *really* nice."

"Good." I moved my hands up to her bare tits spilling out of her shirt. "Keep going." I rocked slowly into her as she rocked steadily back against me. "Keep riding me like that. Just like that. That feels so fucking good."

The sounds of the office faded back in my ears as we found a rhythm.

The phones ringing, the elevator chiming – every sound I heard on a daily basis got me hard as a fucking rock as Sara sat on my lap in the conference room, squeezing the edge of the table as she fucked me under her skirt. She felt incredible, her pussy gripping me, absolutely milking my cock as she bounced on it.

"Oh God, Julian. I'm going to be loud," Sara warned.

"Be loud," I muttered, sliding my hand up to her neck as her pussy clenched around me like a vise. A sharp moan escaped her lips. "Shit," I grinned.

"I warned you."

"I liked it." I dropped my hand to rub her clit.

She cried out sharply again, arcing her body so far back I caught the base of her ponytail and pulled her lips onto mine. My balls churned as I swept my tongue through her open mouth.

"Come on my cock, Sara. I can feel your pussy tightening around me," I growled, stroking furiously between her legs till I felt her sex pulsing rapidly around me.

I clamped a firm hand over her mouth when she came, her cries muffled against my palm as I gazed down at her full tits. They shook hard, those rosy nipples so tight they looked like candy.

The visual sent me over the edge.

"Come inside me, Julian."

Fuck it. Maybe that did.

A low groan tore from my throat as my orgasm slammed into me. The satisfaction continued to roll through my body as Sara kept swiveling gently around me, her eyes peering over her shoulder at me as she drew every drop of my cum out the way she fucking loved to do.

Jesus Christ, this woman was something.

We kept our eyes pinned on each other as we caught our breath. I couldn't stop staring at her if I tried, and just when I thought she couldn't get sexier, she reached across the table to grab the badly wrinkled itinerary.

"I had a question about who would be giving the tour on day two. Is it going to be the staff there or me?" she asked, her little smile acknowledging the fact that she was still sitting on my lap, and my dick was still throbbing inside her.

"It's going to be a bit of both, depending on how well acquainted we can get you with the resort in the time that we're there alone," I answered, barely able to keep a straight face.

But she kept the questions coming as my dick went soft inside her, my hands still playing gently with her tits as we reviewed the schedule. It was insanely hot, and I swore to God at that moment that I could marry this woman.

Unsurprisingly, I was ready to go again within ten minutes.

19

SARA

"Thank God it's finally perfect out." Lia slid her shades on as she tipped her head back, basking under the sun of the breezy mid-seventies weather.

Last week's heat wave was officially over with, making the twentieth-floor terrace lounge at Hoult Tower the new spot to have lunch. It was a gorgeous space with black rattan benches, white pillows and bright, leafy green plants serving as partitions for privacy. Thank God for that, because there was no guessing what might come out of Lia's mouth.

"Maybe your sex life with Julian controls the weather."

And there it was. I adjusted Julian's Persols on my face as I turned my head slowly to her.

"I hesitate to ask, but what in the fresh hell are you talking about?"

"How do you not see it?" she sassed. "The heat wave came when you guys were being cold and mean to each other. Now it's gone because you've been having nonstop sweaty office sex. And it's particularly cool out today because you guys... *really* went for it this morning, I mean damn."

She wasn't wrong about that, and I knew I'd regret telling her, but this morning's romp was way too good to be kept a secret.

"I think he learned that move from Lukas."

"Lia!" I jolted upright. "Ew!"

"What? I'm talking about the location, not the actual positions! But fine, fine, Lukas did not invent fucking in the bathroom," Lia conceded as I buried my face in my hands.

We'd had sex in the restroom of a ritzy steakhouse this morning, and I was getting wet just thinking about it now. I hadn't taken my eyes off of Julian once in that mirror. I'd had the pleasure of watching every second of him – the way his perfect jaw dropped when he first entered me to the way his gorgeous features pulled so tight as he burst to a finish inside me. It was our usual rushed, hot sex, but it also felt different because he'd kissed me deeply for a good two or three minutes after, ignoring the knocks on the door from all the poor people who had to use the bathroom.

"I need to get my fill before I go," he'd explained, grinning.

Thanks to our Biarritz trip on Monday, he was packed with meetings out of the office from eleven till six, so I didn't protest. I needed to get my fill too.

"I take it all the people in the office know by now?" Lia asked, shaking me out of my memory. "That you're sleeping with Julian?"

"I think if you say it any louder, Lia, they'll definitely know."

"I'm pretty sure it's not *my* volume that's giving you guys away," Lia sassed. "Did you not tell me you guys had a moaning contest in the conference room on Wednesday?"

"I'm almost certain I didn't phrase it that way."

"You're starting to talk like him," Lia gasped.

"I take that as a compliment," I replied.

"Oh God, you guys are gross. Your level of admiration for each other is almost self-congratulatory, because you're basically the same person."

I burst out laughing as I chucked a balled-up napkin at her.

"It's true!" Lia giggled. "But I secretly love that about you two. You both are *very* similar in great ways, and that's exactly why I called it in the first place that you'd make an awesome couple. Me. Lia. *I* said it," Lia jabbed her thumb at herself. "I actually made a bet about it, which reminds me that Lukas owes me twenty dollars."

"Lukas bet against me?" I feigned a gasp. "How rude."

"In all fairness, he bet against Julian's ability to feel things," Lia snorted. "That guy. I swear he never has girlfriends. He never even talks about flings or one-night stands, so we're not even fully sure that he has them. He's just so crazy about work."

"Yeah, well... we'll see if this thing between us lasts past work."

"What are you talking about?" Lia frowned.

I groaned as I sat up straight.

"I don't know, Lia, nor do I really want to get into it right now," I muttered, shaking the ice left in my coffee. "My contract lasts three months or however long the Roth negotiations take. After that, I have trouble imagining that Julian is going to think much about me if I'm not at his office and in front of his face every day."

"You don't know that."

"No, I don't know anything for sure, but I do know what the most realistic turnout would be," I said, keeping my voice casual to disguise how much my heart was twisting under my chest.

"And what would that be?" Lia asked, tipping her shades up.

I drew in a deep breath. "That even if Julian Hoult did feel some tiny fraction of a thing for me, he would probably be really good at forcing himself to forget it if he had to. I mean look at who he is, where he's gotten himself. I'm a workaholic, but he's a machine, and a month-long whirlwind isn't going to affect a machine. It's just going to bounce off of him because he's made of steel. That's what it takes to run an empire like his. Right?"

I looked over to find Lia quiet and hugging her knees to her chest, as if I'd just hurt *her* feelings.

"Jesus, girl," she said. "That's not the attitude."

I heaved a sigh and shrugged. "Sorry. I just want to be a big girl about it now, so it doesn't hurt me later."

"I get it," she said in a small voice. "You know I totally get that. I just..." She sucked in a deep breath and let it out. "I wouldn't have snagged Lukas without you pushing me and being the little trouble-maker you were," she smirked. "Sometimes I think about what might have slipped through my fingers if you didn't force me to woman up and just *go* for it with him. He's the best thing that's ever happened to me, and after all the shit you've been through, I just want the best thing to happen to you."

"Daw. Lia." I wiggled my lips to hide the fact that she'd just made me emotional. "I appreciate that," I said as she flashed me a pout that said "sorry," because she knew I didn't like getting mushy or weepy. I smiled. "But hey, have you ever considered that maybe *you're* the best thing that's ever happened to me?"

"Oh, I agree wholeheartedly I am," she said to make me laugh. "But I'm the best thing in a different category. There's a few. Social life, love life and career."

"Jesus, you have it all," I realized. "You dirty whore."

"Ha! Is this a bad time to say that Lukas is texting and wants us to leave now for the Hamptons?"

"No, it's not a bad time, because I'm thoroughly done talking to you," I joked, ruffling her hair as we got up from the benches. "Go furnish that beautiful beach house of yours, you domestic little thing."

"Are you sure you don't want to come with? I can tell Lukas to wait till five."

"Absolutely not. You'd hit rush hour. Also, I'd puke out the window within the first two minutes of watching you two googly eye each other."

"We do get pretty gross sometimes," Lia admitted with a snort. "Alright, woman. Then enjoy your Friday and the rest of your weekend *without* being a Negative Nancy, alright?" she said firmly, narrowing her eyes at me. "No overanalyzing things while I'm not here to talk it out with you. Just..." She held her hands out in some zen meditation pose. "Enjoy the now."

"I'll enjoy the now even more if you get out of here already."

"*Rude*. Hug me goodbye!" Lia demanded, which I of course did, throwing in a bunch of kisses on the cheek before sending her off.

AFTER A LONG DAY of conference calls with Colin and the people from the Biarritz resort, I was exhausted. It felt like the realest day of work I'd had thus far, and it didn't help that Julian was out at meetings since the morning. I didn't realize how much slower time passed without him around to occasionally glance at.

Or, of course, sneak office quickies with.

"Wow. Weather's gonna be nice this weekend," Colin said, looking at the forecast on his phone as we headed for the elevator. "Any plans?" he asked.

"Actually, no," I realized with a wince of disappointment.

"Aw man. Why not?"

I laughed. "Probably because I'm still not used to having weekends. I worked at least six days a week at my last job, and if I had Sundays off, it was strictly for decompressing," I said, silently marveling at how incredibly long ago that felt. "Also, now that I actually have some free time, my best friend is the one who's always busy. She and her boyfriend just bought a house out in the Hamptons, so they're always out there."

"Wow! Very nice," Colin remarked as we stepped in the elevator. "On the bright side, we get to go to sunny Biarritz, France on Monday."

"Yes! God, it came up so fast. I really can't wait. I haven't been out of the country in ages."

"Well, you'll love it there. And Julian's pretty cool about giving employees time to explore when they're on business trips."

"Yeah?" I smiled. "That's nice of him."

"Yeah, he's a great boss. Can't really beat working for him."

I nodded and went quiet.

It was an innocuous remark, but it was yet another reminder that at some point, I would no longer be working for Julian. And as ridiculous as it was to miss something before it was even gone, I was very much starting to do that.

"Alright, Sara, enjoy your weekend!" Colin waved goodbye when the elevator finally opened to the lobby.

"You too!" I called after him as he rushed out of the building, presumably to meet his roommates he mentioned having plans with.

Walking through the lobby, I listened to the thunderous clacking of what sounded like a thousand pairs of shoes on marble. It was the usual Friday dash, when tower employees controlled their urge to just race for the doors and start the weekend already. It made me naturally antsy to walk faster myself, despite the fact that I had gorgeous eighty-degree weather and absolutely nowhere to go.

Balls. I made a face to myself, realizing how bummed I actually was about this.

But when I emerged from the tower, my eyes were immediately drawn toward a gleaming black sedan parked directly in front of its doors.

For reasons I couldn't understand yet, a smile twitched onto my lips.

I had never in my life felt as if a car was watching me, but for some reason, I felt that now as I squinted at the tinted backseat windows. I didn't even realize my feet had gravitated across the sidewalk to the car till I was standing at its passenger door and watching the window roll down.

"Hi there," Julian greeted me from the far end of the backseat.

"Hi," I returned, unable to restrain my smile. He looked so sexy just sitting there with his jacket on but his tie off, and those blue eyes glinting at me with a hint of mischief. My heart skipped because I knew right away that he'd been waiting for me. I read his intentions from the first second I saw him. But for perhaps the sake of amusement, we went through the formality of small talk.

"How was your day?" Julian asked.

"Good," I said, the cool breeze blowing hair out of my face. "And how was yours, Mr. Hoult?"

"Good as well," Julian replied with a smirk.

"Glad to hear it," I nodded.

The same knowing grin curved our lips as I simply stood on the sidewalk, the two of us eyeing each other for another beat of silence before Julian laughed and said, "Do you have plans tonight?"

A smile burst onto my lips.

"Not at all," I replied as I heard the sound of him unlocking the doors.

"Good. Then get in."

20

I stood back on my heels as I enjoyed my view of Sara standing in the middle of the lot, turning slowly around and around in that blue skirt as she took everything in.

"Julian... I don't even know how to react to this right now," she murmured as she floated over to the Hellcat.

From the tower, we had taken the car to more cars – specifically the ones in my garage on Eleventh Avenue. The moment I'd flicked the lights on in the lot, Sara had been locked in a trance. The slow click of her heels echoed in the large space as she wandered in awe, mostly silent with her hands folded in front of her.

"You look like you're on your first field trip to the museum."

"Quiet. You realize this is amazing, right?"

"I do enjoy it." I slid my hands in my pockets as I made my way toward her. "I also enjoy how you've paid no attention to the cars thus far. They were more of what I had in mind when I asked you to pick our ride for tonight."

"But I want this," Sara whispered longingly, running her hands along the hand-stitched leather seat of what was in fact my favorite bike. "Why do we have to take a car? Look how beautiful this thing is."

"While you have impeccable taste, that's an F131 Hellcat Combat, and it has no passenger seat, so I promise you, we're not taking that," I said, giving a laugh as she promptly stalked off to find a different bike to admire.

"Hm. Something tells me you ride motorcycles for the express purpose of being alone," she observed dryly, and correctly, after passing three more with no passenger seat. "Uh-oh. Look what I found," she lilted as she made her way to my Norton Commando. A wicked curl touched her lips as she ran her fingertips along the passenger seat. "Looks like we have a winner."

"Sara. I'd prefer something with doors. And seat belts."

She flashed a teasing smile as she mounted the Norton in her skirt. Christ.

"Why? You ride these things," she pointed out.

"Yes. I do."

"Well, if you're not worried about your safety, then no need to worry about mine."

"We've established I have difficulty with this," I said, but I'd already lost her attention at this point. That curtain of dark hair fell over her shoulder as she tilted her head to look at something.

"Oh. Norton," she murmured with familiarity.

"You know it?"

"Not really. It's just my dad had a Norton belt growing up," she said, her voice lost in memory. "It had this logo and a little British flag."

"He had a bike?"

"Definitely not, but he *was* British. Still is, as far as I know."

I smirked as I watched her lean over and wrap her fingers around the handlebars.

"Not sure why I didn't expect your parents to be Brits."

"They're not. Just Dad. Mom is from a *tiny, tiny,* mountain village that Dad was photographing many years ago during his travels," she said wistfully, sounding as if she were reciting the way the story was told to her growing up. I smiled as I imagined Sara's big eyes on a mini version of herself.

"Was your dad a photographer?" I asked.

"Not at all," she laughed. "He was an eighteen-year-old gap year backpacker when he met my poor, unsuspecting mom. She says she didn't like him at all the first summer they met. He was loud and excitable and a little overwhelming. But despite how young he was, he said she was 'too pretty to just forget,' so he kept visiting her summer after summer till she started finding his quirks charming enough to move to London with him."

"That's some serious persistency."

"Yeah, my dad is... *whimsical*, as he likes to say. He's a lawyer who loves his colorful socks and chatting anyone's ear off. Says 'he's never met a stranger.' He's that guy."

"Mm. Yeah, I'm familiar with that guy."

"Oh, yeah," Sara giggled as she tried the foot pegs on the bike. "Meanwhile, my mom trusts no one in this world. Except him. You'll never see her admit it, because she's as ridiculously stoic as you are," Sara glanced at me with a grin, "but she still finds my dad to be so very charming and 'unbearably funny,' as she says. It's cute."

"Sounds like my parents," I smiled.

"Forever in love?"

"Yes."

Sara let out a breath. "That's the way to be."

"So I hear. You're in heels, by the way."

"What?"

"You're not exactly dressed to ride a motorcycle tonight."

She blinked, as if still processing the topic change.

"Oh. I have a change of shoes in my purse."

"Seriously?"

"Yes. Any girl in heels who's carrying a big purse has flats or sneakers in it. I guarantee you."

I eyed her. "Your pencil skirt doesn't lend well to mounting a bike."

"I've mounted you in this skirt."

I held in a groan. "Listen, everything you're doing on that bike right now is already going straight to my cock, so for the sake of getting to our plans on time, don't talk about mounting me," I said as she tipped her head forward and giggled. "Tell me why you're hell-bent on taking the bike tonight."

"Because you said you're choosing where we go, so I get to choose how we get there," Sara said simply. "And I choose this. Also, I've kind of been obsessed with motorcycles since high school," she grinned dreamily.

"Also unexpected."

"Yeah, well, I fantasized in *great* detail about escaping that place," she murmured distractedly. But I saw the way she blinked when she caught herself. I cocked my head.

"Escaping what place?"

She looked at me. "Save for speedboats, motorcycles are also the coolest form of getaway in heist movies," she said brightly, purposely ignoring my question. "So, a hundred percent, we're taking this bike. And if you're concerned about it being my first ride, it's not. So, done. It's decided."

I had to admire her determination.

"Fine. But you're wearing a helmet, and I'm going to teach you the proper way to mount and ride as a passenger. Most importantly, when I lean, you lean. Don't try to balance me by going the opposite way. Even if you feel like we're about to fall, which you will."

Sara narrowed her eyes at me.

"Are you trying to scare me out of this?" she questioned as I laughed.

"Somewhat. Last chance to back out."

"Never," she whispered dramatically.

"You don't even know where we're going," I smirked. She smiled as she cocked her head at me quizzically.

"What difference does that make?"

21

SARA

To answer my own question: a big one.

The location of our night made a big difference, because apparently, we were off to a place Emmett had recently invested in called Blue Harbor. It was a newly built restaurant and bar styled like a swanky living room, complete with enormous bay windows and an open deck facing the water. It was apparently becoming quite the hot spot this summer.

It was also located in the Hamptons, more than two hours away.

I was stunned when Julian dropped that on me, and very much intimidated. But I had also talked a pretty big game at the garage, so I refused to back down – and I was thankful for that once our ride started.

Because from the very first second Julian accelerated onto the highway, the exhilaration never stopped.

Eyes open or closed, it felt like I was flying.

It was such a cliché, but I really felt wild and free – by far the most alive I'd ever felt in my life. The never-ending rush of adrenaline was almost suffocating as I rode behind Julian, my arms wrapped around his strong torso and my palms soaking in every clench of his core when we leaned into a turn.

We were completely exposed to the elements as we zipped past cars and trucks and *eighteen-wheelers*, but any fear of the road had dispersed the moment I laid my chest against his back. I felt safe with him. Whatever unique, Julian-esque confidence emanated from him on a daily basis seeped into my skin as we sped through the open road, under the pinkish glow of the setting sun.

You're dreaming.

I kept telling myself that. I kept closing my eyes to process it all, but every time I opened them, the amazement hit me again. The deepening hues of the sunset hit me again, and the fact that I was leaving the city with Julian hit me hardest every time. With my chin on his shoulder and the wind in my face, I felt every bit like the luckiest girl in the world.

And considering the thrill of the ride, it was hard to believe that there was more than this planned.

The best was still yet to come.

THE SUN WAS ALMOST FULLY SET by the time we stopped at a gas station for a much-needed break. My ass was actually buzzing from the vibration of the seat, and I had to laugh at myself as I privately spanked some life back into it inside the bathroom.

> **LIA:** *Damn it woman why are your texts always so cryptic? You look very cute but where the heck are you?? Tell me!!*

I snorted at Lia's text. I had sent her a bathroom selfie as a belated thank you for the Daisy Dukes she'd dropped off at the office for me two weeks ago, during the heat wave. I had finally stuffed them into my purse to bring home after work today, and thank God for that, because riding a motorcycle in a pencil skirt would have sucked ass.

Also, the skirt just wouldn't have looked quite as cute with Julian's soft white tee.

I was wearing it on top, and as I smiled at my reflection in the mirror, I swore I could very well wear this outfit forever. It was cute and comfy, especially paired with my red Converses, but more than anything, it served as a reminder that today was real. An hour into the ride, and I still felt like I was in a dream. It felt like a scene from a movie I would've been obsessed with as a teen. Texting Lia was almost a figurative way of pinching myself, just to show myself that this was in fact real.

> *ME: What are you up to tonight?*
> *LIA: Emmett's up here so we're at dinner with him. Super*
> *gorgeous restaurant called Blue Harbor. I seriously*
> *can't wait to bring you. I wish you were here!!*
> *LIA: Where are youuuu*

I was all too amused with myself as I purposely ignored Lia's last text, slipping my phone in my pocket as I walked out into the convenience store, where I spotted two women in big sun hats and striped beach covers huddled over by the window.

Oh, yeah. Totally with you ladies, I laughed to myself when I realized they were staring out the window at Julian. Back at the garage, he had changed into a casual outfit as well – a white T-shirt, black leather jacket and dark grey jeans. It was the kind of casual look that I never imagined him wearing, but obviously, he wore the hell out of it.

He looked even better now with the last of the sunset hitting him as he waited for me outside, leaning against the side of the bike.

"Good Lord," I had to murmur with a little grin to myself. Was it weird to take a picture? Whatever. I did, and with the sound on, too. When a man looked *that* good, this kind of shamelessness was warranted.

"Oh, honey, is he yours?" one of the sun hat ladies asked me, looking my outfit up and down. "Oh, yes, you match *too* well not to be with him," she whistled.

"Yes, I guess he is mine today," I giggled, the door chiming as I pushed through to leave. Sun Hat Lady stopped me with a wagging finger.

"Ah, ah – just today? Oh, no, no, dear. That is not the attitude," she clucked, echoing the exact words Lia had said to me today on the terrace. She even shot me a *tsk tsk* look through the window as I walked back outside. But I caught her little smile and wink as I felt Julian's hand touch my waist.

"Hey." He hooked his fingers into my shorts to pull me close. I blushed when he cupped the backs of my thighs with his hands, his eyes on my lips for two seconds before he looked at me. "How does it feel?"

This day? In general? Being with you?

Oh, you know. Fucking perfect.

"You mean the ride?" I asked quietly, struck by how strangely intimate the moment felt. "It's good. Not bad at all."

"When else have you been on a motorcycle?"

I wet my lips, briefly hesitant to answer.

"With my best friend in college," I answered. I couldn't help the grimace. My heart beat fast when I thought about her, and it was never a gradual transition – it was just sudden, brutal pounding. "Should we get going?" I asked, eager to change the subject.

I could tell from the way Julian studied me that he wanted to ask another question, but to my relief, he handed me my helmet. With his head tilted over his shoulder, he watched with a grin as I mounted the bike.

"Good girl," he murmured as I wrapped my arms around him.

Then once again, we were off.

22

SARA

By the time we got to Emmett's restaurant, we were apparently too late to catch dinner. Fortunately, everyone was still there and gathered around the fire pit by the beach. I smiled when I quickly spotted Lia's silhouette, her hair piled on the top of her head and her arms wrapped around Lukas's neck as she sat in his lap.

"Ridiculous," I remarked as Julian and I walked toward them.

"I agree," he smirked, though it was a semi-hypocritical thing to say, given his hand gently massaging the back of my neck as we walked across the beach. I had mentioned feeling a little stiff from the ride, and since that mention, Julian had subconsciously had his hands all over me – rubbing my back, my shoulders, my neck. I was pretty sure he didn't even know he was doing it, considering his busy eyes scanning the restaurant for Lukas and Emmett.

But whether he did or not, I definitely wasn't complaining.

"Oh my *God!* I knew it!" Lia shrieked, bursting off Lukas's lap and bounding toward me when she spotted us. "Hi, hi, hi, hi, *hi!*" she squealed, slamming into me with a hug that sent me hurtling backwards into Julian. I heard him laugh as he caught me, giving my ass a quick squeeze before he put me back on my feet.

"Hey, crazy," I giggled, kissing Lia on the cheek. She ignored me to point a stern finger at Julian.

"You! You could've told Lukas you were bringing her so I had some warning!"

"I did tell Lukas," Julian replied.

Lia's face twitched with a second of confusion before she gasped and yelled, *Lukas!*"

I laughed as I watched her kick sand up while marching back to him to demand why he didn't share with her the good news. Julian exhaled as he ushered me with a hand on my back.

"It's hard to believe stories that she was ever anything resembling a calm or mild-mannered person."

I burst out laughing. "She really was pretty reserved for awhile."

"I can't imagine it."

"I swear," I smirked as I felt Julian's fingertips slip just under my shorts. "She's from a small, shitty town like me, and that place did a number on her for awhile, so I think when Lukas came around, that was the turning point."

"You're from a small, shitty town?" Julian turned to face me. "Where?"

I paused and blinked up at him, forgetting I'd even said that. My fingers smoothed over the sudden knot I felt in my throat, but I gathered myself quickly.

"You know, it's every bit like you to weed out anything I say about Lia, and just listen to the part about me."

"Yes. I don't like her. I like you. Is that surprising?"

I smacked him so hard on the chest he actually winced as he laughed.

"Don't you dare say you don't like my best friend, Julian. I mean it. Especially when I *know* you do like her as a human being. If you're Lukas's friend, you have to. It's not like she didn't do worlds of good for him, too."

"Fair."

"Say one nice thing about Lia."

"She has the good sense to associate with people like Lukas and yourself."

"That doesn't count!" I feigned anger, pushing away to walk ahead of Julian. But with two hands on my hips, he grabbed me back, and I grinned as I felt his lips in my hair.

"I like how you look when you get defensive of her," he said low in my ear.

"Still doesn't count," I huffed, though in reality, I was far from pissed. I was nothing but pleased with Julian's arms crossed around my body, my hands hanging on his forearms. My heart was beating fast over how good it felt to just melt back into his chest.

I was seconds from drifting off on a cloud when I heard a voice yell, "Oh shit! Look who it is!"

And suddenly, Julian was torn away from me, lost in a crowd of people eager to greet him.

There were more than half a dozen people around him, but I couldn't help noticing the woman in the long emerald dress with the sophisticated, trimmed-to-perfection pixie cut. I had first looked at her because I never failed to be in awe of women who pulled off that hairstyle. To me, it had strict prerequisite bone structure require-ments that very few people possessed. My mother was among them, but I was definitely not, so it never failed to pique my interest.

But then, of course, I started noticing Pixie Cut for different reasons.

Judging from the way she very gingerly rested her hand on Julian's shoulder, and very slowly kissed his cheek, she knew him. And judging from the way her eyes flicked from me back to him before she smirked and murmured something, she probably knew him as more than just a friend.

Oh.

Fuck.

I hadn't expected to deal with this – the situation or the emotions involved – and I wasn't prepared. For starters, I wasn't wearing a damned ball gown like Pixie was, nor was I dripping in gorgeously fine, expensive-looking jewelry like she was. The playing field wasn't exactly level, but at the same time, why did I feel it needed to be? I didn't own Julian. He'd never even called this a date. Realistically, it was – it had to be – but he hadn't introduced me to anyone yet.

Then again, a decently buzzed Emmett had quickly approached to introduce himself to me. He had a big, excited smile on his face as he said, in a strangely restrained voice, "Nice to meet you. Julian has spoken about you." He held his arms out defensively and cried, "*What?*" when Julian shot him a look across the fire pit. "What? I didn't say anything weird!"

I was thankful for Emmett, because I definitely needed that laugh. Also, the mere fact that he was standing near me was apparently good enough reason for Julian to come back, circle an arm around my waist and reclaim me.

"You guys have a nice introduction?" Julian asked with wary amusement, his glare engaged in some sort of silent conversation with Emmett's.

"We had a *perfectly normal* introduction, during which I revealed no more information than was necessary," Emmett grinned at Julian. He pointed his thumb at Julian when he turned to me. "Sometimes I talk like him so he'll understand what the hell I'm saying."

"I still don't understand him for shit," Julian laughed as he brought me away to the two empty seats beside Lukas and Lia.

Lia was wrapped up in a blanket now. It went up to the middle of her nose and made her giddy eyes peering at me look all the more cartoonish. To Julian's annoyance, she asked to switch seats with him for a bit so that she could be next to me. The fire flickered with mischief in her eyes as she sat down, dropped her legs in my lap and leaned into my ear.

"Oh my God, he's being so un-Julian right now," she whispered, putting a big grin on my face.

"He's definitely being... super cute."

"And that is definitely the first time 'cute' has ever been used to describe Julian Hoult. Pretty sure even when he was a baby, his mom called him 'handsome' and 'efficient.'"

I laughed hard enough to attract Julian and Lukas's attention for a second. Biting my lip, I exchanged a little grin with Julian before he went back to his conversation.

"Like *that*. That just now? You guys are acting like a couple or some shit," Lia hissed. "Sara, I swear to God, I am presently over- whelmed with the possibilities of our summer if you start dating Julian."

"Oh my God, will you cool it?" I laughed. "Can I take this a day at a time, please?"

"That's what normal people who practice caution say. You're not that person anymore. You just did two hours on the road as your first motorcycle ride ever."

"To be fair, I've ridden the back of a motorcycle around an empty parking lot before."

"Yeah. Totally comparable," Lia said just before she was pulled into Emmett's conversation. I was too busy exchanging eyes with Julian over Lia's seat to pay attention to the question being asked, so I was lost once I was roped in to give my answer on the topic.

"Sorry, what's happening?" I laughed sheepishly as Lia and Julian exchanged seats again. Emmett nodded toward the restaurant.

"I was just saying how I invested in this place because I did post- prom in Southampton after high school, and these assholes," he gestured around the fire pit, "are telling me post-prom in the Hamp- tons is ridiculous, so I wanna know what everyone did for theirs."

"Post-prom?" I repeated to buy time. I swallowed as I blinked at the flames whipping in the fire pit. "Um, in my town..." *Crap.* My throat felt suddenly so dry. "People went to party venues for the 'after prom party,' and it was adult supervised, but I know that they were able to still get away with bringing alcohol and stuff."

"You don't sound like you went to it," a bright, clear voice observed. I turned to the side to realize it belonged to Pixie. She wasn't being particularly rude, but I mentally cursed her for pointing that out.

"Yeah, I didn't go," I admitted.

"Why not?"

"Um." *Fuck.* The entire circle was staring at me now, and I was so shitty at lying. I could practically hear Lia's mind racing to figure out how to intervene, but she was coming up as short as I was. Damn it. I could lie swimmingly on a regular basis, if I was prepared to, but this question caught me completely by surprise. "I graduated high school a year early," I finally confessed to some impressed looks around the pit. It seemed to be enough explanation for most, but Pixie pressed on.

"So you were a little younger your senior year. That doesn't mean you're not allowed at prom," she said with sympathy in her voice. Whether it was real or not, I didn't know.

"Yeah, I just..." I trailed off, my heart beating too fast now for me to come up with my next thought.

"Emmett, why don't you tell everyone about the fire you started at your prom?" Julian said, causing even me to look promptly over at Emmett for an explanation.

"You started a *fire* at your prom, E?" some guy laughed.

"You're surprised?" Julian smirked.

"I for one am not," Lukas volunteered. "But I definitely need to hear the story now."

And just like that, crisis averted. I was certain no one remembered my lack of attendance at my own prom as Emmett explained exactly how he committed accidental arson at his. I breathed easy again, and I closed my eyes with content when I felt Julian's hand massaging the back of my neck again.

It would've been nice to open them without seeing Pixie staring hard at me.

"Lia, who is that woman?" I had to ask when Lia and I took our customary bathroom break for the sole purpose of asking these kinds of questions. "The one in the green who grilled me about my prom."

"I don't know, but trust me, I was asking Lukas the same question after she pulled that I'm-so-curious shit. Like, couldn't she see that you didn't want to talk about it? Jesus."

"What did Lukas say? Does he know who she is?" I asked.

"No." Lia flashed me an apologetic look. "I swear there's so much even he doesn't know about Julian, and he's by far the closest to Julian outside of family."

Dammit. It was crazy to think that, as much time as I'd spent with Julian of late, I hadn't remotely scratched his surface. If a friend as old as Lukas still didn't know a good chunk about him then I imagined there was no chance for me to get an answer if I somehow dared ask who Pixie was.

"So, Emmett's funny," I offered to lighten the mood.

"Yeah, he's crazy," Lia laughed. "And a party animal. Give him another few hours, he'll turn this kumbaya into a full-on rager."

"Oh God. Looking forward to it," I snorted before we decided it was finally time to go back outside.

"Oh, come on," Lia muttered when our feet hit the sand and our eyes spotted Pixie in my seat next to Julian. Lia peered at me. I must have looked upset because she brushed it off. "It's okay. No biggie. That's probably fair game when people leave their seats for the bathroom. It isn't war unless they refuse to get up."

Funny enough, Pixie refused to get up.

"Oh," she made a little face after I said excuse me. She nodded over her bare shoulder at her own empty chair five seats down. "Can we exchange for a bit? I just need to catch up with this man. It's been way, *way* too long," she said, turning flirty eyes to Julian toward the end of her sentence.

I could feel Lia ready to blow a gasket behind me, but before she did, Julian stepped in.

"Sara, come here," he said to me, hands on my hips as he pulled me to sit on his lap.

"Oh my God," Lia said aloud before muffling her giggle and returning to Lukas.

My heart was beating fast now as I found myself returning Pixie's hard stare while sitting on Julian's lap, his hands resting in my bare lap. I did my best not to squirm as I felt his fingertips grazing the skin on my thighs, but I clearly did a poor job of that because the second Pixie paused their conversation to check her phone, he whispered to me, "Stop that."

"Stop what?" I whispered back.

"Clenching your pussy. I can feel it on my thighs, and I'd rather not get any harder than I currently am in front of these people."

I had no time to reply, biting down hard on my lip when Pixie's eyes flickered back up to us – more specifically, to me.

"So, you rode pillion today," she said.

"Pillion?" I repeated.

She glanced at Julian with a smirk then brought her eyes back to me.

"That means the passenger seat, sweetie."

Oh, hell no. I knew even Lia had heard her bust out the condescending "sweetie" because there was an abrupt halt in her chatter with Lukas.

"Oh. Well, in that case, yes. I did ride pillion," I replied with a smile I refused to let her break.

"I'm a bit surprised you would take someone inexperienced for a two-hour ride," Pixie remarked to Julian. "You're usually so big on following rules."

"Yes, well." Julian stroked his hands up and down my waist in a way that set my entire body on fire. "She can be very persuasive."

The low rasp in his voice made me clench again, which in turn had him giving a low chuckle in my ear.

Oh God.

Lia was definitely eavesdropping, because her sudden, sharp giggle brought everyone's attention to our little side of the fire pit.

"What's up, Giggles?" Emmett asked.

"Oh, nothing. I just overheard Julian calling Sara 'very persuasive,' and I just had to agree." Hanging onto Lukas's neck, she turned around to look at me while still addressing everyone else. "She is unrivaled when it comes to making people do things. Right, Lukas? Let's not forget that this bad bitch over here is the reason you and I got together."

Lukas playfully held out his hand for me to shake. "I do owe you a big thank you," he said. "Thank you for meddling when I was courting this woman. You *are* the best, and any uptight billionaire assholes in this vicinity would be lucky to have you," he added, sliding a smirk over to Julian. I was already blushing hard, but Lia took it further.

"Did everyone hear that? Sara is the best, so don't fuck with her," she announced to no one in particular, though I knew exactly who this message was directed to.

"Yeah, she's fuckin' Superwoman," Emmett chimed in. "Pretty sure no one else could've trapped those Roth assholes as fast as you did."

No. No, no, no...

I stiffened, the knot in my throat instant.

"Emmett," Julian ground out behind me, but it was too late. Someone had already asked what Emmett was talking about, and now, without thinking, he was explaining my role as a professional seductress in the Roth negotiations.

Oh my God. Stop.

The sound of my pulse in my ears drowned out the conversation around me. No one was supposed to know about the nature of my contract. Lia knew. Clearly Emmett knew. But now, all these strangers knew, and I couldn't help but imagine that they were drawing unfairly sleazy conclusions about me. Then again, my job was to dress in skintight clothing to lure a pair of skirt-chasing billionaires to bid on Julian's resort. Maybe the sleazy conclusions weren't unfair.

Maybe this was just a part of me that I had never actually erased.

Too late, I cursed inwardly as I watched Emmett try to backtrack. I couldn't hear what Julian and Lia had said to do damage control. Whatever it was, it clearly didn't work because there were already several guys in the circle looking at me differently now. They were raising their eyebrows at me, their expressions stripped of the respect they had on when they thought I was Julian's girl.

A feeling of filth crawled over my skin.

It was the same exact look I got from guys on campus after the incident. It was exactly this. The girls cringed like they were disgusted, but the guys looked like they were excited. Pleasantly surprised, even, in a dirty, sordid kind of way.

I knew what they were thinking. I didn't look like *that* kind of girl – the crazy, kinky, reckless girl who would probably be an easy lay.

"So, wait, I don't get it." Pixie's sharp voice pierced through my flashback. "You're like... an escort for these men?"

My stomach turned, and my silence made her little red lips fall open.

"Wow, that's..." She peered at a friend to her side and loudly whispered, "*Yikes.*"

My heart pounded out of my chest.

I was up and off already, my feet digging through sand as I paced away from the fire pit. I could hear Julian and Lia arguing under their breaths behind me. I hoped Lia would win the fight about who got to go after me, but I suspected Lukas had held her back, because it was the only possible way for Julian to win that particular matchup.

"*Sara.*"

"I don't want to talk to you," I said between my teeth. "Or anyone."

"My brother is a fucking idiot, Sara, I'm sorry. I'm so sorry," he muttered furiously. I swung my arm out of his grip the first time, but the second, I let him pull me close. "Please let me talk to you."

"I don't want to be here right now, Julian, I feel disgusting," I protested. "I feel so dirty and disgusting right now. Those guys – they were looking at me like I was some kind of..." I shook my head, unable to finish.

I was crying. Apparently, I'd been. I wasn't even sure when it started, but I prayed that the tears had waited till after I ran away from the pit. With Julian gripping me tight, I looked up at the stars to distract myself from the pain of my seizing lungs. I could feel the bad memories coming vividly back to me, and I couldn't take it. They reminded me of all the guilt I'd managed to set aside in the past month with Julian. They reminded me of my mom, and how I knew she still worried about something twisted living inside me. I knew she worried that what I did in college wasn't a fluke, and my recklessness was just waiting to come back.

I felt guilty for ignoring her calls.

I felt guilty for dressing provocatively, and being so sexual.

I had been so good at keeping her away for so long, but suddenly, the girl who hated herself was back, and she could barely breathe as she thought about what she'd done in the past four weeks.

"Come on. You're coming with me." Julian's voice was firm as he guided me away. I wanted to shove him off of me, but I also needed him to calm me down like he had that night at the pool.

Before I knew it, he had me in the passenger seat of a car, the two of us speeding fast away.

23

JULIAN

I forced her to talk to me.

I hadn't realized how badly I'd been needing answers about her till now, and the fact that my instincts were too late had me fucking enraged with myself. I was usually good at this. If I was missing information I needed, I gauged it fast and found some way to get it.

Of course, that was in my work life, and I had Sara confused with something I merely wanted.

I wanted to know about her. I wanted to understand why those dark looks clouded over. They happened rarely, and for barely a few seconds, but I had seen them in her eyes, and I wanted to know why. The problem was that I thought I only wanted it, so for the sake of avoiding indulgence, I didn't press for the answers.

Of course, I was realizing now that understanding Sara was more than just a want at this point.

"You really need to know this?" Sara whispered.

We were closing in on one in the morning, but I wasn't backing down. I had brought her back to my house, and she had insisted on sleeping. As cruel as it was, I refused to let her. I knew she wasn't sleepy – she was avoiding my questions about her past the way she had steadily been for days now.

"I need to know," I confirmed, showing no mercy to the pleading tears in her eyes as she sat at the edge of my bed. "I don't enjoy feeling like I can't protect you. The more you tell me, the better I know how to keep someone from hurting you. So talk."

"You first. Who was that woman in the green dress?" she asked, glaring up at me. "She seemed a bit possessive of your attention."

"That was Madeline," I said. "I met her five years ago while I was out with Emmett one night. I don't know where he found her. He generally collects new friends throughout the night."

"And you two have slept together?" she asked.

"Twice," I answered. "She's just a woman I've slept with before, Sara. Your issue with her should be solely with the fact that she crossed the line in conversation today. You have no reason to feel threatened by any woman I've had a history with, no matter how long or brief."

"No? Tell me why not," Sara said. Her tears had stopped an hour ago, but her dark eyes were still wet, and I found myself unable to say no to them.

"I care about you more than I've ever cared about another woman. That's your answer."

"That's hard to believe," she murmured as she stood up and made a beeline for the bathroom. I clenched my jaw as I followed her in.

"Why?" I asked. "What reason have I given you to doubt that I care for you?"

"None," she answered remorselessly. "I just don't know you. I don't know anything about you," she said, angrily dabbing a tissue at her eyes as her voice started to waver. "I'm obviously feeling things for you. You don't make it easy for me to avoid that, but I want to keep myself at least a little protected from you. Explaining my past to you is just me volunteering to knock down whatever's left of my wall, and I don't know if that's worth it for you, Julian. Not when this little thing here will be done before I know it."

My heart processed her words before I did, because I had barely a warning before my pulse started hammering.

"What the hell are you talking about?" I asked. She shot me daggers over my tone.

"Are you really going to pretend whatever's going on between us is something you're willing to invest your time in?" she demanded. "Look at you. Look at who you are. You don't do this kind of thing. You don't have girlfriends. There's a good portion of your life you haven't revealed to your own best friend. You're guarded, and I get it. It's the best way to get work done. We've both employed that method of living. We both know what it's like, so why are you asking me to expose myself for you when you'd never do the same for anyone else, let alone me?"

Fair point.

In fact, everything she said was so fucking dead on it pissed me off. It only intensified my need to know about her. If she was that much like me, then the work was a distraction from something deep and dark, and I needed to know.

"I'll tell you whatever you want to know about me if you tell me about you."

The offer was out before I could change my mind. But she still didn't bite.

"You won't want to look at me let alone talk to me after I'm done," she said. My chest felt hot as I heard her voice falter, and watched her eyes mist with fresh tears.

"You know that isn't true. I can't stop looking at you. That's been the problem since the night we met."

I watched the storm of clashing emotions flicker in her eyes.

"Fine. If you're so convinced of that, let me go right ahead. I stayed at June Magazine for almost ten years, despite how they treated me, because I was convinced no other company would ever hire me. My mom was convinced June neglected my background check because I was hired directly out of my internship. I was arrested in college, Julian. Can you guess what the charges were?" she asked heatedly, her voice quivering. A tear fell from the corner of her eyes as she shook her head. "It was prostitution. Would you like to run now?" she hissed, her wild eyes flitting all over my expression.

I looked stunned.

I knew I did. I hadn't moved a muscle on my face, but I could tell from the way Sara's tears were falling now that my eyes had given me away. It felt like a dagger had splintered into my heart as I watched her cover her face and crumple to the ground, letting everything out. Every tear, every cry, every shudder. She was sobbing uncontrollably at my feet, and I knew how much it had to hurt for her. Like me, she lived to repress and control. She found her way to bury her past, and she stuck to it, no matter how unhealthy or draining it was. Whatever it took, it was better than letting the emotions swallow her the way they were doing now.

"Look at me," I said, lifting her chin to face me. I was on the floor with her now, and I had no idea what I was about to say. But instead of measuring my every word carefully, I for once let them come out as they pleased. "Look at me, Sara. You see me. You know I'm not going anywhere. I'm right here, and all I want is to know that I can fix the way you feel. I can't stand it when you're unhappy, and I'm going to have you smiling by the end of this night, I promise you that. I just need you to talk to me first, Sara. Please."

She shook her head and cried, but she let me kiss her, and though it took another few minutes, she brought her knees to her chest and forced herself to breathe. Another minute of silence, and she finally started leading in.

"The scar I have... you know what I'm talking about."

"The one Turner mentioned the night at the pool," I nodded.

"That one. You saw it when you were helping me come down from my panic attack."

"Yes."

"I usually have it covered with makeup. It's in the shape of an 'F' because the girls at school wanted to burn the word 'freak' on me with their cigarettes."

I felt my nails dig into my palm but I didn't let on to my fury. I knew she'd stop talking to soothe me. She had that need to completely take care of me. I noticed it awhile ago, in everything from the way she fucked me to the way she calmed me down around the Roths. I loved it. But I wasn't interested in that selfish pleasure tonight.

"You were bullied?" I asked.

"From the start. But what did I expect," she murmured, staring blankly down at the floor. "My dad... he moved us to Texas on a whim. After his mom died, he wanted to leave London, and he picked this little town where one of his travel buddies from forever ago lived. I was already different when we got there – I looked different. I talked different. My dad had an accent, my mom was too nervous to speak to other moms. I was an easy target. But it got so much worse when my dad decided to represent his friend in an assault case. Some bar fight. The defendant was popular around town – he was the high school football coach, and he had a kid in my grade. Also well liked. Also popular." She drew in a deep, trembling breath. "So everyone made my life miserable from that point on. And it got that much worse after my dad won."

Her teary eyes peered up at me as I gently pulled her legs away from her chest, wrapping them around my midsection as I lifted her onto my lap.

"Go on," I said as I found the scar on her arm. It was disguised well, but I saw it now, and we both gazed down at it for a moment.

"It took a couple days for them to finish the F," she mumbled. "The girls would corner me in the bathroom. One time, they even snuck some boys in to keep me restrained while they burned me. I remembered crying, but I didn't make a sound because I felt like that was validation for them. I was just thinking of how to get myself out of the place." She smiled a little. "I fantasized about getaways a lot. That's where the motorcycle thing came in. But that wasn't realistic, obviously, so I just worked to graduate early and start completely anew in college. I already knew where I wanted to go that we could afford, and I knew what sorority I wanted to join. I knew how I would dress and act so I didn't seem different again, like an outcast again. I had dreamt of going to prom since I was a little girl, and wearing that big, poufy dress. But since that clearly wasn't going to happen, I told myself I'd go to frat parties, and mixers, and I'd have that perfect all-American teen life in college."

"Did you?" I frowned. I wanted to believe the pain ended in high school, but I remembered the cloud that cast over her eyes when she mentioned college at the gas station. "You said you rode the back of a motorcycle with your best friend in college."

"Ashleigh," Sara breathed. The sound of the name drained the color from her cheeks. "Ash is what we called her. She was my big. I got into the sorority I wanted, I got all the friends I wanted, and I got her as my big sister, which seemed like winning the jackpot at the time. She was this insanely popular, Barbie-like girl who everyone adored on campus, and the fact that she took me under her wing was like a dream. We were inseparable from the second we met, and suddenly, just a summer after all that torture in high school, I had everything I ever wanted. I had this built in family with my sisters, and I had this girl who would drive me around, take me out, be a shoulder to cry on. I was seventeen, and she was like a god to me. She had me wrapped around her pinky so hard I didn't question anything she asked of me."

I brushed away the hair that fell into Sara's face as she looked down. Her eyes refused to look at me, even after I cupped her jaw and brought them back to me.

"What did she ask of you?"

"She had me..." She breathed for a moment. "She had me perform favors," she finally muttered, peering at me for a reaction I didn't give. "For guys in the frat we were paired with. I knew I didn't feel right, but I didn't really understand what was happening. I was so desperate to believe these girls were my friends. I didn't have coffee dates, or sleepovers, or parties back in high school, and I had all of that with these girls. They helped me study, they met me after class, they defended me to the death if anyone was even a little rude to me at a party. So I was so confused. I was..." Sara shook her head in awe of herself. "So fucking stupid."

"You were seventeen," I said, wiping her tears. "The kids in high school, they were blatant villains. You knew to run from them. But these girls were different. They acted like friends to play into your vulnerability, and what they did to you was heinous."

"That wasn't even the worst part," Sara whispered, staring up toward the ceiling. "Ash convinced me she needed money. Something about her family being in trouble. She reminded me of all the times she drove me, or paid for me, or did whatever for me. And she guilted me into saying yes to something disgusting, because she said I'd be screwed if I didn't do it. That college could be as bad as it was in high school. Worse maybe."

I wrapped her arms around my neck and kissed her as she struggled to get the words out.

"It's okay. Take your time," I said. But she sped on, as if wanting to get the bad taste out of her mouth.

"They found someone – some man who would pay a lot of money to sleep with me. They told me he was one of our friend's older cousins, but when I got to the motel, the man was so much older, and from somewhere else. He said he found Ash online. I remember feeling so betrayed, and I remember how annoyed he got that I cried in front of him."

She cried again, and this time I lifted her off the floor to carry her to my bed. She let out a sigh of comfort when I laid her down and pressed my lips to her forehead, but she didn't let me kiss her.

"I need you to know that I didn't have sex with that man. Okay?"

"Okay," I whispered. "It's okay, Sara."

"One of my sisters called the cops. I told her before we left about what Ash and the other older girls were asking me to do, and I begged her to call the cops. I didn't think she would, but she did. I felt so disgusting for being naked when they found me. I had already tried touching that man. It honestly felt like the cops came at the last possible second. But I thank God for them anyway, and I thank God for the girl who called them for me. I wasn't even mad at her for being like everyone else and ignoring me after the incident."

"Because you called the cops?"

"Yes. Ash and the girls were arrested. Their names were in the paper, and mine got taken out when they realized I was a minor. They dropped the charges on me when they realized what was happening, and the kids at school thought that was unfair. They blamed me for everything – said I was asking for it with the way I dressed, the way I wore makeup. They had already saved the article that came out with my name in it. It's still archived online. I tried to have it taken down, but someone put it back up, even after I transferred thousands of miles away. And it just feels like this nagging reminder that I was once this... little *thing* that existed solely for sex. It makes me feel dirty and disgusting and *guilty* for wanting sex. Especially the way that I want it. A part of me feels like I should be repenting still."

"Do you feel guilty about what we've done in the past few weeks?" I asked, my chest tight in anticipation of her answer that I'd unknowingly hurt her. That she'd partially hated herself every time we slept together. But with her hands cupping my jaw, she studied my eyes and shook her head.

"No," she said with a breath of awe. It was as if she had realized her answer that very second. The crystal sound of her whisper pierced the quiet of the room as she went on. "All I feel is good around you. I feel like I'm doing something a little wilder and crazier than I'm used to, but I don't ever feel bad about it. Not with you. I don't feel guilty about anything between us, and it makes me feel like I'm actually free around you. Like I'm really acting like myself instead of the girl I forced myself to be. I was just trying to make it up to myself and my parents for what I did when I was seventeen."

"That was ten years ago, Sara. It wasn't your fault, nor should you feel guilty about what you want. You're not defined by what those girls did to you. You can't keep blaming yourself."

"I pushed it to the back of my head for awhile," she insisted softly. "I didn't even think about it much while I was at June Magazine. I was so overworked, but I think I liked it. I was always exhausted, too busy to do too much drinking, definitely no dating, and it made me feel like I had successfully transformed into someone new. Someone not filthy and reckless. My mother was proud of me. Everything seemed okay."

"Until you quit."

"Yes." Her eyes were drier, calmer now as they traveled over my face. "I took your job offer because I wanted to be near you. I'm not even going to lie about it at this point. But since I've started, I've felt just... *better* about myself. Like I'm allowed to enjoy the things I used to feel guilty about, and like I'm the one in control now."

She pulled me closer by my shirt till I lowered my weight onto her. I felt the heavy chains around my chest lift the second she smiled.

"You make me feel... happy," she murmured. She paused. "Like I've never felt before in my life," she exhaled. But then she swallowed hastily, looking apologetic. "And I know that's a lot for you to hear right now, so you don't have to say anything. Just nod or say one word to acknowledge you heard it, and we'll move on. Just say 'okay.'"

"How about 'same'?" I asked as she blinked with confusion at me. "I feel the same."

I watched that little smile on her mouth break into a grin.

"But I want to make sure you stay happy," I whispered, kissing her curved lips. "I'm not going to let anyone hurt you again. I promise you that. Okay?"

She breathed out slow, steady now, and closed her eyes.

"Okay."

24

SARA

So he does sleep.

I lay on my side for a minute after waking up. The exhaustion from last night had hit me fast and hard, and I remembered falling asleep with Julian in bed with me. For the first hour I drifted in and out, I knew he was awake, because he would murmur something to me or brush his hand through my hair. In my half-conscious fog, I remembered being convinced the man didn't sleep.

That's how you go from normal hard-working guy to billionaire. Zero hours of sleep a night.

I recalled stirring at three in the morning and being alone in bed. At six o'clock, it was the same thing.

So waking up at eight-thirty next to Julian in nothing but a pair of sweatpants was a bit of a shock. It was like spotting a shooting star. That lean six-pack aside, it was striking to see him simply resting for once, and just being human. There was the slightest, *slightest* natural smile on his smooth, pink lips, and it made me laugh to myself to think that Julian Hoult actually smiled more in his sleep than in his day-to-day life.

To avoid staring at him forever like a crazy person, I eventually dragged myself out of bed. I set my feet carefully on the hardwood, expecting to feel a bit of a lag or a haze, or some sort of emotional hangover from last night.

But I felt nothing.

I just felt... *good.*

Despite going to bed with a smile on my lips, I didn't expect to wake up happy. Confessing everything to Julian last night had been a roller coaster. At some points, I felt dread and fear for what he was learning about me. At others, I felt almost the same exhilaration I felt when I was on the bike with him.

I felt open. And free.

Light on my feet, in his white T-shirt and my blue panties, I wandered the beautiful house I hadn't had the chance to soak in last night. It was actually too big for me to explore every room of, and I had little interest anyway after finding the floor-to-ceiling wall of books in the living room.

There had to be a thousand of them. Maybe more. The shelves stretched even around the corners of the wall, with a polished wooden ladder attached. My hungry eyes scanned over the spines of probably a hundred books before landing upon one that made me smile, because it was the only one with bookmarks sticking out of its pages.

The French Language: Idioms and Phrases.

I couldn't help grabbing it. It was the morning's second piece of adorable evidence that Julian Hoult was in fact human. He didn't know how to speak French, and he wanted to learn. Simple as that.

I imagined it was for the purpose of business, considering the resort in Biarritz, which was of course on the French side of Basque Country. So plucking it from the shelf, I headed for the porch outside, toward the vintage porch swing that had been calling my name since I spotted it out the window. Padding over in my bare feet, I sunk back into the luxurious pillows, a little grin on my lips. The trip to Biarritz was the day after tomorrow.

But within the first few bookmarks I peeked at, I realized Julian had not purchased this book for the purpose of work.

My eyes unblinking, I flipped through, mentally collecting all the phrases he had saved to learn.

I miss you.

I think about you.

I love you more than you know.

I breathed in deep.

Okay, Sara. I reminded myself it wasn't a big deal – that all adults had dating histories. It was just part of life. But then I remembered what Julian had said to me barely eight hours ago, before I allowed myself to tell him everything.

"I care about you more than I've ever cared about another woman."

I couldn't help but doubt that with these bookmarks sitting in my lap. I couldn't even deny they were his. He had notes scrawled around in that perfect handwriting I'd come to memorize in my time at his office. And if that weren't proof enough, a loose piece of pressed flower stationery fell out from the next page.

It was a letter written in neat but swirling cursive, and it was entirely in French.

The only word I recognized was *Biarritz*.

"Morning."

Julian's voice prompted my sharp gasp. Clasping my heart, I looked up to find him standing on the porch in front of me, the sun beating down on his wide, muscled shoulders, and his glimmering blue eyes staring down at me.

"Morning," I returned, a tinge of guilt in my voice. I glanced down at the French book. "I thought it was for work purposes," I explained, my voice tight. "I didn't realize it was..."

"What?" Julian challenged lightly. "What is it that you think you're looking at right now?" he asked. I swallowed.

"Remnants of a very passionate affair."

"No." He gave a short laugh. "For the most part, you're wrong."

"For the most part?" My brow twitched. The porch swing swayed lightly with the faintest squeaking as I sat there cross-legged, gazing curiously up at Julian's unreadable expression. "Will you tell me the story behind it?" I finally asked.

The only giveaway of the deep breath he took was the heavy rise and fall of his sculpted chest.

"Yes," he answered. "But we're going to need to get breakfast first."

25

SARA

I wondered if Julian's story was something horrific, and the stunning Riva yacht he had me boarding was for the sole purpose of softening the blow.

After grabbing breakfast to go at a charming little pastry shop, we took Emmett's truck to a glittering white marina, where I found myself standing before a gleaming, forty-foot black and mahogany speedboat I could've sworn I'd also seen in my dreams before.

"If this is your way of keeping me distracted while you confess your secrets, I don't appreciate it, because it's kind of working," I said, hardly able to help a smile as I gazed at Julian. He had his Persols pushed up, giving me a clear view of those eyes looking bluer than ever. I wasn't sure if they were reflecting the water or his light blue button down, but they were striking enough that I almost tripped while getting onto the boat.

Without flinching, Julian caught me.

"Actually." He squeezed my hand tight till I was solidly on my feet. "The boat is for the purpose of distracting me."

"Oh."

Oops.

I didn't consider till now that it might actually be hard for Julian to talk about himself or his past. It wasn't my instinct to imagine that *anything* was hard for him. That was why the bookmarked French book was so charming and curious to me.

At least it was until I saw the love letters – or whatever they were.

"How'd you learn to drive a boat?" I asked, in the seat next to Julian's as he navigated out of the dock.

"My grandfather taught me." He looked like some classic Hollywood movie star with his hair lightly slicked back, his sleeves pushed up and his Persols back on. I decided on a cross between young Clint Eastwood and prime James Dean.

"Your mother's father?" I asked.

"My father's father. He taught me how to steer a boat, how to line a fishing rod – he also taught all eight grandkids how to use our chest voices when heckling opposing outfielders. So we'd be loud enough to actually distract them."

The sun bounced off Julian's shades as he smiled, his hand on the wheel and his posture relaxed as the boat accelerated to knife through the shimmering blue water. It was a breathtaking sight.

"Your grandfather sounds like fun."

"He was. He was also 'that guy.' Similar to your dad." Julian glanced at me to catch my big smile. "Yeah, he was loud and happy and animated. He asked my grandmother on a date about two minutes after he first spotted her at the stadium, and when he took her out that night, he told her he was going to marry her, have three kids with her, and buy the Empires for her."

"And he did?" I grinned. "I mean the three kids part."

"Yes. That he got right. Same with the marriage part, obviously. He was a lower-middle class kid from Brooklyn, but he wound up making most of his money through property rentals, and he did try to buy the Empires twice before, but his bids were rejected."

"Oh no. Was your grandma holding him to the whole thing about buying her the team?"

"Not at all. She teased him every day about how she didn't believe he'd ever be able to do it, and that he was batting six sixty-seven on promises."

"Lord. Such a baseball family," I smirked. "They sound too cute. Is your dad also 'that guy?'"

"No, my dad would be more like me."

"Serious and scary?"

Julian laughed. "Yes, but less scary. A little nicer. No – a lot nicer."

"Really? Tell me about him."

"Well, he did inherit some of my grandfather's romantic side. To the point that I grew up thinking all kids celebrated Mother's Day with the same fanfare as Thanksgiving and Christmas. We used to spend the entire month before the day planning her surprise. We would get all her favorite foods, decorate the entire house with her favorite flowers."

"Which were?"

"Ranunculus flowers," Julian said, his perfect hair blowing slightly in the wind. "The name is misleading. They're really beautiful."

I exaggerated my surprise to tease him.

"Huh. Julian Hoult likes flowers?"

"Hard not to with the way I grew up. Every April of my life revolved around flowers," he grinned. "Dahlias were also high on the list. Hydrangeas, too. Mom liked all the harder to find colors, so Emmett and I usually started ordering a month before Mother's Day. Dad was in charge of planning and executing the menu for the night, and Emmett and I were on ordering and décor."

"And by Emmett and you, you mean..."

"Just me," Julian laughed, his eyes crinkling adorably behind his sunglasses. "There were these big, chocolate-covered strawberries that were Mom's favorite, and timing that order so they stayed fresh would always cause Emmett to melt down. There was always a point where he got overwhelmed and meditated by coloring and making cards."

"Oh, no! Poor Emmett." I couldn't stop grinning as we zipped fast now under the sun and through the water, my mind filled with images of baby Emmett having a total breakdown while baby Julian made calls and spreadsheets in preparation of the Hoult Family

Mother's Day. "So, is this where Julian Hoult's famous organizing and planning skills originated?"

"Possibly. Though my father did start me on business classes around middle school. He said all my grandfather's real estate was purchased on a whim, when property was cheap, so it was unreasonable to believe that his kind of success would just replicate or fall in our laps. We had to earn it."

"Ah. Now I see how you and Dad are more alike," I nodded, glancing behind us to see how far we'd gone. At this point, the marina was a sparkling white dot far, far away. "I take it Emmett's more like Mom?"

"No, my mom is a good balance of fun and serious. Emmett would be more like my crazy grandfather. Not a surprise at all that he was always my grandparents' favorite grandchild."

"Really? It wasn't you?"

"I was a close second," Julian chuckled. "I was a bit fickle. I wasn't easy to amuse at all, and that just kills the fun of playing with kids."

I giggled at the image of Julian playing with children. Again, not something I'd imagine for him, but clearly, he was full of more surprises than I gave him credit for. Or he was just far more human than I could ever really fathom.

"So Emmett was the happy, smiley kid."

"Shocking, right?" Julian said dryly despite his grin. "I'll admit he was hilariously cute as a kid. Pretty much never stopped smiling – thought anything you said or did was fucking amazing. My grandpa used to bring him around the bleachers when Emmett was a toddler, and he'd just introduce him to complete strangers. He just thought there was no chance someone at an Empires game would prefer to actually watch the game than meet this 'fine young gentleman.'"

"Oh, God. That's actually too cute." I felt like my heart was going to burst out of my chest as I watched Julian. Maybe it was the sun hitting his brilliant smile, but it looked like he was beaming at the mere thought of his family.

"Meanwhile, my grandmother was glued to the game. She loved

her grandkids, but if there was baseball going on, she wasn't taking her eyes off the field for anything."

"So, she came here from Germany, went straight to a game to get a feel of Americana, and then became the most hardcore baseball fan in your family?" I clarified, completely charmed.

"Absolutely," Julian replied. Oh, yeah. The man was beaming. "She likes to pull my President of Baseball Operations aside every once in awhile, and give her some pointers on who to sign during free agency. She's almost ninety now, but still keeps a mental Rolodex of player contracts and salaries throughout the league, just to think of possible trade scenarios. The players think she's terrifying. They call her Rosemarie The Reaper."

"Oh my God." I had to take my sunglasses off to wipe at the tears squeezing from the corners of my eyes from laughing so hard. "Are you sure it's not your grandma you take after, Julian?"

"You know, it's gotta be a mix of both her and Dad," Julian decided with a little smile. "I'm a reflection of them. Emmett's a reflection of Grandpa."

"In that case, your entire family had to be your grandparents' favorites. There's no way they weren't."

"Oh, we were. And we still are. Though for different reasons now, probably."

I stilled as I remembered that there was a reason we were here on this boat. There was a part of this story that wasn't about flowers and baseball and strictly good times. I knew that part was coming as I watched Julian's curved mouth fade back to a line.

"I was twenty-three when my grandpa's cancer spread to his bones. I remember me and Emmett and my parents spending a lot of time in hospice with him and Grandma. We would just play cards, or talk, or watch the game, but it was good. It felt like we were taking our time to say goodbye, and we were leaving off on some laughter and good conversation. We took the time to make new memories instead of just talking about the old ones. Though we did that too. It was just a nice, peaceful time, all things considered. Both my grandparents accepted what was happening, and for the most part, they were at peace with it.

"But my aunts and uncles and cousins visited occasionally to quickly ask how my grandpa was feeling before interrogating him about the will. They were afraid he was leaving his best real estate to my father, because he was the favorite."

"Oh, Jesus," I whispered.

I had only heard about these family battles over wills and money. I didn't have a big enough family myself to see it happen, and I really couldn't process that things could ever get so ugly among blood – especially over something as trivial as money.

"Yeah, they were shameless. And horrible," Julian said evenly.

There he goes.

I could always tell when a topic upset Julian. He always carefully extracted any and all emotion from his voice, carrying on with a calm that was strictly uninterpretable. The only tell was in his eyes, but today, he had those covered. In that sense, shades were like his superhero cape.

"My dad wanted to keep peace with his siblings," Julian said. "He felt like my grandpa deserved to see his family whole before he went. And I resented that. I hated keeping quiet when these people came barreling in during our last conversations with him. We would be talking about something that was making Grandpa laugh when they'd storm through demanding answers about the will. My cousin, Paul, was the worst of anyone. He was the oldest, he was married, and he had his second child on the way, so he was hell-bent on inheriting some real estate. He pushed everyone aside to badger my grandfather till he was in tears. I don't remember what I did, but I snapped. I remembered everyone screaming for me to stop, and I know I at least dragged Paul out of the room before I choked him out. Emmett pulled me off of him before I could do any more damage. But really, the damage was done. Everyone was screaming and crying. My dad pulled me aside and tore me a new asshole for treating family like that."

"But what about the way they were treating *their* family?" I argued, my own voice shaking with the fury I felt over Julian's asshole cousin forcing his grandfather to cry on his deathbed. "How could he possibly care about just the property when your grandfather was about to – "

I cut off because I didn't want to say it. Julian gripped the wheel of the boat tight.

"I know. Nothing made sense to me that day, and I felt like I was helpless for once. Everyone was furious with me, and I couldn't stick around without doing more damage, so I talked alone with my grandfather. He said he loved me, he understood, and he knew I needed to just get away for a bit – to cool off. He said that we'd say goodbye now. Just in case."

I hugged my knees tight against my chest. I knew where this story was going, and I couldn't take it. My heart was twisting and turning as I waited for Julian to just say it, but obviously, he needed time.

For awhile, it was just the silence and the sound of the motor as the yacht continued sailing toward the skyline.

"I took my bike, actually. It was my preferred getaway, too," Julian finally said, and with the kind of strained smile I knew was for the purpose of bracing your emotions. Inching closer to him, I dared to reach for his hand. Before I could tell myself to pull back and give him some space, he took my hand in his. I stared down at our fingers entwined, a little amazed by the notion of my touch providing him comfort.

"Where did you go?" I asked softly.

"Nowhere in particular," he said. "I just rode. I rode for probably five hours to calm myself down. I was close to Martha's Vineyard by the time my heart was beating normally again. But when I checked my phone, I had more than fifty missed calls, texts and voicemails."

I closed my eyes for a second. "Your grandfather passed?" I wasn't sure if he'd even heard my whisper of a question, but then he gave my hand a squeeze.

"No," he said. "It was my dad. He had a massive heart attack an hour after I left."

I covered my mouth.

I couldn't speak for a moment.

Several moments, actually. My heart pounded like it had grown ten sizes, and I could almost feel how rocked Julian had been standing next to his bike all those years ago, in a different state, helpless and broken by the news. I had no idea how he could even go on talking, but he did. His voice was mostly steady, but his grip choked the wheel as he steered and explained everything.

His dad had passed that very night, and by the next, his heartbroken grandfather left them as well. And of course, the Hoults were in shambles – at least Julian's grandma, mom and brother were.

The real estate wound up going to his vile aunt, uncle and cousins. His mother obviously didn't care. She had never wanted it in the first place. And now, all she wanted was her husband who was suddenly gone.

Apparently, she took her grief out on her son.

"She's apologized profusely since, but she blamed me then. She said I drove my father to that point. And I did. You can't deny that," he said, knowing well I was about to try. "You really can't," he repeated with the most faintly detectable tremor in his voice. "I shocked him, and I angered him so badly it killed him. I didn't get to say goodbye to him. We just left off. It still feels like we're up in the air, and wherever he is, he's always wishing he could say something to me."

My heart was completely broken for him. I could tell from the way he cleared his throat that he was choked up, and more than anything, I wanted to just crawl into his lap and give him the biggest hug, but he was still driving. I took a moment to sort through my fractured jumble of thoughts.

"You have to know he's proud of you, Julian," I murmured. "How could he be anything but that? You put his early business lessons to work, you founded your company – you even followed through on your grandfather's promise to buy the New York Empires. That's crazy, Julian. You and the people around you might be used to your success and achievements at this point, but as an outside party, let me tell you that I am constantly in awe of you. You are unstoppable, and considering the unreal accomplishments you've had so far, I can't imagine a greater honor than being the motivation for your success, the way your family is."

Julian said nothing but squeezed my hand hard, rubbing his thumb over my palm.

"You told me yesterday to stop blaming myself and trying to repent for the past," I pointed out gently, "so I'm telling you now to allow the same for yourself. A part of you has to know you deserve it. You gave your grandmother the opportunity to be Rosie The Reaper to a bunch of big pro ballers. Your grandfather is definitely somewhere laughing with your dad about that," I said, a little smile touching my lips as I watched Julian grin.

"They're definitely pleased about that."

"Exactly."

Julian smiled for a bit, and I let myself enjoy it. But I knew there was more.

"My guilt doesn't end there," he finally broke the silence. I took in a deep breath.

"What else happened?"

"I was estranged for years from my mother and Emmett."

I raised my eyebrows. Judging from his relationship with Emmett now, it was hard to believe that Julian was ever anything but close to him. But evidently, there was a period where they had gone years without speaking.

"I went home for my father and grandfather's funerals, but I moved overseas shortly after. Just weeks after. There was a sudden wall between me and the rest of my family. My mom couldn't look at me. She didn't want to. Emmett claimed it was because I reminded her too much of our father, and not because she blamed me for his death, but I knew that was a lie. So, I moved to Stockholm."

"Stockholm? As in Sweden?" I said with surprise.

"Yes. People don't associate the city with being the tech hub it is, but it was there that I wound up starting the company that would become Hoult Communications. It was Hoult Media at the time, and it offered mobile content like news, sports scores, et cetera. Once we developed a mobile payment technology, the company surpassed a billion dollars in value. I was twenty-seven when I sold it."

"Holy shit." I let it all process for a bit as the boat slowed significantly, humming along the water now. "So you spent four years away from your family," I murmured. My mom was exhausting, and my dad was a lot of talking to handle at a time, but I couldn't imagine going even a year without seeing them.

"It wasn't easy. But as time went on, the wall between us just got higher and higher. More and more miscommunications built up. My mother can be incredibly proud and hard headed, and when I asked if I could send her money, she took it as a slight. She thought I was trying to buy her forgiveness for abandoning them when this entire time, I swore she was the one who abandoned me. I was so angry for so long, and I missed my dad. A lot. I had always grown up telling myself I would be exactly like him, so with my mother and my relationship on the rocks, and Emmett just doing whatever he could to keep her afloat, I filled the void with a woman I worked with. Elizabet. Or Liz."

"I'm going to guess she's French."

"Yes. She was something of an assistant to me at Hoult Media."

"You were in love with her?" I asked, doing my best to sound casual despite how fast my heart was beating.

"I thought I was. In reality, I just wanted to replace the family I lost, and I was hasty. I picked someone I thought was important to me because I conflated her significance to me with the success of my company. She was in the office every day watching me grow it from a startup, and my perception of her was skewed thanks to that. After we split for good, I made a rule for myself."

"Zero tolerance. Never sleep with or date an employee," I recited so dryly Julian looked at me with a laugh.

"Yes."

"Split for good?" I recalled what he said. "What caused the final split?"

From Julian's pause and the way he drew a palm over his jaw, I knew we'd reached another painful peak in his story.

"Liz said for a long time, it was easy to pretend I loved her the way she loved me. But then Lucie came along, and she saw what real love looked like in my eyes."

I swallowed. "Lucie?" I repeated, a small chill running over my arm just before Julian answered.

"My daughter."

It felt like my organs had all crashed to my feet before he clarified.

"She isn't biologically mine," Julian said, looking at me. "Liz got pregnant with her around the time of one of our breaks, but I specifically didn't do anything to confirm paternity when Liz said the child belonged to me. I wanted a kid. I wanted that family. I raised Lucie till she was four years old."

"Oh my God," I breathed. It was a much more significant amount of time than I had thought. "How old were you?"

"Twenty-five," Julian replied. "From the ages of twenty-five and twenty-nine, I was a dad. And a fucking good one. I was the father my own father raised me to become, and I was proud of myself. I adored Lucie in a way I didn't know was possible. But Liz couldn't handle it. Lucie and I were closer than she was to either of us. Lucie had anxiety. Panic attacks."

Julian glanced at me, and my reaction to the explanation I now had for that night. He had been able to put air back in my lungs the night at the pool with Turner and Carter Roth, because he'd spent years using the same tricks to soothe the girl he raised as his daughter.

"I was the only one who could calm her down, and Liz resented that," Julian said. "She resented that she was second best to the both of us. She resented that the love Lucie and I had together upstaged anything we had for her, and it was a painful daily reminder."

"That sounds hard," I couldn't help but murmur. It really did. There was nothing more hurtful than being unloved and unwanted, and I knew well that being reminded of it every day was like torture following torture. A revolving door of pain.

"It had to be hard. I didn't even realize myself how much it had to hurt," Julian said, remorse in his voice. "I was just so hell-bent on having a family again. I was transfixed with Lucie, and with being a father. It felt like through the universe, my dad and I were somehow sharing a connection again. I knew exactly what he had felt when he was raising Emmett and me." Julian paused, as if suddenly losing his breath. I squeezed his hand. "Lucie would look at pictures of my dad and say 'Grandpa,' and it was the best feeling. I was so over the moon, I didn't know Liz was unhappy. I had no idea I was hurting her constantly." He swallowed. "And I had no idea that she was plotting to hurt me back."

A pang of fear hit my chest. "How?"

"I woke up one morning in December, and they were gone. Bags packed. Just gone. Liz didn't tell me where she went with Lucie, and it wasn't till months later that I found out they moved to France, where Liz is from."

"Biarritz?" I guessed.

"No, but close by. She had always talked about going there with her family growing up, and how it was always a dream, and she wanted to raise her children there."

"So you built the resort," I murmured, staring ahead of us in pure, stunned awe.

"Yes. Before all the renovations and additions, it started out as a home. A big one. Liz said if I somehow showed her my love, maybe she would come back. Just maybe. So I designed a fucking mansion for her. At least I said it was for her."

"But it was for Lucie."

"Yes."

The heat of the sun was almost unbearable now.

I was speechless.

I had been so sure Julian Hoult was unfeeling, made of steel. But for this little girl, he had turned himself inside out and worked tooth and nail – all for the fighting chance to perhaps see her again.

And apparently, he did. But it was short-lived.

Liz had returned to Julian, and they had spent all of four months in the Biarritz home before she detected the lie of his love and disappeared once again.

"They live somewhere outside of Paris now. Liz told me she would make sure I'd never be close to Lucie again. She promised me she would stop speaking English to her, and place her in a strictly French-speaking school."

My jaw dropped at the unbelievably calculated cruelty of it all.

"So Lucie would be unable to communicate with you?"

"Yes. She writes letters here and there, and I provide financial support here and there. But the relationship we once had is gone, and now that she's almost nine, I doubt she really remembers it. Which is okay. It's less painful for her."

The anguish in his voice was more than evident now, so I let him be for awhile. I needed the quiet myself, too, because my image of Julian had just been completely rocked. He wasn't just cold, hard and efficient.

He was a million layers of complexities that made my heart actually ache for him more. He knew grief and suffering all too well – he just kept it always locked tightly inside of that ironclad exterior.

Except for now. With me.

The wind tousled my hair as I climbed halfway into his lap.

"Hey." I wrapped my arms around his neck and kissed his cheek. He turned his eyes to me for a few seconds, studying me with a look of unfiltered relief that made my heart swell. "I know it was hard to say all that."

He gazed at me another few seconds before leaning in to kiss my lips.

"Not as hard as it could've been."

26

JULIAN

I woke up in the morning when I felt Sara stir, but I didn't open my eyes even after she climbed onto my chest, feathering sleepy kisses over my lips.

"You're awake," she murmured with a soft giggle. "I can see it."

I smirked. "I'm awake. But I'm still recovering."

She knew well what she'd done to me last night.

We were content to be quiet during the boat ride back to the marina, and after getting home she had gotten wordlessly into the shower. Just as wordlessly, I followed her in. I had jerked off on the marble bench while watching her soap up that beautiful body, her hands taking extra time on her tits when she heard the way I groaned.

Christ, I was content to just watch her all night.

She was just so damned beautiful. She had a way of hypnotizing me without even trying, and entrancing me with just the way she spoke or moved. I had been under Sara's spell from the moment she pulled me up to stand in front of her in the shower, her eyes shimmering up at me as she took her time to lather my body with soap. We spent awhile standing under that rainfall, content to just watch each other as she drew her hands all over me.

I was hard, obviously, but I didn't want to break the moment to get a condom.

I was happy where I was. We both were.

Of course, our bodies entwined the moment we stepped out of the shower. We didn't make it three feet to the bed, but the love seat worked fine, and I went briefly blind after bursting inside her and fucking drowning the condom in my cum.

At night, I lie there next to Sara, so sweet and beautiful as she slept right next to me. As fucked up as it made me feel, I jacked it hard while gazing at her lips. They were pink and perfect, parted lightly a she breathed. I studied the way her thin top stretched over the full mounds of her breasts, and I swore I could've come just from watching her sleep.

But with a sweet little noise, she woke up.

She was groggy, smiling, half-asleep when she tugged gently on her tank top, till one of her breasts sprang free. I had every muscle flexed as she reached over and wrapped her fingers around my cock, taking her time, sighing with bleary content as she helped jerk me off.

It was surreal.

"You came all over my hand last night," Sara whispered when I opened my eyes, a grin of content on my lips.

"You were a very sleepy, sexy girl last night."

"Mm, well, I'm not going to lay there doing nothing if my man needs to come."

I raised my eyebrows. "Your man?" I repeated, enjoying my view of her blushing furiously as she lay on top of me.

I let her stammer for a bit. It was cruel, but she was cute, and I needed time to figure out what the hell was going on with my own heart.

I felt different this morning – awake in a way I hadn't felt in awhile. And I was under no illusion that our conversation on the boat yesterday had nothing to do with it.

I hadn't spoken about any of that since it happened – not about my father, Liz or Lucie. The only people I had told the story to were

Mom and Emmett, and then, it was for the sake of explanation, and defending my side of the story as to why I left for so long. There had been tears, yelling and questions demanded mostly by Mom. It wasn't a peaceful conversation, but it was the first step in breaking down the wall. So of course it was hard.

But yesterday with Sara had been easy. In fact, it felt surprisingly good. Relieving. I hadn't felt the need to ever revisit that story, but it felt oddly natural to do it with her.

And I was repaying her for that this morning by forcing her to stutter about how she didn't mean to call me her man. I grinned.

"Easy," I murmured gently. "Tell me what you want for breakfast. I'm going to cook for you."

She blinked. "You are?"

"Yes. But that requires a few things first."

"What?"

"We need to pack so we're ready to go after we eat. But even before that, we need to go on a grocery run."

"And even before that?" Sara grinned, writhing on my chest as my hand went from cupping her ass to fingering her slick pussy from behind. I smirked as she flattened her hands on my chest and pushed up till she was straddling me.

"I think you know the answer to that."

"Mm-hm." Sara wet her lips, flattening her hands against my bare chest as she sat up to straddle me. Her mouth lightly parted when she felt my dick twitch under her pussy, and she giggled as it twitched again in response to the way she teased me with her tank top.

She pulled it up slowly, using the bunched hem to lift the underside of her chest. When she finally peeled her top off, her tits bounced so hard I growled and gripped her waist to reclaim the top. I swirled my tongue over her taut nipples, sucking on them like candy as I reached down to free my dick. I enjoyed her little gasps as I rubbed my naked head against her swollen clit.

Fuck, that feels too good.

Before I even reached to find a condom, she read my mind.

"I'm on the pill, Julian," she breathed. "And I'm clean."

I looked at her. I had barely returned her last two words before we were kissing so deeply it bordered on violent. She cried out as I ripped her panties clean off her body, tossing them aside to grip my dick and push deep inside her.

I groaned like I was already coming.

I fucking could.

She felt impossibly good. Her warmth, her breath, her skin on mine – nothing in my life had ever felt as right as this. I was grinding deep as it was, but she met me halfway on each thrust, pushing me so far inside her that the pleasure had me feeling fucking drunk. Her pussy was so wet I could hear it, and I knew she had to be dripping onto my sheets as she cried my name.

I couldn't think. I never felt this way, and on the off chance that I did, I didn't enjoy it.

But right now, I let myself go. Because the deeper I sunk into Sara, the more I could breathe – the more I actually *wanted* to breathe. For so long, I hadn't minded that suffocating weight in my chest. It was just something I carried with me every day, and I accepted it. It kept me accustomed to pain. But now that I knew what lightness felt like, it was all I ever wanted.

It felt better than anything I knew.

And I was pretty sure I could never go back.

SARA

I FELT Julian's eyes on me even as I moved around the kitchen, drying the dishes he'd hand washed. I'd reasoned that there was no sense in running the dishwasher for six dishes, and he lazily argued the opposite point just to rile me up, pretty sure.

He had a different look in his eyes since the morning. I didn't recognize it, but I loved it. He looked... dare I say *relaxed?* I was almost sure that was it.

"Let's just stay another night. We'll leave for the airport from here," Julian said, crossing the kitchen and kissing the top of my head on his way to the fridge.

"What? You just told me you had somewhere to be at two. I'm all packed. Once I finish drying this glass, we're good to go," I said, watching him grab a water bottle from the fridge and smirk at me as he twisted it open.

"You're cute when you're mad at me for something small."

"Versus?" I reached high to put the water glass back in the cupboard.

"When you're mad at me for something like forcing you to change into work appropriate clothes."

I tipped my head back and laughed. "God, that feels like forever ago."

Julian squinted. "Wasn't it?" he asked in a way that didn't require an answer. He was just breezy this morning, and despite our time crunch, I enjoyed watching it as he ambled around the house in a white T-shirt and blue jeans.

"Hey, aren't you always getting on Emmett for being late?" I teased, drying my hands on a blue-striped cloth napkin. "Julian. Get up off the couch."

He laughed. "Come here."

I tried to resist but failed when he patted his lap. Going over to him, I grinned, enjoying the feeling of his chest pressed against mine as I straddled him.

"What's up?" I cocked my head. "Are you idling because you don't want to go?"

"Yes."

I gave a sympathetic smile as I ran my fingertips along his chest. "I can imagine how hard it is to have to smile and fake nice for the rest of your family. I couldn't forgive them either. But it's only one day a year. It's for your grandma. And for Grandpa and Dad."

"I know." Julian collected my hands and kissed my fingertips. He didn't look at me when he said, "I want you to come with me."

My eyes fluttered. "What?" I bit down on my lip when he looked up at me. "Really?"

"Yes. Will you?"

"Of course," I blurted. "But... won't everyone think I'm your girlfriend?"

"Yes. But you can fake it, right?"

"I haven't had to fake it this entire last month, so I might be out of practice."

Julian rubbed my thighs. "Are you trying to turn me on or get me out the door?"

"The latter," I smirked, hopping off his lap so fast he groaned. "Come on, Hoult. Let's get our asses on that bike. We got this."

27

SARA

"Oh my God. I'm seeing things. Rosie, am I seeing things?"

Standing before me, literally clutching her pearls was Audrey Hoult, Julian's beautiful mother who apparently needed her mother-in-law to confirm that I was in fact standing there, and not an illusion.

"Mom," Julian said with what could only be described as charmed exasperation. We were in the middle of a busy restaurant, and he had warned me she might have this reaction, so I did my best not to giggle. I also made sure to wait till Audrey was visibly breathing again before I introduced myself.

"Oh, no! No handshake. I need to hug the first woman my son's ever brought home," she insisted as she wrapped her arms around me. I laughed over her shoulder as Julian stood there, hands in his pockets and eyes locked on me while nodding as if to say, *yep, exactly like I warned you.*

"Well, technically – "

"Oh, I *know*, Julian, technically, we're not home, this is a restaurant, but *still*. Sara, please. Come meet Rosemarie."

I couldn't help looking completely delighted as I shook hands with the very minuscule Rosemarie Hoult. I felt like I was meeting a celebrity, and it probably showed on my face, because Rosemarie proudly said, "Has he told you my nickname?"

"Rosemarie The Reaper," I said, prompting laughter from several of the cousins.

"That's right," Rosemarie beamed at Julian. "Those boys are terrified of me."

From there, Rosemarie introduced me to her two children, who I managed to smile for as I shook their hands. I knew they were the ones who had fought like animals over Julian's grandfather's property. But I also knew from Julian that Rosemarie, despite deploring her children's behavior, wished for them to simply be a family again.

So once a year, on their once-customary Sunday, they came together.

"You did better than I did," Julian murmured to me after I greeted the infamous cousin Paul. He was a balding man in his late thirties with a baby strapped to his chest. He smiled brightly at me and didn't look particularly villainous, but I knew too well that villains didn't always look the part.

"Thanks. Are you okay?" I asked Julian, standing close as I held his hand loosely in mine.

"I'm pretty damned good right now, actually," he said, eyeing something behind me while leaning in to kiss my forehead. "Well. Now I'm just okay," Julian smirked in a way that told me Emmett was behind us.

I peeked over my shoulder to see him standing there in a black skinny tie and a grey button-up stretched over his big, muscled frame. His adorably deep frown looked like it had no place on his normally jovial face.

"Hi, Emmett," I smiled.

"Hi. I... think I owe you an apology," he said, eyeing Julian. "Mind if I borrow her a sec, brother?"

"I do." Julian's quick reply made Emmett laugh. "Where are you taking her?"

"Julian," I flashed a teasing look. Clenching his jaw, he relented.

"Fine, borrow her. But return her to me as soon as possible, please."

"You got it, lover boy."

I almost heard Julian's eyes roll as Emmett walked me out of the bright dining room and into a little greenhouse of a hallway that led to the garden patio outside. I tried not to look too charmed or amused as Emmett struggled with how to start his apology.

"Look, I..." Emmett cleared his throat. "I don't even... well, first of all – "

"Emmett. Don't worry," I relieved him. "I know it looked pretty bad that night when I ran away. I'm not going to try to explain why I reacted so strongly, but what I will say is that your brother took pretty damned good care of me that night. I'm fine now. You slipped up, but it's not the end of the world. I had a great weekend, and I'm not angry at all."

Emmett blinked, silent for a second.

"Wow. That went a lot better than I thought."

"What, you thought I was going to be a raging bitch about it?" I teased.

"No, but Julian tore me a new one all night after you guys left. He really didn't let it go, he was beyond pissed for you. I was about to offer him my truck as an apology."

"Well, we did take your truck home that night," I laughed.

"Yeah, but I mean for keeps. Anyway, thank you, Sara. I'm so fucking grateful that you're not pissed at me," Emmett exhaled, running a hand over his short-cropped hair. "You probably know this, but my brother likes you a lot. I can tell."

I smiled. "How can you tell?"

"Man." Emmett drew in another deep breath as he looked down the hallway and into the dining room. "It's kind of crazy, but I can *see* the difference in him. In just the way he looks and talks. Sometimes he can be kind of... vacant. Like he's on autopilot. And it just feels like he hasn't been lately." Emmett squinted as he studied his brother from afar. I turned over to find him sitting with his mother, the two of them laughing. "It feels like he's actually in the moment, and present, and reacting. Like you flipped a light switch in him. Does that make sense?" he winced.

"It makes perfect sense. And it's incredibly flattering to me."

"Well, I'm actually not trying to flatter you," Emmett grinned. "It's just the truth. And listen, I know you guys are leaving for Biarritz tomorrow, and I just wanna say, when you're there with him... if you see or hear anything that mentions the name Lucie, don't... jump to conclusions. It's not what you think."

I grinned at Emmett's need to protect his brother while trying, for once, not to spill the beans on a secret.

"You're very sweet, Emmett, but Julian already told me about Liz and Lucie."

"Jesus fuck, seriously?" Emmett looked bowled over. "Wow, that's..." He looked at me as if I'd just told him I was secretly the Queen of England. "That's really fucking amazing. That's really cool, 'cause I didn't think he would ever – " He cut himself off again. He rubbed his chin and cleared his throat. "Look, I'm supposed to stop blowing up his spot, but I just gotta say – whatever he feels for you, Sara, I think it's pretty big. Right? It's gotta be. It took me two years to get the full story about Liz and Lucie out of him. Lukas doesn't even know most of it, so... thank you for being someone my brother feels like he can talk to. He's never really chosen to have one of those."

I bit my grin. I knew Emmett wasn't trying to flatter me, but somehow, that simple statement had me more honored than I could ever remember feeling.

"Alright." I heard Julian's voice shortly after his distinct footsteps started ambling over. "I'm sure whatever you've said by now, the damage is sufficient," he said to his brother. "I've come to collect her if you're finished here."

"Sure am."

Julian looked at me with a smile. "I know you might have just reached your limit of Hoults for today, but my mother is requesting some time with you, if that's okay."

"That's more than okay," I replied.

"Shit, hold on," Emmett said. "Actually, I have one more thing to say to Sara, okay?" he said, laughing at Julian's *are you shitting me* look. "Just go, J. She'll be right there. I promise," he insisted.

He kept his eyes on his brother till he turned to leave. Once Julian was out of earshot, Emmett faced me with a grin.

"Look, I just wanted to say... in case he ever pisses you off, because Lord knows he pisses me off a lot... my brother's a really good man. The best I know. And when he cares about someone, he'll stop at nothing to make sure that person is happy, and safe, and completely taken care of for the rest of their life," Emmett said earnestly, completely serious for once. "There's really only a few people he regards that highly outside his family – Lukas being one of them, and I guess you being the other."

"Sure you're not trying to butter me up right now, Emmett?" I teased to disguise the fact that my heart was fluttering.

"Yeah, I'm not smart enough to blow smoke up people's asses," Emmett snorted, making me laugh. "What you see is what you get. And honestly, I was just telling you that because sometimes Julian... he can hurt people without realizing," he said, making my smile falter just a little. "He doesn't mean to – he's just so focused on some-thing else, usually work. And if he somehow hurts your feelings during this trip because say, he's really busy, or distracted, or just plain being himself – just know that it's worth it to stick around with him. Even if you don't know what the hell he's thinking half the time, and you can't stand that he doesn't say much. He's still a good man who's going to take care of you. I mean he's definitely the best guy *I* know. I'm still kind of hoping to be him when I grow up," Emmett smirked, putting the smile back on my lips.

"Thank you, Emmett. I appreciate it," I said, giving him a hug.

"Alright. Go talk to my mom now," he said. "And sorry ahead of time if she brings up grandkids!" he called after me.

28

SARA

The last time I was out of the country was when I was eighteen.

It wasn't quite summer yet. I had dropped out of school, and I already had a new college lined up to transfer to in the fall.

But that wasn't for another five or six months, and I hated every minute of being home in my shitty little town.

My father had a thriving law firm about ten minutes away now, so there was no chance of us moving. I was stuck at home in the place that the misery first started, and worse, many of my classmates from high school still lived there. They knew I was back, they knew what I'd done, and it delighted them. They left printouts of the article covering my arrest at our door. They taunted my mother if they saw her at the gas station or grocery store.

I myself didn't leave the house.

I was terrified.

So eventually, Mom started taking us on mini road trips. She worked part-time at the local library, but she quit the job in order to be home with me every day. And if I had the energy, or found myself in a good enough mood, she'd take me driving to explore the other parts of Texas.

"There's more than where we live," she said behind the wheel of her old Camry, wearing sunglasses too big and boxy for her face. "Daddy taught me that," she added, beaming as much as she could for someone as reserved as she was.

"Yeah, he taught you that by bringing you to London and then forcing you to live *here*," I had griped.

"Yes, but now I have a car. I have these big roads. I can go anywhere I want."

"You never do."

"What am I doing now?"

"What, it took me getting in trouble for you to start exploring? That's sad." My surly teenaged pessimism was a force to be reckoned with.

"Maybe that's sad," Mom conceded. "But sometimes it takes a tragedy for us to get moving. To find the strength to look for better things."

"So I'm a *tragedy* now?"

Again, the pessimism.

I was definitely not in a particularly charming or likable phase of my life. After the bullying in high school, then the entirely different kind in college, I felt like the world was against me. Sometimes, I felt like even my mom was against me. I could see and feel how much she loved me with every fiber of her being, but sometimes I would catch her gazing at me with almost a fearful look. Like she didn't quite know who I was, or who I'd grown up to be.

I spent a lot of time in my room just watching movies and TV. Mom offered to sit with me, but she was awful at sitting still, and she always lectured me on my taste in sappy romantic movies.

But the road trips helped us.

They started small, with little half-hour drives to Dallas. Then they got longer. I'd take my Una Magazines with me for those rides. For the three-and-a-half hour journey to Austin, my dad joined us, and he sang the whole way. My magazines were of particular comfort for me that time as my mother and I switched back and forth between being amused and enraged by him.

In Austin, we went to the botanical garden, and despite my dad's protests for his weak knees, we hiked Mount Bonnell. At the top, I met two women in their mid-twenties who offered to take a picture of us in front of the view. They wound up inviting the three of us to watch their roller derby bout that night, which we did. Dad loved it. Mom not so much. But she did appreciate that one of the girls spotted me in the stands, and dropped by to say hello.

It was fun. I felt like I made more memories during those trips than I did in all my years at school. I was noticeably brighter after the travels. My mom noticed that. It just made me feel like there was so much more out there than I was giving the world credit for, and that I did in fact have the potential to start over again – for real this time.

For my birthday, my dad suggested we all take a trip back to London. It would be my mom and my first time back since moving to the States.

I didn't remember much. I realized now that I was four when I left – the same age Lucie was when her mother took her away from Julian. Four years was a significant chunk of time, but apparently still easy to lose grasp of in memory.

The plane ride to the airport was cramped and uncomfortable, and I didn't feel any kinship to London when our taxi finally arrived into the thick of the city. I felt disappointed that a place that was supposed to be a part of my identity was as much a stranger to me as any other European city might be.

But within two days, I was in love.

I loved how big the city was. I loved the architecture. I loved the way everyone sounded like my dad. Somehow, I felt less like an outsider there than I did at home.

There, it felt like anything was possible.

"You should have found a school to transfer to in London. Your mother would have moved back here with you in a heartbeat," my dad said as we sat in a café one morning, my mom still asleep.

"Yeah, right. Like you'd survive being away from her so much."

"I would fly to see you two every Friday. And then I'd return to work on Monday."

I laughed. "We don't have the money for that. Sorry. But one day, I'll earn it for you. Promise."

"I believe you." Dad clinked his cappuccino cup to mine. "You're hardworking enough, and the fact that you chose New York to start over tells me you're not scared of anything. But let me tell you something. Some people with your brains and your talent still get lost in a city as big as that one, because there are so many people and so much to do. But I believe in you that you'll look temptation in the eye, walk right past it and make yourself proud."

"And you and Mama proud."

"Us too," Dad said. "No matter what you think sometimes, we could never stay mad at you. Sometimes, the heartbreak will hit us out of nowhere, because you're our daughter and we wish you never even had to experience what you did at that school. We get angry that you were hurt. You might see us during those times and think we're angry with *you*, but we're not. We're just going to take time to forget what happened, Sara. But eventually, we will. Your mother and I just want you to be safe and happy. That's all any parent wants. We're proud of you, Sara, and we believe very much in you."

I couldn't forget those words, or that trip.

It put me in awe of my parents' forgiveness. My mother, in particular, had sacrificed her entire life and everything she knew to create and raise me. She then watched me make a mess of her hard work by getting myself into the trouble I did, and even after that, she continued sacrificing to simply ensure that I was happy, and encouraged. She had only just begun acclimating and hitting her stride in Texas when everything happened with me at college. She had given up every one of her dreams just to give me the *chance* to meet mine.

So it was from that point forward that I swore to myself I'd repent for what I did. My parents deserved everything from me, and I would stop at nothing to make their hearts swell with pride for me.

My mom cried the day I snagged that job at June Magazine out of college. My dad booked tickets to New York for that very weekend, so he could take me to a celebratory brunch.

It was hard not to conflate their happiness with my happiness at the job. I associated my job with us moving on from what happened.

The drama my freshman year of college became a distant memory we didn't speak about. It still hung over our heads every day, but higher now – barely noticeable except for when certain topics came up, like wanting to look for a new job. My mom would ask what was covered in background checks, I'd quietly Google it, and neither of us would talk about why she had asked. We both knew, but we didn't need to say it aloud. It still hurt too much.

So over time, I told myself I was happy to stay with the same company. Perhaps I could've left, but the process of even thinking about it sent me back to the bad memories, and I preferred staying where I was – in a state of comfort. Predictability.

For so long, I was sure I liked my life that way.

"I wish I'd found you earlier," Julian murmured as I sat on his lap, both of us entwined in one seat on the private charter. "I would have hired you to my company in a heartbeat."

I smiled. "Yeah, but that's the point. You wouldn't have found me earlier, because I felt too safe there," I whispered. "And after everything I'd been through, there was nothing more important to me than feeling safe. Like there's nothing to worry about, and I can just relax."

"Understood," Julian murmured, running his fingers through my hair. I closed my eyes as I reveled in the feeling of his calm blending into mine.

I couldn't wait to touch down in Biarritz, but shortly after our conversation, I drifted off to sleep against his chest.

29

We arrived at night, and the view of Biarritz visibly took her breath away.

It was fun for me to watch.

The buildings along the coast were illuminated, glittering gold against the pitch black of the sky. It was a good preview to the glamour of the city in the daytime. Without a full view of it though, Sara was already enamored.

"It's so crazy. There's old castles, but there's Art Deco, and there's this *water*," she murmured as I let her walk ahead of me, taking everything in on both sides of her. She stopped for every building on her left and every jagged rock in the water to her right. It crashed gently against the shore, sweeping over our bare feet as we carried our shoes. "If The Great Gatsby took place anywhere but West Egg, it would be here," she decided before finally turning and giving me the chance to look at her face.

Her excitement was unbridled and it had her eyes brighter than I'd ever seen them.

But she closed them and smiled when I held her cheek. With the moonlight shining down on her, she was as beautiful as I'd ever seen her. It made it hard for me to reconcile that at nine at night, we still had work to do. All I wanted was to take her into my hotel room and fall into bed with her. To hear more about her little road trips with her mom around Texas. I wanted to find out everything I possibly could about her, and the fact that I didn't have all the time in the world to do that infuriated me.

I asked myself how I hadn't planned this trip better, and given myself more time with her before the Roths arrived.

All I wanted was to touch Sara in every way that made her smile. I wanted to show her all my favorite parts of the town and let my memories with her serve as the last I left Biarritz with. I wanted to ask her a million simple questions I somehow didn't have the answers to yet.

I didn't know where her favorite restaurant was back home, and that for some reason bothered me.

I wanted to be the one who had all the information, all the elements to make her the happiest woman in the world. But with the Roths and their advisors arriving in twelve hours, and Sara far from brushed up on how to give a tour of the resort, I didn't have the time. I had work to do, and for once, I fucking hated it. For once, I just wanted to relax.

I just wanted to be with Sara.

"What are you thinking?" she asked when she finally opened those glimmering eyes again. I smiled down at her as I replied.

"Nothing."

IT WAS difficult leaving Sara's room in the morning while she was still asleep, but I had just gotten word from Colin that he'd arrived, and so had the Roths with their team.

I let Sara rest. We'd been up late after arriving at night yesterday, and spending the next three hours touring the property before going back to her room.

I asked some more of my questions last night as we relaxed in the bath, my front to her back, her head resting against the crook of my neck.

Shamelessly, her favorite restaurant in the city was a West Village spot that sold only French fries and, apparently, "a glorious selection of condiments." Her dream vacation was to either Tuscany or Monaco.

"Why Tuscany?" I asked.

"Because wine."

"Fair enough. Why Monaco?"

"Because Grace Kelly."

"Your best friend once said my mother looked like Grace Kelly."

"She so *does!* I totally thought that yesterday. And Lia totally went on her Grace Kelly kick because of me. She'd never watch old Hollywood movies without me bugging her to."

So I'd collected some answers in French fries and Grace Kelly. Unsurprisingly, I wanted more.

"Biggest goal?"

She hummed against the ridge of her wine glass while thinking.

"The thing I dreamed for longest about was definitely going to prom and feeling like a princess in some big, puffy ball gown," she snorted. "Since I was five, I fantasized about every detail down to the big reveal of my dress, and the walk down the stairs, and my date putting on my corsage as my parents took pictures."

"Jesus."

"Don't blame me. The stupid movies ruined me," she giggled. "But anyway, since that ship has clearly sailed, I'd say the big goal is making enough money in the future to buy my parents a home in London. So they can fly back and forth between there and Texas. A three-bedroom, preferably. For when I visit."

"Why three bedrooms? Do your parents sleep separately?"

"My dad does snore like a beast, but no. I imagined for like, my kids."

"Yeah? And how many kids do you want?"

"Three." She twisted around to face me when she asked, "Yourself?"

"At least one. No more than three," I'd replied.

This morning, I was still thinking about the wistful little *hmm* sound she made after I gave my answer. It made me grin even after I shut the door of her room behind me, the sound tugging at heartstrings I didn't know I had.

A moment after, I spotted Colin in the hallway.

He was coming from knocking fruitlessly on my door down the hall. Turning from it, his eyes shifted from Sara's door behind me to my wrinkled shirt. His smile was surprised but delighted, and much less restrained than I expected from him.

"Sorry," he apologized hastily before going straight into work mode. "So, Turner and Carter are here, and they're... clearly not accustomed to working straight off a flight. Carter is going to sleep in his room right now, but Turner insists he'll come for your meeting with the advisors." Colin smirked. "He made it a really big deal that he was bestowing us with his presence, considering his jet lag."

I laughed. "Jesus. I don't even need him here anymore. His work is done."

"Yes, well, now he just needs to be babysat and ego-stroked while you talk to the guys with the brains. Speaking of them, they're early for the meeting in the salon, but I had the kitchen set up coffee and a breakfast platter in the meantime. Is, um, Sara joining?" Colin asked, eyeing the door of her room not too far behind me. That kid-like grin reappeared on his face.

"I would say it's not what it looks like, but it is," I said as I nodded for us to start walking. Colin adjusted quickly to his surprise for my candor.

"Oh. Well, she's extremely smart, kind and capable, so if a rule were to be broken for anyone, it should be her."

"I appreciate it," I said. We exchanged one amused look before returning to business. "To answer your question, Sara won't be joining this meeting. She needs to meet with members of hotel staff to prep the Roths' tour after breakfast," I said as I got to my room. Colin stopped me as I opened the door.

"Uh, sir – I know the itinerary is clear, but Turner specifically requested that she join us at breakfast," he said. I exhaled.

"She's busy right now, so I'll have her join late. See you down there in ten."

30

SARA

I had mentioned wanting a second just to walk around outside the resort last night, so despite Turner apparently waiting on me in the salon, I snuck out of the back of the hotel to check out Biarritz in the daytime.

Greeting me at the door was the green 1958 Cadillac Eldorado Julian had called to take me on a fifteen-minute drive. With the top down, it particularly matched the glamorous vibe of the town. I had to giggle to myself, thanking the driver who held the door for me before whipping out my phone to text Julian.

> **ME:** *Are you trying to make me feel like old Hollywood in this car?*
> **JULIAN:** *Whatever puts a smile on that face*
> **ME:** *Trust me there's a big one right now.*

I couldn't stop grinning as the driver whisked me down the street, providing his charmingly accented tour of Biarritz, the "gem of the Basque Coast" that once served as the exclusive holiday spot for European nobility.

I was so very in awe.

Every street felt like a mix of styles I never knew coexisted. There were bright colors and pastels, as well as stone castles and cliffs. It was trendy surf town meets fairytale kingdom, and I could hardly believe it was real.

Though we had stopped a few times for me to wander and snap pictures, I didn't at all feel like I'd had enough time. Of course, my consolation in going back to the resort was seeing Julian. A part of me already missed him. He'd snuck out early this morning while I was sleeping, and somehow, having only woken up next to him the past three mornings, I was already spoiled. I needed more.

My cheeks were still flushed pink with excitement when I returned to the hotel, and by the time I got to the ritzy checker floored salon, I spotted Julian at a table with Colin, Turner, and four other men. Turner, despite looking deathly hung over with his sandy blonde hair in his eyes, spotted me first and rose quickly to throw his heavy arms around me in a bear hug.

"This one!" he boomed. "The party doesn't start till this one arrives. Gentlemen, meet the star of the show, Miss Sara Hanna."

I smiled graciously as I went around the table shaking hands and making introductions. All of the advisors were at least ten years older than Turner, but at least a few of them had the same wandering eye that he did.

My outfit this morning was a striped top with flowy, high-waisted pants and espadrilles. Topknot. Headband scarf. Simple, sexy and not too showy. I was going to be in a swimsuit around these guys later, so I figured I'd pace myself.

Of course, this outfit alone was causing Turner's hand to linger for longer than necessary on my lower back. I could tell Julian noticed because his eyes were glued to Turner's arm, and his posture was noticeably rigid under his white shirt.

"Man, I can't wait to take you surfing later," Turner grinned as his advisors engaged Julian in some talk about inspections.

"Turner, I think we made it clear that I'm actually not very good at that," I said, giving him a laugh. He grinned and lowered his voice.

"Well, I thought it was clear that my enjoyment came less from watching you succeed, and more from watching you splash around in a bikini."

Oh.

What was left of my smile was stiff as Turner and I simply stood there for a moment, wearing amiable expressions for each other to maintain the guise of a seamless meeting.

But I had expected this at some point. I had prepared myself for Turner to get handsy and inappropriate, and I wasn't afraid. We were baiting him, after all, and this was expected. All I had to do was maintain pleasant enough to keep his ego stroked and his attention still piqued. Once the paperwork was in progress, my job as a professional seductress would require much less tolerance for Turner. Once the paperwork was *finalized*, I could very well tell him to fuck off if I wanted to.

We were close. And I was confident.

That said, I was still somewhat relieved that the weather took a turn when it came time for our surf and boating trip. We'd waited it out for a half hour, but with the rain still going, we canceled our beach outing and opted for what was originally scheduled for tomorrow – a tour of the spa.

It was an oasis hidden in the very center of the resort with brilliant white pillars, sparkling pools and Turkish baths, as well as views of the sweeping coast. I had barely finished talking about what had been added during the renovations when Turner decided he needed a massage.

"My back is stiff from the flight," he said, wincing as he reached over his shoulders and rubbed himself.

He locked his eyes on me as he did so. I cocked an eyebrow, and he grinned in response. I didn't know exactly what he was saying, but I had a feeling it was lewd, and that feeling was confirmed shortly after.

"Sara looks like she needs a massage," Turner announced, his eyes still on me as he interrupted his advisors. "Maybe we should get a couple's massage. You look like you're probably very tight," he said with a smirk.

"Jesus, Turner," one of his advisors laughed nervously as Julian offered an easy smile despite the fire I caught in his eyes.

"Turner. Let's get you an hour-long Swedish massage. Shall we?"

"Trying to get me out of your hair, Hoult?"

"Absolutely," Julian said to the raucous laughter of the advisors. "Come on. Let me introduce you to our spa manager."

I WAS INITIALLY hesitant about staying at the spa while Julian went on to talk with the advisors, but he said he preferred some time alone with them, and I'd have Colin with me as well.

"Sara, he's paying us to get *massages* right now. Come on," Colin laughed under his breath as Julian waited for me to relent.

"I just want you to have some time to enjoy yourself while you're here," he murmured, ushering me aside. "And I do like keeping elements of my business to myself. I hope you understand."

I nodded though I didn't quite.

But then I remembered how Julian had associated Liz with the success of his first billion-dollar business, and how that had too positively skewed his perception of her. I chewed my lip as I considered that by excluding me from this meeting, Julian was trying to put a barrier between his career and me. I wasn't sure if that was a good thing or a bad thing. I felt like it was possibly the latter, but I told myself not to think about it too hard.

So I distracted myself with the tranquil music playing as I got undressed in the women's locker room, eventually emerging in a robe to find a girl named Anaïs waiting for me.

For someone so small and petite, the woman was strong. Incredibly so. I had still been vaguely bothered by Julian's request before entering the dim massage room, but barely a minute later, I was mentally thanking him for the treatment. It struck me only then that, save for the complimentary shoulder rubs at the manicure place, I'd never had a massage before in my life.

And it felt amazing.

My skin was slathered in natural coconut oil, and slippery enough to make it easy for Anaïs to rub the heel of her palms against as she massaged my back then my legs. Even the pads of her fingers were strong.

God, this chick is good. I honestly wished I could afford her on a daily basis, just to help massage away all the stupid, overanalyzed thoughts in my head. Forty minutes into the massage, and she had yet to get tired or lose an ounce of strength.

I was practically asleep from the deep relaxation when a knock sounded at the door.

"Oh." I could actually hear Anaïs frowning. She sounded as surprised as I was by the sudden interruption, quickly apologizing to me before slipping out of the room.

Soon enough, I could hear a low, male voice joining hers just outside the door.

It was a mutter I couldn't quite make out, but it sounded too low to be Colin. Lying naked on that table, I stiffened at the thought of who it might be. My stomach tightened with a dark suspicion, but before I could analyze further, the door slid slowly back open.

Eyes on the floor, I froze.

I was staring at men's shoes walking in. My heart slammed like a rock against the table, and before I knew it, a hand was lifting the towel off my naked ass.

From the mere graze of the fingers, I knew it wasn't Turner.

"Oh my God – *asshole!*" I hissed, lifting my head to find Julian standing over my body, a crooked smile on his lips.

"Lay down."

His command was a low murmur, but it still packed more authority than I could deny. Lying back down on the table, I peeked up to watch Julian gaze down at the coconut oil.

"Are you going to finish my massage?" I smirked. "I did have twenty minutes left."

"You'll get your twenty minutes," Julian said as his dexterous fingers flicked down the front of his shirt to unbutton. When it fell open, I got a delicious, two-second view of his six-pack before he said, "Head down."

Biting my lip, I put my head down, watching his feet round the table to stand at the very front, just above me. I was still giggling as I heard him oil up his palms.

But I closed my eyes and moaned when I felt his strong hands press down on my shoulder blades. My mouth parted as he began rubbing down to my back, then the small of it before he leaned over enough to grab handfuls of my ass. Though he squeezed a bit for his own pleasure, he still massaged me, pressing the heel of his palm against all the right places.

His touch was distinctly different than the masseuse's. It was firm, relaxing yet undeniable sexual. The pads of his fingers stroked me in slow, almost circular movements – like he was savoring my skin.

Oh God, this is too good.

Lifting my head, I could see Julian getting hard through his slacks as he hovered over me. I parted my lips. I was only inches from being able to cup his package with my mouth, and the thought alone made me so incredibly wet.

It also made it particularly torturous when Julian started massaging my thighs.

Sliding his hand between them, he gave long downward strokes, scooping my pussy on the way up every time.

"You're so ready for me," Julian murmured, gathering more and more of my wetness on his palm with every stroke of my thigh. I bit the edge of my fist as I tried to muffle myself, but the anticipation was killing me.

"Put your fingers inside me," I whispered pleadingly.

"I thought you wanted a massage," he teased as he spread my legs, propping one knee slightly up to expose my pussy. Then with just his index and middle fingers, he rubbed between my thighs, teasing my slick folds and getting them impossibly hot with every stroke. "Your ass looks so fucking good like this," he murmured. I gasped when he spanked it, his other hand still massaging my pussy. "Look at how hard you have me."

I tilted my head up again, gasping at the steel rod straining against Julian's slacks.

"Take them off," I begged softly.

"Lie on your back," Julian countered as he rounded to the side of the table, presenting me the delectable view of his shirtless body.

I felt another surge of wetness in my pussy as he gave those three swift jerks to undo his belt. I'd become addicted to that sight.

"Massage the oil onto your tits," Julian said as he unbuttoned and unzipped his pants.

I reached over to dip my fingers in the oil, holding my hand above my chest to watch the liquid drip onto my hard nipples then slide down my naked curve. The sight was tantalizing even for me. I had to gaze down and watch as I rubbed my own breasts, letting out a giggle for the fact that I was practically shining them for Julian.

But he didn't share in my amusement. In fact, as he watched me, his jaw tightened. He actually looked turned on to the point of being pissed off when he approached me, running his hand over the length of his clothed erection.

"I don't think you realize, Sara," he pulled my hands away from my body, "just how much of a fucking animal you turn me into," he finished in a murmur, pushing my tits up and together. They were so round and reflective they looked almost fake, and I never in a million years thought I'd find that arousing, but right now, I was so wet I was pooling onto the table. "Do you have any idea how difficult it is to carry on with a meeting when all I can think about is you? When all I can see is your perfect fucking body getting rubbed down by hands that aren't mine?"

"I'm sorry I ruined your meeting," I smirked.

"You'll make it up to me," Julian said, sending a chill over my skin. With gravel in his voice, he murmured, "Spread your legs for me."

As soon as I did, he cupped under my left thigh, pulling me to the edge of the table and lifting my leg. Resting it on his naked chest, he pulled out his cock, stroking it twice in his hand before sliding it into my pussy.

"Oh my God."

I clawed the silky sheet on the table as Julian leaned forward, penetrating me fully. His eyes were like steel as they took me in. He looked so unbelievably gorgeous in the warm lighting, yet so dauntingly serious. His lips were pressed into a line even as he wet them. But he allowed himself a low growl when he leaned forward to play with my breasts again, squeezing and pinching as he pushed in deep.

I could barely make a sound. I was filled to the hilt, my pleasure tinged with just the right amount of pain as Julian furiously pumped his hips. His every muscle flexed, and his every tendon twitched as his tempo steadily increased inside me.

"Tell me how that feels, baby," he whispered, his electric stare shining bright in the dark room. I struggled to speak. "Does that feel good?"

"Too good," I breathed in awe, my eyes following his every move.

I felt more exposed than ever as he lowered my leg from his chest, gripping under both my thighs and holding them apart to give himself an unobstructed view of his cock driving into my pussy. His bottom lip tucked just under his teeth as he watched himself fuck me. *Holy shit.* There was something so carnal and erotic about his rapt focus on the image. It felt as if he were claiming me – showing himself that when he had me like this, I belonged to no one but him.

He looked absolutely entranced by his view.

But when I came, his mouth was promptly on mine – like he wouldn't miss my orgasm for the world. His kiss was deep, fast and lush, and with his cock still buried inside me, it felt like he was devouring me. Owning every inch of me.

And I wanted him to.

I watched with wild-eyed fascination when Julian gnashed his teeth and finished inside me, his fingers digging into my body, his hard muscles slowly relaxing as he groaned my name. As we caught our breaths, it felt as if I breathed in what he exhaled.

It was a miraculous feeling.

I didn't ever want to let it go.

31

JULIAN

The first meeting of our second day in Biarritz was streamlined to include only Colin, two advisors and myself. It was just before noon, so as far as I knew, Turner and Carter were both asleep. Sara was on another drive around town that I'd arranged in the same green Eldorado.

I knew she was displeased when I left for the meeting this morning from my hotel room. As I knotted my tie, she sat at the edge of my bed in a yellow dress that went off her shoulders. She had her ankles primly crossed and her hands folded in her lap while looking thoroughly pissed at me. It was oddly charming, and I couldn't stop glancing in her direction, but I didn't change my mind.

I wanted to go to this meeting without her. The topic of discussion for today was well beyond the study materials Colin and I had given her about the resort, and it didn't make sense for her to attend.

On top of that, it was probably time to start separating her from the project.

So I sent her on a little adventure for the day, hoping that by night, I could listen to her talk breathlessly on and on about it.

"Now this is quite the view," Turner's advisor, Irv, said as we sat on the wide terrace of the resort's fine dining restaurant overlooking the coast. "To be frank with you, Julian, the Roths have long made up their mind. I think you know that," he chuckled, holding his hands up in slight apology. "At this point, we really only need to go through formalities. Then we'll get into the extensive paperwork, but as you know, we're all very pleased with how well this suits Turner and Carter's endeavors. I realize it's barely noon, but we should toast to that."

"Just in time," Colin remarked as the servers came back with the bottles of champagne I'd ordered.

"Of course, you're always a step ahead," Irv laughed, waving the server off to pour the flutes himself while his colleague, Robert, gazed out at the ocean. It looked particularly blue under this morning's sun.

"Do you surf, Julian?" he asked.

"I do."

"Ah, of course you do. What don't you do?"

"I haven't in a long time," I admitted, squinting in the sun since I'd given my Persols to Sara. "I'm not sure how well I'd fare out there after so many years."

"How many years has it been?"

However many years it's been since I've seen Lucie.

"Probably five now. Maybe six," I replied, peering out at the water.

I could see the exact spot where I'd spent dozens of mornings with Lucie. I could still remember those ridiculous golden pigtails wagging in the wind. Her hair was short. To her mother's dismay, it refused to grow. But Lucie was never bothered by it. She loved ribbons and bows, so she still did her own hair in the morning, securing two inch-long pigtails at the top of her head that I called her hamster ears.

Every time I said "hamster," she would oink. And every time I told her that wasn't the sound a hamster made, she'd laugh. In that way, she reminded me a lot of Emmett. She did things just to amuse herself with my reaction.

Their sense of humor was such a striking resemblance that one morning I caved and called Emmett to introduce him to Lucie.

They talked easily and exchanged goofy stories for over an hour, which surprised even me. While still on the phone, Lucie asked me when she would meet her uncle, and Emmett and I looked at each other, took a breath and just like that, overlooked the wall between us to book him a flight to France. Lucie was so thrilled she darted off to make him a welcome card despite the fact that his flight was two weeks away. At least it was till he canceled it.

Two days after our great conversation, Emmett texted and said he couldn't come, and not to call him anymore – that Mom was hurt over how he was trying to embrace the family I had replaced them with. I did my best to explain, and I think he tried to listen, but the call ended before any good could come of anything.

And just like that, another brick cemented itself to the ever-heightening wall between us.

So I spent as much time as I could with Lucie.

We loved watching the surfers together in the morning, before Liz even woke up. Despite how often she asked, I was hesitant about teaching Lucie to surf. But after seeing so many fathers out there with kids as young as two years old, I yielded. She was an absurdly good swimmer, anyway, with no discernible fear of the water. Paddling out was always my biggest challenge on a board, but Lucie aced it like it was nothing.

Staring out at the water this morning, I spotted a boy a little older than her out there, and I wondered how Lucie stacked up against him now. She had said in one of her letters that she still surfed when she could, but that was awhile ago. Realistically, she'd forgotten surfing the way she had English. Remembered the basics. Not well enough to want to practice.

"Hoult, Turner told me great things about the hot stone treatment here."

Returning my eyes to the table, I eased smoothly back into the conversation. Irv and Robert were talking about the spa that Turner had apparently raved about. I offered to schedule them appointments there before our dinner tonight.

But despite my convincingly undivided attention on them, I was thinking about the distance.

I was probably an hour-and-a-half away from Lucie by plane right now. I could actually take the jet and be there faster than that. I'd ask a trusted member of the hotel staff to join me, and that person would serve as my translator, so I could explain everything to Lucie.

I had no idea what her mother had told her about me.

I didn't want to think about it, but knowing Liz, it was something cruel – probably that I had willingly left them because I was too busy for a family. That I had asked them to move out. I could tell from the waning excitement in the letters Lucie sent that her image of me was changing as she grew. I imagined she could better understand the stories her mom told her. Whatever the French words were for "abandoned" and "unavailable," she probably heard them a lot when Liz spoke about me. If Lucie badgered her enough, I wouldn't put it past Liz to mention that she wasn't biologically mine. She was ruthless when it came to hurting people. She said she'd learned that from me.

So I believed fully that she would hurt Lucie for the sake of dragging me through the mud. And for that reason, I wished badly for a chance to explain myself. I'd considered the short plane ride about a thousand times during this lunch alone.

But as much as I wanted to and technically *could* see Lucie, I knew well that reappearing in her life now would only hurt her.

In her letters, she mentioned friends and school, and all the new memories she was creating in place of the ones we once had. She was moving on. Kids did that well. They were quicker than adults when it came to looking at a different reality and accepting it as their new one.

It wasn't to say Lucie didn't hurt over me. There were probably many nights of questions and crying shortly after they moved out of the house. But over time, that heartbreak subsided, and by now, Lucie had hit her stride in terms of forgetting about me. The decreasing frequency of her letters, and the way they spoke happily of friends showed me that much. Now, she was simply focused on being a happy little girl.

So as I sat at this table with Turner Roth's advisors, I decided to finally let her go.

If there was a bright side, it was that I had my own new chapters ahead of me.

32

SARA

I'd covered everything from the beach to the aquarium to the Musée Bonnat by the time I returned to the resort around five.

For excluding me from the meeting this morning, I was hell-bent on staying at least grouchy with Julian, but that didn't work. He had texted me all day during my adventures, asking for updates on what I'd seen. After a good deal of badgering, he even caved to my request to download Snapchat, an idea he was fervently against till about 2PM.

But from that point on, I sent him picture after video after picture of where I was. And wherever I was, I stopped and grinned to read whatever he promptly sent back. For shots of scenery, it was usually "very nice" and a suggestion of something cool to see or peruse nearby. But for selfies, Julian's replies grew increasingly urgent, starting with *"you look gorgeous"* to *"damn it Sara,"* before finally reaching *"come back now so I can take your dress off."*

> **ME:** *If you actually have the time between meetings to do that, I will happily skip the Casino Barrière*
> **JULIAN:** *Come back to me please*
> **ME:** *Everything okay?*

JULIAN: Not bad considering I haven't had to deal with
    either Turner or Carter all day
ME: Not bad but not good either?
JULIAN: Everything's fine. Just need you right now.

I stopped in the middle of the town square, my heart skipping a beat as I read that message. Then without wasting another second, I turned straight on my heel to go back to the resort.

I was on my way up to our floor in the vintage elevator when it stopped halfway, opening to present me with Turner. His shirt was half unbuttoned and twisted askew, thanks to a similarly haphazardly dressed girl hanging off his body.

"Holy shit, enough," he laughed, peeling her off of him before stumbling in and noticing me. "Oh, shit! Look who it is. Quick, press door close so she doesn't follow me in," he said, hitting me with the stench of sex and sweat as he jabbed the button.

"Hello, Turner," I finally offered my greeting.

"Hello yourself. Jesus, look at you. I just wanna pull on this," he said, tugging at the tie of my bikini top at the back of my neck. I shirked away.

"Please don't."

"That's fine, I can see plenty as it is," he laughed, looking down at the outfit I'd changed into for the beach – a white V-neck tunic dress over my light blue swimsuit. Turner kept his eyes pinned to my cleavage. "Listen, Sara, what can you tell me about the age demographics in this town?" he asked with a serious frown despite still staring at my chest.

"The residential population or the tourist population?"

Turner grinned. "Whatever."

"Well, starting with the population on a regular basis, it's about twenty-five thousand with a median age around – "

"Honestly, all I really want to know is why I'm having trouble finding girls as pretty as you."

Ugh. I stretched my lips in a smile to avoid retching in Turner's face, which I really did want to do considering he'd just baited me with work talk for the sole purpose of leading into a shitty pick-up line.

"I think that's above my pay grade, Turner."

"You're funny. Seriously though, Sara – what does it feel like to be the most beautiful woman in Biarritz right now?" Turner pressed on, almost buckling my knees with his sheer level of cheese. "Don't laugh! Trust me, I've been looking around, I've given it a few shots here and there, but so far, the talent is surprisingly bleak for a surf town," he said as the elevator approached my floor.

"You never pressed your floor, Turner," I smiled as the doors opened on mine. I pursed my lips when he followed me out.

"I have a question about the age demographics. Business stuff." He strode behind me with a grin in his voice. "Can you help me out?"

"Absolutely. Would you like to schedule for all of us to meet a little early before dinner? I'm sure Julian's on the premises, so that can be easily arranged," I said, slowing to a stop in front of my door. Turner smirked down at me.

"Nah. I've already got you here. Let's just talk in your room," he said, nodding behind me. He was aware as usual that I saw right through his bullshit – he just didn't care. He was confident it would still work.

"No, Turner, we should meet in the salon," I said politely.

"Oh, come on, sweetheart. Don't be so rigid." *Oh, pleeease.* I did my best not to roll my eyes. I honestly wished I had a hidden camera live streaming all this entitled douchebaggery to Lia. She'd love it. "Just humor me, Sara."

"Alright, Turner," I said, watching his eyebrows wiggle in anticipation of my key on the door. But I didn't give him that satisfaction. "Hit me with your question right here. About age demographics? Is that what you wanted to ask?"

I did my best not to laugh as Turner's face fell flat. But just as quickly, it returned to life with that signature shit-eating grin of his.

"Jesus. You really don't trust me enough to come in your room?" he asked, giving a little chuckle.

"My room is not a space for a business meeting, Turner."

"Fine, then let's do something besides business."

Okay, so you're clearly just going for it now. I crossed my arms.

"Considering business is precisely what we're here for, my answer is going to be no."

"Let's be real – your business here is a little different than that of the guys."

"Come again?"

Turner rubbed his chin and laughed. "Oh, no... you think I don't know, do you?"

My heart thumped but I cocked my head to play it off.

"Know what?"

"Why you were hired," he said, stepping close to me. I was sure his chest was entirely too close to mine, but I didn't give him the satisfaction of looking down to confirm. I kept my stare pinned right back on his, refusing to look anything but undaunted.

"And why do you think I was hired, Turner?"

"Come on, Sara," he whispered mischievously. "Girls like you get jobs like these because they're pretty. Because their asses look good in little skirts. You're hired strictly to make deals go more smoothly for guys like Julian. It's why he hired you to oversee the changes at this resort," he said, letting me know that he didn't actually have the information I thought he did. I let out an inaudible breath of relief as Turner smirked. "Julian put you out here because people are more inclined to do what you say, Sara. You're sweet, and friendly, and pretty, and they subconsciously want to please you. Hell, I know I want to please you."

"Turner, from what I observed before you joined me in the elevator, you have your choice of women here," I said calmly.

"Well, they don't do it for me. I tried using them to scratch the itch – it didn't work."

I was quickly reaching my limit of being able to even fake laugh this off, so with the same polite smile I'd been giving him, I said, "Turner, I do have to get ready. I'll see you at dinner."

His voice was smug as I turned to open the door.

"That ass of yours is telling me to come in."

"I assure you it's not," I fired back without glancing behind.

"Christ. So why even dress like that if you don't want me to react?" he asked. I was halfway in my room when I froze in utter disgust. "You're asking me to fuck you and then telling me you don't want it. Is that not what's going on?"

Lord, Turner. Seriously?

His questions were appalling. Undeniably so. Still, I waited for myself to feel that rush of shame or guilt. I waited to feel the need to cover up and tell myself I'd asked for it, but the feeling didn't come.

Firmly blocking my open door, I turned to face him.

"Mr. Roth, as it turns out, women sometimes do things for their own pleasure and happiness. I wear my clothes because I like them, and because I feel good in them. I enjoy feeling attractive, and if that catches your attention, then you are welcome to look. But unless I invite you, do not ever touch or assume you're entitled to. Using the way I dress as an excuse for your lack of respect or self-control is not justified or sufficient." I tilted my head. "Okay?" I asked with a deliberate brightness that could only be interpreted as friendly.

Turner gazed at me for several seconds, his eyes glimmering.

"You know, you're different than all the other girls."

"I'm not. I'm just different from the ones you pursue. Cast a wider net and you'll meet plenty of women willing to speak their minds."

The shit-eating grin was back. "Why look for them when I've already got you?" Turner asked, looking me up and down. "Come on, sweetheart. Just let me in for a second," he persisted. "I'll keep it strictly business – pinky swear."

I stared at him. "We can discuss anything you want right in this hall."

"I don't want to discuss it in the hall, Sara, and considering I'm the one making all the final decisions on this trip, you should probably think twice about being so difficult to work with," he asked, his teasing tone tinged with an iciness now. He smiled at the slight falter in my expression. "You know Hoult needs this deal. I'm by far his highest bidder for this resort, and Roth Entertainment is the only, and I mean *only* company that can launch Empire Stadium into becoming the most lucrative stadium in New York. Considering the competition, that's a big fucking deal in that town. And it's a big deal to his family – I'm sure you know how important his family is to him. Right?"

"I do," I muttered, my heart racing.

I swallowed hard as I thought about this deal coming down to a chance run-in with Turner, and his stupid, egotistical need to get his way and come in my room. I couldn't stand the thought of Julian failing this venture solely because of me, or the thought of becoming another woman who came between him and his family. I considered that letting Turner into my room could be quick – that I could text Julian the moment I got in and let him know to swing by ASAP. If Turner's intentions were in fact as lewd as I imagined, then I'd just have to stall for ten, fifteen minutes before Julian arrived.

For the sake of this entire deal, those fifteen minutes seemed potentially worth it.

At the same time, while I took more risks these days, I'd decidedly stopped taking ones like these.

I respected myself far too much for it.

"I'm sorry, Turner. But you're not coming in my room," I said, heading inside and nearly shutting the door in his face. My heart pounded when Turner pushed his hand against it, but to my slight relief, he only held it open enough to say one last thing.

"Come work for me." He was quiet for a moment, his eyes curiously studying mine. "I'll triple the salary you've got with Hoult."

"I appreciate the offer, Turner, but no thank you."

He laughed. "You barely gave it a thought."

"I didn't have to. See you at dinner."

I flashed another perfectly nice smile before tightly shutting my door and locking it.

33

JULIAN

In the bustling dining room, with live jazz floating around us, I sat with Irv to my left and Robert to my right. Well across the table from me was Sara, sandwiched between the Roth brothers, looking so beautiful I could barely think straight.

My heart rate hadn't gone down since she arrived at dinner in a light beige dress with thin straps I could barely make out against her glowing skin. The material looked soft, and it hugged tight all over her body while dipping loosely across her breasts. Her plunging cleavage made an appearance only when she reached or leaned in certain positions, making the night a game of silently anticipating Sara's every movement, no matter what you were doing. Like everyone else, I was guilty of looking every time that neckline dipped.

But unlike everyone else, I was too far from Sara to speak to her, which made looking at her physically hurt.

I wanted to be next to her.

Fuck that – actually, I needed to be.

I was genuinely unsure that I could sit through this dinner. I'd seen Turner and Carter salivate over Sara before, but something was different tonight. To start, I hadn't had the time to see or touch her since early morning. I ached for the chance to hear her breathlessly recount her stories from the day, but thanks to Irv and Robert's cease-less questions, I couldn't make it to her room after she got back to the resort.

It was a technically small hiccup in an otherwise seamless day of great meetings, but it felt huge to me.

I could admit that I wanted her comfort. There was a dull ache in my heart today. I knew it had to do with Lucie, and I knew I needed only a few moments with Sara for that ache to fade away. Just a second or two of her arms wrapped around my neck and her head resting against my chest was all I needed to breathe.

"Another glass of champagne for you, sir?" the server asked as he glided by. I was in the midst of declining when Turner yelled across the table.

"Another round for everyone. We're celebrating," he told the server jovially. "Turner Roth." He held his hand out. "This is my brother, Carter. Remember the names, 'cause we're buying this resort, so you'll be seeing a lot more of us soon."

For fuck's sake. I prepared to apologize on his behalf, but the server was quickly gone, and Turner was quickly back to murmuring in Sara's ear.

Under the table, my fingers fired a quick text.

> *ME: You alright?*
> *SARA: Yes.*
> *SARA: But I miss you.*

Fucking hell.

We locked eyes as Turner leaned his arm onto the table in front of Sara, caging her in like his prey. Her steady gaze confirmed she was still fine, that she had this under control, but it didn't ease my heart. My patience for being apart from her had been wearing thin all day, and now, as I watched her remove Turner's hand from her bare shoulder, it was officially gone.

"Gentlemen," I said suddenly, facing Irv and Robert while shooting another quick text.

> *ME: We have a meeting with the resort's marketing team*
>   *tomorrow at 8AM, before the final meeting with the*
>   *Roths at 10AM.*
> *COLIN: Oh God we do?*
> *ME: No. But go with it*

"You're kidding. You have to go already?" Irv seemed genuinely disappointed. I knew well that he disliked being around the Roths as much as I did. "But Turner just ordered a round of champagne."

"Yes, unfortunately, the three of us should be wrapping it up soon. Colin," I looked to him a few seats down. "Remind me the time of our meeting with the marketing team tomorrow?"

"Eight in the morning, sir."

"Oh, wow," Irv muttered, removing the napkin from his lap to stand and say goodbye. "Well, we look forward to seeing you tomorrow at noon," he said, shaking my hand before Robert got up to do the same.

Across the table, Turner practically fucking pouted.

"You shitting me, Hoult? You gonna let Uncle Rob and Grandpa *Irv* outlast you tonight?" he demanded incredulously. "At least let Sara stay. Girl just wants to party. Don't you, Sara?"

I could tell from the way she flinched that he'd squeezed her knee under the table. My heart felt like a brick as it hammered in my chest, my eyes blazing on Turner as Sara rose from the table.

"No, Turner, I think I'd just like to sleep," she said with an admirable calm. "Gentlemen." She faced Irv and Robert with a tight but convincing enough smile. "I look forward to our final meeting tomorrow."

"As do we, Ms. Hanna," Irv said. "You have a good night now."

"You as well."

With that, the three of us left, pacing briskly and in unison out of the busy dining area. The room was big but the air still felt hot as I strode alongside Sara, both of us wordlessly aching to touch one another.

It wasn't till we were out of the Roths' eyesight that Sara's eyes glimmered over at me, the corner of her lip between her teeth. I dropped my eyes to see her hand reaching cautiously for mine. Apparently, she couldn't wait.

Apparently, neither could I.

Instead of taking her hand, I touched Sara's back and led us in a sharp turn down the stairs toward the restrooms. She didn't ask what we were doing. She didn't so much as hesitate as side by side, we descended the stairs.

The moment we got down there, I pushed her up on the wall.

"I need you now," I hissed, catching her jaw and holding it firm as I kissed her deeply.

Her energy immediately matched mine. With two hands gripping my belt, Sara yanked me tight against her body, eagerly parting her mouth for my tongue.

"Julian," she gasped as I pushed us into the men's bathroom. I had no way of knowing it was empty, but it was, and thank God for it, because I couldn't wait another second to feel her. "You're crazy," she whispered breathlessly through the smile she pressed against my lips. Her giggle bounced off the marble of the empty room as I pulled her into a stall and locked us in. "*Julian.*" She moaned as I rubbed her palm against my fully hard cock. "You're so fucking crazy."

"You're the only one who gets me like this."

"I know," she whispered.

"Pleased with yourself?" I smirked, licking a wet line up her neck. Her breasts trembled in my hands as she shuddered. "Are you happy that I have no control around you?" I murmured, cupping her in my palms and thumbing circles over her nipples till they pebbled tight. "You make me feel like I'm losing my fucking mind, Sara."

"You do it worse to me," she breathed. Her fingers moved quickly, undoing my belt as I kissed the straps off her shoulders and watched her dress tumble down to her waist. I dug my fingers into her hips as I kissed the round tops of her breasts, groaning as she freed my erection and stroked it in her soft hands.

My forearms crashed against the stall, caging her in as I braced myself. The head of my cock was throbbing as she rubbed it against her naked stomach and whispered, "I want you to fuck me."

I had every intention of doing so. But just then, the doors swung open and we heard a gratingly familiar voice.

"Seriously, man. Fuck Hoult for leaving right after I ordered champagne."

∼

SARA

My mouth hung open for several seconds, my heart pounding in disbelief.

Topless in the men's bathroom, Julian's cock pulsing hot in my hands, I found myself suddenly standing two yards away from Turner and Carter Roth. Thank fucking God for the stall doors that reached all the way to the floor. They shielded Julian's shoes and my heels as the Roth brothers pissed at the urinals.

They were like middle school girls. Even after they were done with their business, they stuck around to talk shit about none other than us.

"He's just mad you might fuck his assistant before he does," Carter laughed, washing his hands. My eyes locked on Julian's, I saw the fire return behind them. It burned hotter as Turner chimed in with his usual bullshit.

"That dude's got such a stick up his ass. If she worked for me, I'd be smashing every day at the office. I'd fuck her right in front of everyone. I wouldn't care."

"The guys would love that," Carter chuckled. "She's got some fuckin' tits on her."

Julian's neck was tight. I noticed a vein in his forehead that I hadn't before. I willed him silently to calm down, but that was impossible with Turner escalating his idiocy.

"Yeah, I'm pissed I didn't get to see those things that night at the pool. I swear she was shaking them around on purpose to get my dick fuckin' hard," he said, prompting my lip to curl in a sneer. *How delusional are you, Turner?* My chest heaved as his blatant lies continued. "Should've fucked her right in front of Julian."

Julian's hand formed a fist against the wall above my head. He looked a second from losing it so with a hand on his jaw I turned him to face me, my eyes urging him to breathe as my free hand resumed stroking his cock.

"Baby," he whispered his tortured warning. His eyes closed as I slowly picked up my pace.

"I fuckin' tried getting in her room today. She shut me down."

I bit down hard on my lip as Turner revealed what I had yet to tell Julian. My eyes were big, unblinking as Julian stared into me, his eyebrows pulling tight in silent question about what happened today before dinner. I didn't know how to calm him. My pulse was fast as I watched the hollows of his cheeks flex as he clenched his jaw. His shoulders went rigid again, and his chest expanded under his shirt, looking so tight I swore I could bounce quarters off it.

He was livid, but his anger wasn't for me. It was for them.

"Just kick the door open next time," Carter joked.

"For her I might have to. I'm gonna fuck her one way or another."

That was it.

Shit.

My breath hitched in my throat as I watched the last of Julian's composure flicker out of his eyes. But instead of flying out and slamming Turner's head in the wall, he yanked my leg up against his body, pushing my panties aside with his cock.

Holy fuck.

Shock rippled my body as Julian's hard cock pushed inside me. Electricity crackled between us, our stares locked unblinkingly on each other as he entered me inch by solid inch.

"We'll find a way to get her clothes off," Carter snorted as I dug my nails into Julian's shoulders, lifting myself to give him more leverage to rock his hips inside me.

I soaked in his wordless intensity as I grinded against him, my body flooded with a mixture of anger, satisfaction and vengeance.

The Roths could suggest all they wanted that I could be theirs, but the truth was in front of me and inside me, and it fucked me hard the moment the brothers left the room.

"Mine," Julian growled, his lips on mine as he shook the stall, his hips thrusting tirelessly inside me. "You belong to me." He kissed me with a hunger that grew by the second. "Only me, Sara."

"That's all I want," I whispered tremulously as he kept the tempo of his stroke while sucking the tips of my breasts in his mouth. I rolled my head back against the stall, my breaths growing jagged as he flicked and swirled his tongue over me, my pleasure building so high so fast I only vaguely sensed Julian lifting me like a feather off the ground.

Pinned against the wall, his cock pierced me deep, and his abs rubbed against my clit for barely five seconds before the sensation became unbearable.

"Come for me, baby," Julian murmured fervently.

My body obliged and took him with me, my lips gasping for air as Julian finished inside me with an echoing roar. We were entirely too loud for the setting, but we didn't care – couldn't even if we tried. We were too hot, angry, and eager to stake our claims on one another tonight.

And we were both too far gone to stop ourselves.

34

SARA

From dinner, we went straight back to our hotel room – rather, *my* hotel room that we were apparently now sharing.

After grabbing his bag from his suite down the hall, Julian returned to me. Standing in the doorway of the bathroom, he quietly unbuttoned his shirt, getting leisurely undressed while watching me shower through the glass door. I could see behind him into the living room, and out the windows at the moonlight glimmering over the water.

For once, I enjoyed the partition between Julian and me. I wiped at the fog steaming the shower door as I continued watching him drift in and out of the bathroom while taking his clothes, his watch and his shoes off. Without something separating us, I was pretty sure I'd climb all over him again – it was hard not to, even when I was still catching my breath from what he'd just done to me at the restaurant.

Plain and simple, there was no looking at Julian without wanting him. But I forced myself to just pause and take this time to gaze at my current reality.

A little over a month ago, I spent between six and seven days a week in a windowless part of my office at June Magazine. I worked unpaid overtime every day in order to complete my superiors' assignments, I went through my ritual of sex with Vanilla Jeff in his cluttered office, and my idea of vacation was thirty minutes at a coffee shop with Lia.

Now I was in Biarritz, France, in the most beautiful hotel room I'd ever seen overlooking the stunning Basque coast. To top it all off, I had Julian Hoult winding down with me after a long day out. Just watching him get ready to sleep was fascinating. Just *sleeping* in bed with him was fascinating. Seemingly everything about that man made me feel better, happier, more hopeful, and while I had been doing a great job of it up to yesterday, as I watched Julian now, I couldn't deny it.

I was falling.

Hard.

I didn't feel anything close to secure about it, but it was happening, and try as I might, I couldn't stop it anymore.

"Hey," I smiled as he got in the shower with me. I laughed as he gave a crooked grin and leaned his tired body into me for several seconds. I giggled, closing my eyes as he kissed my neck. "You're almost there," I murmured. Tomorrow was our last day before going home. Somehow, it felt like forever ago that we were in New York.

"Thank you, by the way," Julian said when he pulled back. My eyes followed my hands as they ran over his solid pecs then slowly down the ridges of his abs.

"For what?" I asked softly.

"Making this trip easier for me."

"I hardly did anything with the Roths this trip."

"I don't mean in regards to the sale," he said, taking the little round of soap and running its smooth surface along my side. "I mean just... being here. In Biarritz. It's not usually an easy trip for me."

I blinked, water trickling down my hair and into my face. How had I not even considered that? This resort I was having the time of my life in had begun as a home – the one he'd built to bring back Lucie.

Of course it hurt to be here.

"I didn't even think about how hard it was for you to come back here," I murmured, frowning at myself.

"It usually is, but it wasn't this time. I barely recognize this place when I'm here with you. It just feels like another beautiful French city when I get to see it through your eyes," Julian said earnestly, oblivious to how incredibly sweet I found his words. He looked up at me and grinned. "That said I hope you didn't enjoy your time here too much, because I have no intention of ever coming back once we're gone."

"I can always come here alone," I teased.

"It would be a waste to let you go somewhere alone," Julian said.

"Why's that?"

"Because you're so beautiful when you see something for the first time," he answered straightaway. "I wouldn't want to miss all those faces you make."

I grinned wide. "Are you trying to make my cheeks hurt?"

"I'm not. But I've become pretty dependent on seeing that smile, so whatever makes you happy, I'll keep doing it," he laughed, letting water trickle over his head as he leaned in to kiss me.

At night, I drifted off to sleep while Julian sat next to me in bed, looking over some notes. He asked if I wanted him to move into the sitting room so I could turn the lights off to sleep, but I said no. I felt way too much at peace lying there with him reading next to me. I loved every second of it, even in my sleep.

I didn't even mind that I woke up around two in the morning to find him still up, and still reading, though his material had changed since I was last awake.

"What's that?" I asked, my voice cracking from the grogginess. Julian looked down at me and frowned.

"Hey. I'm sorry I woke you."

"You didn't. I just stir here and there," I murmured, eyeing the pressed flower stationery in his hand. "Is that from Lucie?" I whispered sleepily. My lips curved in a smile when Julian took my hand and nodded for me to crawl up against him. Only when I had my head resting on his chest did he softy answer.

"It's the last letter she sent where she wrote that she missed me, and she still didn't understand why she couldn't see me."

"How long ago is it from?"

"About two-and-a-half years ago. She had just turned six. She's thanking me for the birthday presents in this," Julian said, running his thumb over the paper.

"Oh. You... know where they live?"

"Yes."

"And you don't ever get tempted to go there and find them?" My voice was small when I asked the question – as if that might lessen the pain of his answer.

"I thought about it every business trip I've ever taken out here. I thought about it today," Julian admitted in a murmur, pulling my leg over his lap. I leaned closer into him, smoothing my hand up his chest to his shoulder. I rubbed it gently as he spoke. "Figured it was almost like a last chance. But I decided against it."

"Why?"

"Because she's perfectly adjusted now. She's moved on from her memories of me, and it would be selfish for me to barrel into her life now and ruin the peace. She's still too young to fully understand the situation. She wouldn't know how to handle the fact that her mother has fed her lies about me. She'd just feel confusion and resentment, and all I want is for her to be happy. I don't want her to feel what I feel."

I gazed up at Julian, his stunning profile highlighted from the soft glow of the lamp. My heart ached for him, and I wished so badly that he could just see Lucie, but I understood exactly what he meant.

"You're a good man to give her the peace to move on," I said. "Most people would just indulge their impulses without thinking about how it might affect the other person." I cupped the back of his neck and rubbed gently. "I think it's noble for you to take on the hurt for her. Not everybody would do that," I said, thinking about the nights I heard my mother's muffled crying in her room. She was broken up over me, the arrest, and everything I'd been forced to do in college. A couple nights, she caved and came to my room, demanding what the hell I was thinking, and how I could let those girls treat me that way. Didn't I respect myself?

Those nights hurt.

But they were few and far between considering how many other nights she just held it in, crying into her pillow.

"Maybe in the future, you two can reconnect, and you can give her your side of the story," I said.

"I hope she understands by then why I eventually stopped trying to see her."

"She will," I whispered. "Everyone finds out eventually how fragile the healing process is. Maybe she'll figure it out after her first big breakup, and she'll understand that even after the wound's closed, it's still delicate, and sensitive, and it still needs time."

Julian looked me in the eye. "What about yours?" he asked.

"What? My wound?" I offered a little smile. "It's been healing since we left the Hamptons. It's in pretty good shape so far."

"Good." Julian put the letter on the nightstand, pulling me fully onto his lap. He pressed his lips against my forehead as I straddled him. "By the way, you're good at this," he whispered.

"What?"

"Making me happy."

I closed my eyes and let out a sigh of pure content.

"You have that touch with me, too," I murmured, cutting myself off right there, because there was so much more I could say.

You make me happy.

Happier than I ever thought I deserved.

And I think I'm falling in love with you.

My heartbeat rose in my chest as Julian tipped my chin up to kiss me. I wanted so badly to say the words, and to just get them off my chest. But I didn't.

I told myself to save it for another time.

35

SARA

Julian and I had fallen asleep together a few hours after he had accidentally woken me up.

But I thought I had dreamed him sitting up in bed again in the middle of the night, the glow of his phone illuminating his silhouette in the dark of the room. I remembered blinking sleepily at him, and I could have sworn that twice, I reached for him and murmured his name.

But he didn't respond, and for that reason, I was sure I had dreamt it.

This moment, however, I wasn't dreaming.

"Julian?" I was foggy, already halfway panicked when I woke up to see him striding into the room in a grey suit, both his and my bag fully packed and set on the chest at the end of the bed. I grabbed my phone off the nightstand and blinked down at the time. Barely eight in the morning. "Where did you just come from?" I asked.

"The last meeting. They wanted to move it up, and I didn't want to wake you. You were smiling in your sleep."

"Was I?" I couldn't help smiling again now.

"You were. It was cute," Julian smirked at me. "But we have to go now. We have a flight to catch in less than an hour."

My eyes fluttered. "Really? So it's... all done? Everything?" I was so disoriented for some reason. Perhaps the lack of sleep, though I usually functioned fine on minimal rest. I sat at the edge of the bed, processing everything at a delay as I watched Julian move around the room. But he finally stopped to tend to me when he saw how very lost I looked.

"Get dressed, Sara," he said, gazing down at me as he cupped my cheek. "I need you ready to go as soon as possible."

"Is everything okay? Did you finalize the deal?"

"All but. Everything will be finalized back in New York."

"Aren't you happy it's done?" I grinned, rubbing the sleep from my eyes.

"Very," Julian answered, taking my hand and leading me to the closet. "But we can celebrate on the plane. We really do have to leave soon."

I blinked at a lone dress of mine hanging in the closet, everything else apparently packed. I couldn't help feeling strange and slightly thrown off by the unexpected rush, but when I glanced at Julian, I caught that devastatingly handsome smile as he knotted his tie. And suddenly, I forgot my worries.

"Okay," I said brightly. "I'll be ready to go in ten."

From Teterboro Airport, Julian's car picked us up and brought us straight to his riverfront penthouse in TriBeCa. All he'd said as we walked across the tarmac was, "Stay with me tonight," and I was sold.

The fact that he lived in what looked like a high-rise palace was just a bonus.

From the cobblestone road, our car turned into a private drive-in courtyard, stopping in front of a towering arched entrance, where we got out. A warm glow greeted us when we walked into the double-height lobby boasting sculptures and artwork more beautiful than I'd seen in museums.

"Of course this is where you live," I murmured mostly to myself as I walked beside Julian toward the elevator.

It required a key to even move to the top floor of the building, and when the doors opened, they did so directly into Julian's stunning triplex.

"Whoa."

I felt him watching me as I wandered in awe under the twenty-plus-foot ceilings, in the nighttime glow of the downtown lights sparkling in from the windows. They stretched from ceiling to floor, facing north, east, south *and* west. The panoramic view alone pumped my heart with adrenaline.

"Meet me on the terrace," Julian said, nodding toward a glass door. "I'll pour us some wine."

I didn't need to be told twice.

Floating out onto the terrace, an almost tearful smile burst to my lips.

God. I'd lived in New York for almost ten years, and never had I seen a view like this. After my trip to Biarritz, this view was like a final reminder that there was in fact so much more out there.

Three times, I'd been stuck thinking *this is it, so deal with it*. The first time was in high school, the second was my freshman year in college, and the third was my backbreaking tenure at June Magazine.

I kept letting myself think that I'd seen it all, and I knew all my options.

Never had I been so wrong, and never had I been so happy to be.

"Enjoying the view?"

I turned to find Julian holding two glasses of red as he came out to join me.

"How could I not?" I asked, nodding my thanks when he handed me the glass of wine. "Please tell me you're not too jaded to ever come out here, because if that's the case, I might actually have to smack you."

Julian laughed. "I'm out here often, actually. Generally when I can't sleep."

"So, what, you come out here in your velvet robe with a glass of Scotch and gaze out at Gotham like Bruce Wayne?" I grinned.

Julian smirked. "More like a pair of sweatpants, a book, and a glass of water."

"Mm. That's an even sexier image," I said as Julian gave me a low, sexy, kind of tired laugh. Something about it compelled me to snuggle into his chest and close my eyes. It was quiet for a moment as we just breathed against each other, both of us exhausted, but neither of us sleepy. Julian was first to break the silence.

"I have a proposal for you."

I peered up at him. "Hm?"

"I want you to stay home from work tomorrow."

I frowned and pulled slightly back. "Why?"

"Because I want you to stay here," Julian said, his mouth curving into a grin when I arched my brows in surprise. "I think I took a page from your book and developed a vivid fantasy while we were in Biarritz."

"Oh? What fantasy?"

"Coming home to you after a long day of work."

My heart practically sang.

"Julian Hoult," I feigned shock. "That is filthy."

"I'm aware." His gorgeous lips spread into an irresistible grin. "I'm a bit of a sick fuck, in case you haven't noticed."

"Mm, totally. So, tell me more about this fantasy. What am I... what am I *wearing* in it?" I asked scandalously, sipping my wine. Julian laughed hard enough to give me the eye crinkle. God, I loved the eye crinkle.

"Honestly, I imagined everything. A robe. One of my shirts over a pair of your panties. One of my hoodies – "

"*You* own hoodies?" I gasped teasingly.

"Two."

"Let me guess, one is an Empires American League Champs hoodie."

"Correct," Julian smiled. "The other is from my days at Columbia. Probably haven't worn it since I was nineteen."

"It's weird to think that you were ever nineteen."

"Not at all sure how to take that."

"You just seem like you were always a wise, ridiculously hand-some grown man," I giggled. "So in some way, that was a compliment."

"Thank you then," Julian grinned, pulling me back into his chest, wrapping his arm around me and kissing the top of my head. *Gah.*

Another tiny thing I fucking loved.

At night, when we slept, we did the same dance we did our last night in Biarritz – Julian sat up reading while I lay next to him, our pillow talk winding down to a sleepy murmur as I slowly dozed off, lulled to slumber by the sound of his flipping pages.

Again, I woke in the middle of the night to find him still sitting there, awake and reading with one knee up and his arm resting over it.

"Can't sleep?" I murmured, my eyes still half-closed. I felt his fingers gently comb through my hair.

"No."

"Isn't this when you usually go to the terrace?" I asked.

He chuckled. "Yes."

I said nothing more as I waited for him to get up and leave, but he didn't. So with a smile on my lips and his fingertips gently massaging my head, I drifted back to sleep.

36

SARA

I didn't go out at all the next day.

It was sweltering hot, and even if it weren't, I had way too much house to explore and enjoy.

Julian had left for work early in the morning, around seven. I heard him murmur and laugh softly in my ear, probably over whatever sleepy gibberish was coming out of my mouth, and then I felt him kiss my neck down to the tops of my breasts before his footsteps went out the door.

When I finally woke up and checked my texts, I found a single one from Julian.

> JULIAN: *Please make yourself at home. Might be difficult*
> *since the entire home is run by automated controls, but*
> *I left you some instructions downstairs. Enjoy your day.*
> *I'll see you tonight.*

I was already vaguely amused as my bare feet wandered slowly downstairs, but I broke into a full huge grin when I found Post-It notes stuck to each fancy control system, from the automated blinds to the lighting to the steel and glass appliances in the beautifully sleek kitchen. As it turned out, I really needed those instructions. The first hour of my day was dedicated to figuring every system out.

But once I did, the day was a breeze. It felt like more of a vacation than Biarritz did. I wound up spending the whole afternoon and evening just cooking, reading, and wandering the building's luxury amenities before returning to the penthouse around seven – right in time to meet Julian.

I was in one of his shirts, the sleeves folded up and the buttons half done. I had my hair piled loosely at the top of my head, and just black panties underneath. He texted me when he was around the corner, so I stood at the elevator, waiting to greet him and put that big, crinkly-eyed smile on his face.

But I was surprised when the door opened.

Standing there was Julian, stunning as ever in the usual crisp white shirt and dark grey suit, his silk tie still knotted perfectly straight. I wanted to grin at how gorgeous he was, but I instantly felt the dark cloud hanging over him.

"Hey." I cocked my head, my voice light and quizzical as his blue eyes found me. Finally, a smile touched the corners of his lips. Not the big one I was expecting, but still damned gorgeous. "Work okay?" I asked gently, frowning as he set his briefcase on the ground and came straight toward me to cup my face in his hands.

I felt a heaviness in him as he kissed me, and an urgency that had me quickly struggling to catch my breath. His tongue was rough on mine as his hands dropped down to my chest. Despite my surprise, I made no noise as Julian squeezed his fists over my shirt and ripped it open, stepping over the scattering buttons and letting the cotton fall in a heap to the floor.

The sheer heat of his intensity made me dizzy.

I had yet to catch up to what was happening. I was only vaguely aware of his strong arms moving me over to the couch and laying me down. The weight of his body on top of me prompted my soft moan against his lips. They were still locked on mine as he reached between our bodies to jerk at his belt and free his cock, letting its weight fall onto my stomach and drag heavily over me as our tongues continued exploring each other, as if it was our very first taste.

"Julian," I whispered questioningly, but he kissed my confusion away.

His mouth never left mine, even as he reached down to tear my panties down my legs. My arms hung around his strong neck as he guided himself between my legs, parting my folds with the tip of his cock and running it up and down the length of my wet pussy, over and over and over till I was dripping wet. The deepest grunts escaped from his chest as he felt my sex pulsing around his tip, already begging for him.

"Sara," he murmured, the sound of his voice like air to me. His hand firmly cupped the back of my neck as he sucked on my bottom lip, letting it rake hard between his teeth.

A hoarse, ragged cry escaped my lips when he finally sank into me, stretching me and filling me with the most delectable pain. Gasping sharply, I swallowed the hot air he breathed into me as our kiss grew deeper, angrier. Almost forceful.

My tongue fought back as I locked my legs around him.

My abdomen clenched. Our bodies were tight, compact as we used just a small corner of the huge couch to rock into each other. Our skin was already sticky, slippery with sweat, and our mouths were swollen, hot and frantic as the same pleasure built at once inside us.

"Julian," I moaned. "Oh my God. Don't stop."

"I won't, baby," he murmured. "There's nothing I want more than you." Hoarse frustration tinged his voice as his breath quickened. "I think about you every night," he deepened his push inside me, "every morning when I wake up. I don't know what you've done to me," he whispered. "What did you do to me?" He hardened inside me as he whispered his demand on repeat.

I couldn't answer that, but I had something else at the tip of my tongue. I didn't know what was happening, but I suddenly felt like I had to say it.

"I love you," I whispered to Julian, holding his face, looking into his eyes as I said it. They were a wild, ferocious blue, but the moment those three words escaped my tongue they softened. His grip on the back of my neck tightened, and his body shuddered in such a way that I felt its violent tremor inside me.

"Julian..."

He kept his blue eyes pinned tight on me as he undoubtedly felt my pussy pulsing, clenching tight around him. Our chests were slick against each other now, our limbs more tangled than ever. My pleasure was seconds from his peak when I'd convinced myself he wasn't going to say it back. But then I felt his nails dig into my skin.

"I love you, Sara," he growled barely a second before he erupted a hard jerk inside me.

I gasped for breath – or maybe from shock. I wasn't sure. All I knew was that I was in pure ecstasy as I felt Julian's weight still slamming inside me as his heat flooded my pussy. His teeth were gnashed, his muscles quivering as he exhausted the last of his energy to keep fucking me, giving a wild, guttural grunt for every short, powerful thrust between my legs.

"Oh God, Julian!"

When I came, he grabbed my ass and yanked me to the very base of his cock, giving his every inch the full pleasure of my shaking climax. I was limp in his arms as he claimed every shiver and quake in my body, holding me tight against him and murmuring in my ear.

He said it back, I reminded myself, my bliss sending me off on a post-orgasmic cloud.

I wasn't sure I'd ever come down from this one.

JULIAN

As usual, she fell asleep before me.

Her lips were lightly parted as she lay on her side in my bed, looking so fucking perfect and peaceful I felt like I could watch her forever. I kept my eyes on her even as I peeled my shirt over my head and pushed my sweats off my hips.

I checked my phone before I climbed into bed with her.

I had Colin's text from hours ago waiting for me, but I'd wanted to wait till she fell asleep to open it. I wanted to enjoy the dinner she cooked for me, and the way the wisps of hair fell from her high pony-tail as she danced around the kitchen to the old jazz playing on my speakers.

A part of me still held out hope despite the fact that I knew what kind of news Colin was going to report back to me.

I told him to just keep it short and sweet – that I knew what the outcome of my last-minute changeup in Biarritz would result in. I just wanted to give a last-ditch effort, just in case it might work.

My lip curled as I finally opened Colin's texts.

COLIN: Sorry. No dice.
COLIN: Carter vetoed.

Thought so.

After what I'd done our last night in Biarritz, I knew well this was the direction we were heading in. In fact, I'd prepared myself for it all day, and I'd come up with a fallback plan once everything went to shit.

But after coming home to Sara, I let myself hold onto some idiotic glimmer of hope.

It was hard not to with her.

I never imagined preferring anything over the life I made for myself when I moved back to New York. I enjoyed my days at the tower, my nights at the stadium, and Sundays with my family. In between, I fit in drinks with my friends, and some women here and there. That worked fine for me for a very long time. In fact, after everything that happened in Stockholm and Biarritz, I was convinced that this was as good as it got

But then Sara came along, and I realized my life could in fact get better. Worlds better.

Unfortunately, there was no way to make it work.

37

SARA

I wasn't sure if Julian expected me at work the next morning, and even less sure when I awoke a tad before seven to find that he was gone. I frowned as I sat up in bed, my eyes floating about the room as I tried to remember him leaving. I didn't, and I didn't recall feeling him touch me in any way before he went.

Thankfully, when I checked my texts, I found one from him.

> *JULIAN: Good morning. I'll be needing you to come in to work this morning. If you could meet me in my office by 9, that would be great.*

I rubbed my eyes, smirking at the stiff professionalism of his message.

> *ME: Yes sir. Will do. ;)*

There was no response from Julian by the time I'd finished getting dressed, and in all fairness, I hadn't asked a question.

But I couldn't help feeling strangely on edge.

I didn't want to admit it to myself as I got dressed and ready for work, but by the time I'd squeezed myself on the packed rush hour train, I had to admit that I was paranoid he'd woken up and regretted it.

Those three words.

They hadn't been easy to say either, but I'd been consumed by the moment – by the palpable emotion stirring in the air between us. It felt good to get off my chest. It felt even better when Julian looked me in the eye and returned the words.

But today, something felt undeniably off.

I couldn't explain it, and I still hoped I was imagining things, but any hope of that was nixed the moment I walked into the bright offices of Hoult Communications.

I was greeted by the usual hum of fast typing and murmured chatting. That was normal.

But the way Colin avoided me was not.

I had gotten out only half my question about how he was doing before he muttered "sorry" and some hasty excuse about needing to meet with Tori. That was strike one.

Strike two came when I got to Julian's office and found him sitting and chatting with a young but silver-haired woman I didn't recognize. He had the jacket of his sharp blue suit off and draped over his chair. The sunlight streaming through the window bounced straight off his watch and into his face, forcing me to shield my eyes even as the woman across from Julian turned and flashed me a warm smile.

"Oh! This must be Sara."

"Indeed it is."

I cocked my head, smiling politely despite my confusion, and despite the odd feeling churning in my stomach. I didn't recognize the look in Julian's eyes this morning. Despite his friendly, cordial tone as he facilitated my introduction to the mystery woman, his eyes were oddly vacant. He looked cold and steely – nothing like the man who had grabbed me the moment he laid eyes on me last night, and kissed me like it was his last chance to ever feel my lips.

Then again maybe it was.

"Who was that?" I asked the moment the woman left. Her name was Grayson Short, and she knew all about my journalism major, as well as my work with June Magazine. But by the time she walked out, I'd discovered nothing about her besides her name.

Julian nodded for me to take a seat before him.

"Grayson works with Hoult Publishing. She's the person who is arranging your move to Una Magazine."

My eyebrows shot up high. I was still suspicious, on edge, but I gave a big grin. The corners of my lips trembled a bit as I tried to figure out what was going on.

"So... I'm not going to stick around for the Roth negotiations?" I asked.

"No," Julian replied. "You're not."

"Why not?"

"The opening for this position with Una is time sensitive. It's a spot people are vying for, and if your goal is to work with the company, I would suggest you jump at this chance."

I couldn't reconcile the way I was feeling. The fact that I might actually work for Una Magazine made me want to twirl through the air and text every person I'd ever met the good news. At the same time, I fucking hated the sterile manner in which Julian was speaking to me. It felt cruel and insulting, and I tried telling myself he was just in work mode, but I wasn't convinced.

He could've flashed me a little smirk or some knowing smile. He could have texted and given me a warning about maintaining a work appropriate relationship the moment we were back at the office.

But he did none of that. He launched straight into the strict professionalism, and it felt like a statement.

My fury went from zero to sixty as he went on about Grayson, her work, her credentials, and a million things that didn't come close to acknowledging the sudden wall between us. I sat patiently through half his talk, because I still had the annoying instinct to mirror professionalism in an office setting.

But then I remembered I wasn't sitting across from my boss.

I was sitting across from the man who only last night told me he loved me.

"Julian – what the hell is going on?" I demanded, finally snapping when I heard him mention Hoult Publishing International for the third time. "Why are you talking to me like this? And why do you keep mentioning Hoult International? What do they have to do with this conversation?"

Julian didn't even flinch.

"There were no open positions at Una Magazine in the States," he said, his expression blank. "The position I'm setting you up with is for Una U.K. Based in London."

My heart slammed against my ribs as I stared at him.

"What are you talking about?" I asked, my voice reduced to a harsh whisper. "Julian, what are you trying to do to me right now?"

"I'm telling you the truth when I say there was no available position in the States," Julian said. A slight frown appeared between his brows as he looked at me. "I can't have you working here anymore, Sara. I'm sorry."

"Don't do this to me, Julian," I said between my teeth. "I know you're in there, and I know you recognize how fucked up this is right now." The anger in my chest boiled, rising to my throat as he continued sitting there, a statue in a suit, giving me absolutely nothing. "At least give me the explanation," I demanded, wishing I didn't sound as shaky as I did. But at least I was talking. Julian continued with his silence as he sat there, studying me with the eyes that usually gave away his emotions.

Right now, they were empty. Like he'd flipped the switch back to being the unfeeling person he was before we met.

I didn't realize it would be so easy for him. I thought like me, he had changed gradually. That together, we'd found a new side of him the way we did with me. At this point, there was no way I could get rid of what I'd discovered about myself – about how much I could open myself up, and how deep I could actually feel.

But apparently Julian was wired differently.

And I should've fucking guessed.

"What happened yesterday?" I challenged, refusing to back down without a straight answer. "Tell me what happened, because I know you meant it when you said it, Julian," I hissed, my heart hammering as I watched his blue eyes spark to life. "I know you did. And yes, I entertain a lot of dreams and fantasies, but I'm not the type to imagine things, or see something where there's nothing. I'm not by nature a hopeful person – you know that by now," I ground out. "So if you refuse to let yourself feel for me anymore, then fine, I won't grovel. But at least, explain to me what happened here, because you said you loved me last night, and a day later, you're trying to get me as far away from you as possible. You know how cruel you're being right now. And you know I deserve an answer."

My hands were shaking. I didn't know when I rose to my feet, but I did. And now I stood waiting for what felt like ages, because as always, Julian took his time to reply.

"This company is and always will be my priority, Sara," he finally said, sinking my heart like a stone. "This company is how I found my way back to my family. It takes all of me to run both this place and the stadium the way I see fit." He paused, the sharp lines of his jaw tightening. "I've never wanted something like I've wanted you, Sara," he said, his voice a low murmur. "But what I want and what I need are two very different things."

"I don't feel like you mean that," I whispered.

"I do," Julian countered, his frown deepening. "I'm content around you, Sara. Borderline complacent, and I can't afford that. We both need to focus on ourselves right now, Sara. We both have a lot of work to do."

It was a last slap in the face, because all I heard was, *"You're a work in progress. Too far from together for me to bother with."*

My entire body trembled as I stood there staring at the shell of Julian Hoult – the person Emmett had warned me about. He was back on autopilot, content to simply sit there without saying another word. I shook my head in sheer disbelief. I couldn't bring myself to accept this reality, but after another minute of silence, it was clear this was the only option I was getting.

And like I'd told him, I refused to grovel. If there was anything I was vehemently against, it was being that girl again – the one who'd do anything to be wanted, when clearly she wasn't. I absolutely refused.

So with one last look at Julian, I turned on my heel, and I forced myself to go.

38

JULIAN

"You're not allowed in my suite if you don't have a beer. At least hold it, for Christ's sake."

I looked up to find Emmett trying again to make me drink. It was his fourth attempt in as many innings, and this time, his last ounce of patience was gone along with his usual grin.

"Yeah, yeah, yeah," he spoke over me when I opened my mouth. "Technically, it's your suite because you own the stadium. Got that. Don't care. If you're gonna sit with me, you're going to at least try to have a good time," he said, holding the beer in my face till I took it. "Atta fuckin' asshole."

"Not sure that's the saying."

"Yeah, well it is for you."

He left me alone for the next few innings, though I heard him talking about me to one of the many girls he'd brought in tonight.

"Yeah, he's fine. No, don't tell your friend to come over – trust me, that'll be pointless. He's just getting over a girl." Emmett glanced at me. "She's moving to Milan today. Or was it Paris?"

London, asshole.

Emmett knew exactly where Sara was going. He'd gotten it wrong on purpose to bait me into talking, but over a week later, I wasn't interested. It was easier to let Emmett assume the reasons I offered Sara the job in London. Like everyone else, he figured it had to do with my particular relationship with work.

I preferred that than telling him about Turner.

He'd find out eventually anyway, once he realized that no deal went through, I still owned the resort in Biarritz, and the stadium was not partnering with Roth Entertainment, now or ever.

Thanks to Turner's drunken 4AM calls that pulled me out into the hall during that last night in Biarritz, we were right back to where we started.

"For such a hard ass, you don't have proper control of your subordinates, Hoult."

"Do you even hear yourself, Turner?" I asked as we stood down the hall from my room. He was wasted, and I shouldn't have considered meeting him out here for this conversation, but the last thing I wanted was for Sara to hear this. "Do you honestly believe that I would ask this of anyone who works for me?"

"You could. You know well that you could," Turner slurred. He was swaying, red-eyed, and reeking of every liquor in existence, but he stuck fervently to his point. "You're Julian Hoult. You're like me. You have resources. You have money, possessions and connections that people won't ever get in their lives even if they work their hardest," Turner sneered. "Now, come on. Think of one thing you can hold over Sara's head. It could be as simple as her job. Just tell her you'll fire her if she doesn't say yes. I mean for fuck's sake, I'm asking for a weekend. One weekend. And I'll be taking her somewhere nice. I'm not going to fucking lock her in a dungeon — I'll wine and dine her and all that jazz. You just need to make it clear that I expect her to reciprocate."

"You are out of your fucking mind, and that's not going to happen."

"Then I'm pulling out of this deal and blacklisting Empire Stadium from all future Roth Entertainment events," Turner grinned like the fucking Joker. "Don't believe I'll do it? Try me," he laughed. "But before you do that, ask yourself if it's really worth it for some girl. I'm not fucking buying her from you and turning her into my sex slave. I want to fuck her a couple times over a weekend and move on. You know me. I like the chase."

"Then you'll love the fact that you'll never in your life lay a finger on Sara."

"Hoult. Don't talk about her like she's some precious little sweetheart. Trust me, she has experience in this kind of thing. You don't know what I'm talking about?"

Evidently, Turner's curiosity had compelled him to give Sara's name to someone at his office in New York. And apparently, that person had found the article detailing Sara's arrest when she was seventeen.

I felt fucking sick when I realized it.

I knew well that I was solely to blame for putting Sara on the radar of someone like Turner. His obsession with instant gratification was dangerous on its own – combined with his wealth, entitlement and resources, and you had this fucking shitshow.

It was revolting, and it took everything in me to keep from strangling him right there, especially when he called Sara an "itch" he needed to scratch. For his own fleeting want, he was willing to send her hurtling back to the most painful time in her life.

Then again, he didn't know about her past.

But I did.

I had opened that old wound of hers that night in the Hamptons. I'd made Sara face the past she had swept under the rug because I needed to know more about her. I needed to protect her.

And in sending her to London, I hoped I was doing just that.

Even if he tracked her down, Turner's impulses were unlikely to follow Sara to London. I had a hunch that that gratification wasn't quite instant enough for him.

I also had a hunch that between Turner and myself, the worst was yet to come. He was unlikely to just forget and move on from the fact that I'd knocked him out during our last night in Biarritz, and left him to be tended to by hotel staff. He was proud, way too egotistical to leave things where they were, and whatever bullshit he had planned for me, I didn't want Sara around to see it.

I didn't want her to feel guilty the way I knew she would – like she had something brand new to repent for. I just wanted her to be blithely oblivious, like Lucie.

And if that meant the end of us then I'd have to deal. She would eventually move on. Her new life in London would make sure of that.

I would move on as well.

I'd go back to focusing on my work with everything I had in me. I would hunt for new ways to launch my stadium to the top, and I would fall back into my routine of spending every day at the office, some nights out with Emmett and Lukas, and every Sunday with my family.

I would transition seamlessly back into that reality.

That was what I told myself at least.

39

SARA

Three weeks in, and I was still stuck in a cruel loop. I waited every day for it to be different, but every day it was the same.

From the moment I woke up every morning in my little flat, I felt disoriented.

Some days, I jolted up from bed, my heart pounding at the prospect of being late for June Magazine. Other days, I rolled over expecting to see out my hotel room window overlooking Biarritz.

Those mornings were obviously worse. They never failed to start my day off all wrong, throwing me off so badly I'd have to sit at the edge of my bed for five minutes, taking in my surroundings so I could fully grasp where I was.

I blamed my dreams.

They were so damned vivid, and they refused to let me forget either New York or Biarritz, or the man who, at this point, felt like another one of my fantasies. Even after particularly good days at work, I'd come home, have dinner, watch some TV, then sleep and promptly dream again about him. It was ridiculous considering how many wonderful new things I had going on.

For starters, the job at Una was good. Great, in fact. I adored

Grayson and all the other women at the office. We brought each other snacks and coffee, and stuck notes and doodles on each other's computers. We helped each other with research and writing, and we waited for one another to walk out of the building at the end of the day. At the bar after work, we happily continued talking shop because we genuinely loved what we did.

It was a stark contrast to the competition and cattiness that June Magazine fostered among its staff, and it was technically everything I'd ever dreamed of in a job.

I even had my mother staying in London indefinitely. She didn't tell me how she afforded the hotel room so close to my studio. She didn't talk about how much it cost for Dad to fly in and visit us last weekend, and she told me not to ask, so I didn't. I was just grateful to have her, and to feel some sense of home since there was so damned much I missed about being back in New York.

I missed Lia, obviously. Even at my busiest at June Magazine, I still talked to her every day, and saw her at least once a week at our little coffee shop on 18th Street.

I missed my apartment in Little Italy. I'd lived there for so long, and had personalized every inch of it to my liking. Breaking the lease I'd had since graduating college at twenty-two was, as dramatic as it sounded, kind of horrifying. But Lia did her best to comfort me on that front.

"It's okay, because *when* you move back, you can live with me," she had said at the airport, acting as if her bright smile disguised the tears actively streaming down her cheeks. "Lukas will move into the Hamptons home full-time. He won't even mind. And if he does, then tough. That's what he gets for staying friends with that guy."

She refused to say his name, like he was Voldemort. She encouraged me to follow suit, and I did.

But it didn't stop me from seeing him everywhere I went. In the busy streets, during the early rushes, I convinced myself daily that I saw him. On the tube, I fantasized that the wisp of brown hair behind the trio of women was him. When my phone rang, at work or at home, I imagined I'd pick up and hear his gorgeous voice.

I was pretty sure my refusal to say his name was what drove me to dream of him so vividly. It was like my mind rejecting Lia's idea to forget him. It felt as if it was working harder to produce images of him when I was asleep, unable to distract or defend myself.

Hence the disoriented mornings.

But I was only three weeks in. I told myself to wait it out till five. That was how long I'd been at his office, working his job, and sometimes going to bed next to him. Five weeks was apparently what it took for my body to adjust to a new reality, so in five weeks, I promised I'd check up on myself and make sure that I was doing just fine.

After all, he had probably already moved on.

He was probably working hard every day, and seeing Lukas and Emmett at night. While I had not even gone on a date, he had probably slept with at least half a dozen new women.

It killed me to think about, which I hated, because that meant I still cared. It meant I still pined for someone who didn't want me. It was the same as pining for approval from the kids who tortured me in high school, and the girls who ruined my life in college. It was completely fucking wrong, and against everything I stood for in order to respect myself.

So I made myself hold out.

Five weeks, Sara. It was my magic number, and the star of my new fantasy that someday soon, everything would fall into place and be perfectly fine.

40

SARA

"I heard a thing," Lia said cryptically as I dried my post-dinner dishes. Polishing a plate, I narrowed my eyes across my tiny kitchen counter, at the stool I'd put my phone on. We were on speakerphone, but Lia's voice was oddly hushed.

"Can you talk louder?" I asked.

"No. I'm at Lukas's office. He was in the conference room, and I was right outside the door when I realized he was talking to Julian."

"Oh my God, you said his name."

"Omigod! Shit," Lia cursed. "Damn it. We had such a streak going."

"It's fine," I said with a laugh – or at least my attempt at a laugh. I hadn't succeeded at a real-sounding one in awhile.

Five weeks in, and I wasn't feeling better.

I slept fewer hours now, but I wasn't seeing him any less in my dreams, in the streets, on the tube – even in the elevator at my office.

According to my mom, my voice was weary these days. I had bags under my eyes from staying up late at night. The women at work whispered about me in the corner, racking their minds to brainstorm ideas with which to cheer me up. Three days in a row, they took me somewhere beautiful for lunch. When that didn't work, they took me to a male strip club in hopes of at least making me laugh, which I remember kind of doing.

But they knew I was breaking.

I had arrived in London with some hope of starting over. There was a bit of brightness in my eyes. But over a month later, I had officially withered like a new plant that had been watered only once. I'd run out of energy. I missed home, and I still felt thoroughly disoriented – like I didn't know what was real or not.

Since our daily calls continued, I knew Lia could tell. She could sense a difference in me from just how many rings it took for me to pick up the phone. So when she said that she had "heard" a thing, I knew it was more likely that she had, for my benefit, "deliberately eavesdropped" a thing.

"Did you know…" she started, keeping me on edge.

"Did I know what, Lia?" I asked.

"What was the name of the place you went to in France again?"

"Biarritz," I replied, my heart giving a twist. "Why are you asking about Biarritz?" I asked, my pulse suddenly uneven.

"You were there to sell Julian's resort to those guys, right?"

"Yes. They're in negotiations now. They'll probably finish soon," I mumbled, going back to polishing my plate. I heard Lia rustling on the other end.

"Um…"

"Lia. What?"

"I overheard today that that deal never went through."

I paused. "What?"

"The deal with the Perv Bros? It got nixed while you guys were still in, um, *Bi… Buh…* how do you say it again?"

"Biarritz."

"That. Anyway, I may or may not have threatened Lukas for information when we got home, under the promise that I'd never tell you –"

"Did he really believe you wouldn't tell me?"

"No, it was probably for his own conscience," Lia said hastily. "But anyway, what Lukas said was that Turner said something 'indecent' to Julian that resulted in Julian 'knocking him the fuck out' the last day you guys were there. And whichever Perv Bro he knocked out, that guy's still harassing him. So I guess right now, Julian and Lukas are putting their minds together to fight fire with fire. I swear to God, you give those boys a grudge to hold against someone, and they'll team up to annihilate you. Their brains together are scary."

"Hold up, Lia – focus," I pleaded, my heart beating fast. "So Julian hasn't been doing business with the Roths this whole time I've been gone?"

"Girl, no. Unless by doing business you mean plotting ways to kill each other."

"Shit," I whispered, practically dropping the plate on my counter with a loud clatter that made her curse. "I'm sorry," I apologized hastily as my mind tried to piece things together.

I couldn't help but imagine that Turner had said something about me.

I remembered the rage in Julian's eyes when he watched Turner whisper to me during that last dinner. I remembered thinking he might actually kill Turner when we overheard him trashing me in the men's bathroom, and I had a strong feeling now that the Biarritz deal had fallen through entirely because of me.

"Fuck. I screwed him," I whispered.

"You sure did, girl. On every surface at his office."

"Lia."

"Sorry, sorry. But please, *please*, Sara, don't punish me for telling you this by blaming yourself and spiraling into some dark place. I know I'm biased here, but if this is anyone's fault besides those nasty Perv Bros, it's Julian's."

"Lia, stop – "

"I'm serious. He chose to hire you when he already had feelings about you – even if they were just minor then, he knew the risks that came with this. He was just cocky that he could stay professional as always. He had no idea what the fuck he was up against with you," she said, a grin in her voice.

"You're taking way too much pleasure in this conversation right now."

"Only because I feel the wheels turning in your brain right now, and it's giving me this strange best friend ESP," she said.

"Really. And what am I thinking right now?" I challenged.

"That you need to talk to him in person."

"Fine."

"In New York. Right?"

"Yes." My stomach churned at the thought of going home. The idea alone snapped me out of the five-week daze I'd been in. "But just thinking about it scares me right now. I can't handle the thought of going there, getting to his office and being told by reception that he has no time for me. Or worse, being told by Julian that he has no time for me."

Lia sighed.

"Look, Sara. None of this would've blown up if Julian didn't get emotionally invested in you. He could have closed the deal easy if it weren't for the fact that he fell for you. Do you know how many other times he's done business by looking the other way when someone got screwed? He's a ruthless *asshole*," Lia said.

"I don't know where you're going with this."

"I'm saying he probably still cares about you. At this point, we both have reason to suspect that this deal fell through because he was in some way defending you. So why are you afraid to just fly home for the weekend and get yourself some real closure?"

"Because I've seen how easily Julian can flip the switch, Lia, and it's as hurtful as it is scary. He can go from loving one second to completely unrecognizable the next. He acts cold and distant, like he's never even met you. It's not something you can forget easily, and I'm afraid to see it again. I'm afraid it's going to hurt me all over again."

"Well, you stayed at June Magazine longer than you wanted because you were afraid that no other job would ever take you. Maybe you'll stay in London longer than you want because you're afraid of ever coming back to New York."

"Jesus, Lia," I said, unsure if I was impressed or pissed over the tough love.

"You know I'm right."

I clenched my jaw. "I also know you're doing something sketchy right now. Why are you typing so fast?"

"Searching flights."

"Ugh."

"Humor me. Tell me one good thing about Julian. Your favorite memory."

"Why?"

"Just do it."

I had floated over to the couch without realizing it. The dishrag was still in my hand. I tossed it aside and sat down so I could think.

There were actually too many good memories to choose from. I wasn't even sure how we'd made so many in just a span of five weeks. I smiled just thinking about the way he cupped the back of my thighs as he leaned against his bike at that gas station. The sun was setting behind him, and he studied me like he was trying to figure me out. I thought about the nights we spent in bed, when I slept and he sat awake, tenderly stroking his fingers through my hair.

I wasn't sure why those memories popped up, and I had a feeling Lia wouldn't quite appreciate them the way I did, so I went with a different story for her – the first lunch he took me out on at the office. She said she was unimpressed with the story and asked for a new one. I rolled my eyes and told her, for the first time, actually, about the night Julian comforted me after the blowup at the fire pit.

"Does that suffice?" I asked Lia when I finished.

"You tell me. I was only asking you to tell me all those stories so you'd remind yourself what a surprisingly good guy he is," she said, making my cheeks go hot. "Are you still convinced he'll give you the cold shoulder if you come back?"

I heaved a sigh. "No. I think he'll at least hear me out. Maybe even over lunch."

"He'll probably use that corporate voice you love."

"Ugh." I rolled my head back. "Fuck it. Send me the links for the flight. I'll suck it up if he goes Corporate Julian on me. I just need the answers."

"You got it, girl," Lia said.

I heard her fingers clicking away, and once I received her email, we spent the next ten minutes comparing flights to figure out which was best. I wanted to go for the one seven days from now, on Friday.

Of course, Lia preferred one leaving tomorrow morning.

"That doesn't give me time to mentally prepare," I protested.

"Mentally preparing leads to you backing out of this," she argued. "Also, I just booked it."

"Are you kidding?"

"No. Happy birthday."

"It's not my birthday."

"Happy Fourth of July then, I don't know! Aren't you excited to see me as soon as tomorrow?" Lia demanded. "It's been five weeks since I've smelled your hair."

"Creepy."

"Girl, you don't even know how creepy I can get. I've missed you too much!"

I laughed – a real one, almost. Of course it wound down to a sigh.

"Oh God. It's happening," I murmured, staring at the flight confirmation Lia forwarded me. "Departing tomorrow at seven forty-five in the morning? Are you joking, Lia?"

"Again, not giving you time to think twice about this. Still scared?" she asked.

"More so, actually."

"Don't worry about it. Just start winding down for bed now, because you gotta get up early. And no matter what you do, don't freak out. Whatever happens with that asshole, at least you'll get closure. And at least *I'll* always love you."

I snorted, and after another few minutes of conversation, I went to brush my teeth. I had my toothbrush dangling out of my mouth as I packed a weekend bag, questioning myself for the hundredth time if this moment was really happening.

When I went to bed around midnight, I forced myself to relive the last day I saw Julian. It was for the sake of thickening my skin. I wanted to be prepared in case I'd see it again, because chances were that I would. Julian had sacrificed his business for me. There was no way in hell that he didn't resent me, as well as the fact that he had to work even harder now to make up for all the time he lost with the Roths.

Unsurprisingly, I tossed and turned all night, catching barely a wink of sleep between my dreams of Julian sitting at his desk, refusing to say a single word to me.

41

SARA

Like most of the other early morning travelers around me, I was on autopilot as I moved through security, removing my purse and my bag, and watching both items float ahead of me down the conveyer belt.

After a restless night, going through the airport motions practically lulled me to sleep. But I jolted awake every time I remembered why I was even taking this trip.

I needed to know what happened in Biarritz. Even if explaining made Julian hate me all over again, I needed to at least hear it and close that chapter of my life. At this point, I'd do anything to stop dreaming about him already. I wanted so badly to just move on, but I was stuck. So this was my last hope to get Julian forever out of my mind.

"Would you like a seat, miss?" a man offered when I arrived at my packed gate.

"Oh, no, thank you. It's not heavy," I said when he mentioned something about the duffel on my shoulder.

It was in fact heavy – packed with a bunch of snacks and trinkets I'd collected for Lia over the course of five weeks. But I didn't feel like sitting. I preferred standing by the massive window and staring out at the crowd milling under the enormous concourse. It was oddly comforting. It made me feel less alone, and less crazy for coming here in the first place.

Not that the crazy ship hadn't already sailed.

The lack of sleep had me seeing things more than usual today. Every man in a suit reminded me of Julian, despite the fact that none of them looked remotely like him.

There was no looking like Julian Hoult, especially not Julian Hoult in a suit.

I still remembered the head to toe impact he had on me the first time I laid eyes on him in that elevator.

Staring blankly out at the crowd, I remembered the blue of his eyes, the way they pierced easily right into me. I remembered the way his lips curled in the slightest bit of a smirk, and I could see it now as I stared over the hundreds of heads at my gate.

I could actually see Julian.

"Miss?" The man who'd offered his seat stood up.

My pulse was racing. I didn't realize I'd dropped my bag to the floor till he picked it up and offered it to me.

"I'm sorry," I said hastily, blinking hard and murmuring something else about being fine, though I wasn't sure I was.

My eyes were wild as they returned to the spot they'd seen Julian. It was empty now, but through the crowd, a silver glint caught my eyes. It was low – below hip level – but I followed it like a shooting star, confirming to myself that it was his Rolex before my eyes traveled up the sleeve of his suit, my heart jumping out of my chest when I finally looked up and saw him walking toward me.

In a tailored blue suit, parting the dense crowd of travelers and flight attendants, Julian Hoult was walking toward me.

Oh my God.

I didn't blink. I didn't want to lose him, and I didn't even realize I was pacing toward him till I saw his lips faintly turn up.

Oh God.

That smile.

I felt the same adrenaline I felt my first time on the back of his bike. It rushed through me so fast and so forcefully I couldn't breathe. Our steps quickened and slowed in unison as we closed the long gap between us, and I dropped my bag at our feet when I was finally close enough to confirm I wasn't seeing things.

He was real, right in front of me, and for several moments, I held my breath and just stared.

"You're here," I said finally.

"I'm here," he murmured, the sound of his voice rolling like a blanket over my skin. I drew in a deep breath, closing my eyes when I felt tears burning them. I shook my head when I felt his hand touch my cheek and reduce my voice to a whisper.

"How did you...?" I opened my eyes and studied every inch of his face to ensure myself that this was Julian. *My* Julian. The one who loved me, and not the one who sent me away. "What are you doing here?" I asked. His answer almost buckled my knees.

"I came to take you home."

The tears fell despite the soft laughter escaping my lips. "Did Lia...?" I asked.

"Send me your flight information? Yes," Julian chuckled, pulling me close and letting my tears seep through his shirt. I felt eyes from every direction on us as I cried, but I didn't care. I was so fucking relieved I just didn't care at all.

"I didn't realize the deal fell through, Julian. I would've –"

"Don't worry about that," he said, cupping my face with both hands and thumbing away my tears. "That was the last thing I wanted you to think about."

I shook my head. "You worked so hard for that deal, Julian," I said, my voice breaking. "It couldn't have been easy for you to let go of. I know that."

"It wasn't. But it was still easier than letting go of you."

Julian's chest rose and fell under my palms as he let out a breath. It was short, barely there, but I heard the sound of his pain and guilt in it. I saw the same in his eyes when I looked up at him.

"You had to know I didn't want to let you go, Sara. I wanted to keep you for as long as you'd have me. I swear," he laughed softly at himself, brushing his thumb over my bottom lip. "I got so fucking addicted to that smile," he murmured. "I hated watching you leave. I just thought it was for the best."

"I've told you a million times you don't have to protect me," I protested. "I don't know what Turner said to you that night, but considering what I've heard him say about me, both in front of me and behind my back, I can guess."

"He wanted me to force your compliance, Sara. He wanted me to threaten your job unless you agreed to spend a weekend with him," Julian said, shocking me silent for several moments. That much I didn't know. And he wasn't even done. "People who work for him found out about your arrest. I was afraid he would hold it over you, and harass you. I didn't know how that would affect you, Sara, and I wasn't going to assume. Not when it involved something that hurt you so bad in the past," Julian said, a deep frown in his brow. "I just wanted you to keep healing. You said yourself it's a fragile process."

"It is. But it's even harder without the man who helped me start in the first place."

Julian drew his bottom lip in as he smiled. It was the closest thing to a shy smile that I'd ever see on him, and it prompted my first real laugh in five weeks.

Goddammit, that beauty. I just wanted to skip this whole damned morning and be in New York with him already. I wanted to climb in bed with him, and kiss him and remember what it was like to feel good again, and *whole* again.

"I promise you I'm going to be okay, Julian," I said, and I meant it. "I can do anything on my own, but with you, I do it that much better."

The way he glowed down at me was contagious, apparently, because a trio of passing women grinned wide as they gazed at us. It reminded me a bit of the sun hat ladies at the gas station, who barely had to know me to tell me to make Julian mine. I laughed to myself as I thought about them, and I hoped that wherever Sun Hat Lady was right now, I was making her proud.

"God, you have no idea how much I've missed you, Sara," Julian said as his fingers wove into my hair. He kissed the top of my head. "I dreamt of you every day that you were gone."

My tears hung on my lashes as he hugged me tight against his chest.

"Trust me. I know how that feels."

JULIAN

I TOOK off of work for the first week that Sara came home. We exchanged the same knowing grin when I offered her my place to stay since she'd given up her lease. She was moving in with me. We were both well aware of that – we just didn't say it quite yet.

But within the first three days, we fell into a perfect little domestic routine. I woke up early to go for a run, come home to shower then make us breakfast. I'd let it cool on the counter as I crawled back into bed and kissed Sara awake. We generally let breakfast go cold while having sex anywhere from the bed to the bathroom, but it didn't matter because anything tasted good after the appetite we worked up.

During the day, we went shopping for things that she needed, that got lost or thrown out during the move. We exchanged that same knowing smirk as we purchased everything from a toothbrush to a little silver tray to hold her earrings on my dresser. After that particular purchase, she couldn't hold her tongue.

"How long do you think I'll be staying at your apartment?" she asked as we walked out of the store. She giggled at the smile on my face.

"My guess is awhile."

During the night, she cooked dinner while I read or took calls from work. I could never actually be completely off, but it was certainly nice to conduct business with a view of Sara dancing in the kitchen, her ass wiggling around as she tasted her red sauce over the stove.

Like we'd established during that trip to Biarritz, she went to sleep before me at night while I sat beside her in bed, reading or preparing notes for work.

It was a routine every other couple had, and it was apparently everything I needed to be perfectly happy and content.

My favorite nights were the one when Mom or Emmett dropped by, either to drop off some home cooked food or, in Emmett's case, to eat it. I loved those nights, because I got to hang back and watch Sara sit with them on the couch as I poured some wine. I got to listen to her talk and laugh breezily with them, as if she'd known them for years.

I'd lived in this apartment for years now, but somehow the bells of her voice were what it took to make it really feel like home.

Then again, she had a way of carrying that feeling with her wherever we went. The first time I'd felt it was when I brought her to my house in the Hamptons. I felt it more in Biarritz, and I felt it strongest now that I had her in the place I returned to every night after work.

She was my sense of home. My sense of family. She was everything I had tried to work for and pushed myself to find when I was younger. I wish I could have told myself then to save myself the pain – that if I could just wait long enough, the answer to every one of my dreams would come in the form of a girl named Sara.

She was the glue that pieced everything together for me, and she was the motivation behind my new top priority in life:

No matter what, keep her happy.

Keep her parents happy. Keep even Lia happy.

Do whatever it takes to lift even the slightest weight off her shoulders, and keep that beautiful smile on her face.

That was the new goal, and it was a lofty one. But I was known to work my ass off for something I truly wanted.

And plain and simple, she was it.

EPILOGUE

SARA

Twelve Months Later

"What... is going on?" I asked, slowing down at the top of the steps when I spotted Julian at the bottom, looking dashing as ever in his black suit and grey tie.

It wasn't unusual for him to wait for me there when I was taking too long to get ready for dinner, but tonight, he had music playing, and he wore a crooked little smile as he held what looked like a white rose in each hand. He didn't answer my question, simply saying, "Come here, baby."

It was hard to say no to that.

When I got to the bottom step, Julian stopped me, taking my hand and slipping what I thought was just a rose on my wrist. In reality, it was a small but intricate corsage. I was still a bit lost, but I broke into a huge grin when he pinned the other rose next to his lapel – his boutonniere.

"Julian Hoult. Are you taking me to prom?" I asked, giggling my ass off as he helped me down the last step.

"We covered the motorcycle ride on your wish list. We've been to your french fry spot about a dozen times now," he said, his gorgeous lips curving up. "Figured we should cross off prom before we get to the rest."

"Fair enough," I smirked as he brought me to the floor between the open kitchen and living room, both of us laughing as "You Are The Best Thing" by Ray LaMontagne played over the speakers. "But you realize you've set a bad precedent for yourself here, right?" I teased, my lips close to his as we danced.

"How so?"

"You remember that wish list right? Now you have to take me to Monaco and Tuscany."

"Not a problem. Remind me what else is on that wish list? Because I'm actually going to get to another part of it tonight."

I raised my eyebrows. "*Really*, Mr. Hoult. That's interesting, since the rest of that wish list is entirely up to me to complete."

"Something about buying your parents a three-bedroom in London."

"Yes. And trust me, I'm saving," I said, giggling as I took a look at my corsage next to his boutonniere. From the white roses, I looked up at his beautiful face – at all those perfectly sculpted features that, once upon a time, rarely bothered to move. It was funny to think about now considering I got at least one of those crinkle-eyed laughs every day. The Miracle Worker. That was what Lukas and Emmett called me for bringing life to Julian in a way they'd never seen.

Since busting my ass to get my job with Una Magazine in the States, I'd achieved quite a lot. But being Julian's miracle worker was perhaps still my proudest achievement thus far.

"So where are you taking me tonight? Monaco or Tuscany?" I murmured my question against Julian's lips as he kissed me softly. "And do Lukas and Lia know about the trip?" I giggled. "Because they're kind of expecting us at our reservation in thirty minutes."

"I'm sorry, baby, but we're not leaving the country tonight."

"But you said we were covering another part of the wish list tonight, and I don't see myself buying a house for my parents before midnight."

Julian laughed, slipping the corsage off my wrist and unpinning his boutonniere as Ray LaMontagne faded out. I watched with amusement as he set the flowers onto the kitchen counter, returning to me with a hand reaching in his jacket pocket.

The grin dropped off my face as I watched him pull out a little velvet box.

"Julian..."

His blue eyes glimmered when they looked at me.

"You said you wanted to buy a three-bedroom for your parents, so you could visit with your kids. And I kind of imagined from the day you said it that they would be our kids," Julian said softly, laughing at my instant tears. It was just a few at first, but the moment he went down on one knee, they poured. "Sara, you've been everything I've ever wanted from the moment I laid eyes on you, and every day I spend with you, I find myself wanting more. I want to bring you to Monaco and Tuscany. I want to see you walk down the aisle to me in a big white dress. I want to see the way your eyes light up around our children. I think you rubbed off on me," he chuckled, "because all I do these days is fantasize about you, and us and the life we're going to have together. You make me want to be a better man, and the best father in the world. For all the ways you've changed my life, and all the happiness you've brought me, you deserve nothing short of that."

I could barely see through my tears, and my knees were weak enough that Julian read my mind and returned to his feet, laughing as he held me tight against his chest and kissed my forehead.

"Making you happy has been by far my proudest achievement, Sara. And I'll never stop working to keep that smile on your face," he murmured, his lips spreading in a grin as I let out one more sob. "So marry me. I've been waiting for awhile to call you my wife."

"Of course I'll marry you," I whispered, bringing my wet eyes to our hands as he slid the most beautiful ring on my finger. His face lit up just as much as mine as we watched it slide perfectly in place. "Sara Hoult," I breathed in pure awe as he feathered kisses along my cheek.

"Sounds perfect."

"It does."

Like a dream, actually.

I couldn't have imagined it this well as a girl. I couldn't have pictured someone as perfect as Julian, who could take away every ounce of my pain by simply wrapping me tight in his arms.

I lived for just the way he just looked at me – for the way he kissed me in the morning when I woke, and the way he said "I love you" as I drifted off to sleep every night. He was both my fantasy and my reality, my actual dream come true.

The only crazy part was that the best was yet to come.

The End

THE IRRESISTIBLE SERIES

Thank you for reading Bad Boss! If you enjoyed Julian and Sara's story, be sure to check out the rest of the Irresistible Series on Amazon and Kindle Unlimited!

CONTACT STELLA

Facebook: stellarhysbooks
Twitter: @stellarhys

Also Available By Stella Rhys
IN TOO DEEP
TOO FAR GONE (IN TOO DEEP #2)
HAVOC
DAMAGE (HAVOC #2)
DARE ME
WRONG
EX GAMES
SWEET SPOT (IRRESISTIBLE BOOK 1)
DIRTY DEEDS (IRRESISTIBLE BOOK 3)
HOTHEAD (IRRESISTIBLE BOOK 4)

Turn the page for a preview of Dirty Deeds!

DIRTY DEEDS

PROLOGUE

ALY

I tried to see what others saw in him.

I'm sure the height hit them first. Six feet and two inches of pure athletic muscle was bound to grab attention. I got that.

I got that the stupid thing he did with his hair made all the girls and even teachers swoon. Of course, I wasn't convinced he didn't know exactly what he was doing there. I mean who honestly ran both hands *slooowly* through their hair in the middle of talking to someone? It was ridiculously sensual – especially when it always left his hair so perfectly tousled, like he'd just rolled out of bed.

Then there was his voice. Low and kind of gravelly. The dark hair, light eyes combo – that was a thing too. I got that.

But I just couldn't get past what a prick the kid was. Our dads were best friends, and having grown up with Emmett Hoult, I couldn't see the appeal that everyone saw. All I could see was what they couldn't.

When the world looked at Emmett, they saw confident, devilish, sexy.

I saw cocky, spoiled, arrogant. Your typical all-American jock.

I saw the kid I was forced to spend every weekend and vacation of my childhood with – the one that Xeroxed the worst photos he could find in my family albums, just so he could tack them all over my crush's locker.

I saw the kid who got away with literally everything, no matter who I complained to. Teachers, coaches, even the school principal looked at me as a nuisance. A thorn in their side. All they wanted was to adore Emmett Hoult in peace – to be completely charmed by his playful, laid back nature. The last thing they wanted was to have to acknowledge me, the surly buzzkill whose griping would get him undoubtedly pulled from practice, something the football team *"just couldn't afford."*

Even my parents defended his every move.

"It's just a sibling rivalry," Mom would brush it off. "You grew up together. You're practically family. But give it a few years, Aly, and I'm sure you'll get on great."

Right. I gave it a few years, and all Emmett did was get worse.

In high school, all it took was one evening of his mom comparing his bad friends, bad grades or bad behavior to mine, and I'd wind up paying for it with a week of torture at school.

His teammates snickered at me in the halls. He spread the nickname "Baldy" when I botched my haircut sophomore year. By the time I was a junior, I was down to just three friends who didn't worship him or use me to get close to him, and he told me – "just for shits and giggles" – that he'd hook up with every one of them so I'd have no allies left to gripe to.

And he did precisely that.

In short, with very little effort involved, Emmett Hoult took over my entire life.

At home, Dad raved nonstop about his athletic achievements. At school, he ruled every last hallway and classroom. Even at night, in the privacy of my bedroom, I couldn't escape the constant texts from friends he'd "mysteriously" ghosted. They sobbed for me to help figure out what went wrong, or begged me to subtly bring them up to Emmett when we saw each other that weekend. They didn't seem to realize he'd never hang out with them again – that he only hooked up with them to get under my skin. He didn't even remember most of their names.

Simply put, the kid was an asshole.

He always got what he wanted, he didn't have to try, and he never even knew how much his antics made me cry every night. While I was completely miserable, he just carried on with his perfectly charmed life.

And so I hated him.

For all the many stunts he pulled on me, I despised Emmett Hoult. But amazingly, all that crap happened *before* the last week of junior year.

That was the week he truly ruined my life.

~

CHAPTER ONE
ALY

Unbelievable.

Of course his 'summer cottage' is more like a frickin' resort, I thought as I walked through the house.

I had arrived at Emmett's East Hampton home a good ten minutes ago, but I wasn't over it yet. It was going to take awhile to get over this four-bed, six-bath masterpiece of a dream house that Emmett apparently visited just a few weekends per summer. Seriously. This place looked like an ad for Ralph Lauren Home. It had its own wine cellar, pool and outdoor kitchen. It was more beautiful than any home I'd be able to afford in my life, yet it was basically just his side piece home – the bonus one he dropped by if he happened to find himself in the mood.

This frickin' guy. What the heck does his apartment in the city look like if this is what his summerhouse looks like?

I wasn't sure if I wanted to laugh or scowl as I imagined the life Emmett Hoult probably led these days. Over the years, I'd tolerated some Emmett-related updates from my parents, but never enough to get a clear picture of who exactly he was now.

Honestly, I didn't want to know.

Because thinking in depth about Emmett Hoult generally led me down a road of jealousy, bitterness and countless what if's. It made me think of all the bad memories I'd swept under the carpet and tried to tell myself I was fine with when I wasn't, so I staunchly avoided the topic.

That is until now.

"Um... Aly?"

Evie was unblinking when she finally caught up with me in the guest room, dragging my last suitcase in behind her. Her wide eyes went wider as she drifted inside, stopping in front of the door to fully soak in everything from my canopy bed to the lush, white curtains framing the window overlooking the pool.

"So... you said you were crashing at a family friend's *house*," she said slowly, narrowing her big eyes at me. "And I just wanted to inform you that this is not a house. This is a baby mansion."

I wrinkled my nose. "I know. I mean I didn't know before I walked in here with you, but I had a feeling it would be something ridiculously nice. That's just... Emmett Hoult. His life is awesome."

"No wonder you hate him," Evie murmured with fascination as she floated into the bathroom across the hall. The echo of her gasp had me guessing it was pretty big in there. "Aly! Holy *fuck,* this shower is bigger than my apartment!"

I laughed as I crossed the hallway into the bathroom, my eyebrows arching high at the marble luxury that lay within.

"Jesus, Emmett," I muttered under my breath, taking in the absolute spa of a bathroom. "We could actually throw a decent party in here," I snorted, opening the shower door to peek inside at the ceiling showerhead and waterproof speakers.

"Or you could just let me move into your bathroom for the summer," Evie said as we returned to the bedroom. "I mean Mike might not even notice that I'm gone," she cracked, though I could tell from the way she winced that she found nothing funny about her own joke.

Mike was Evie's fiancé of ten months and her boyfriend of eight years. They'd been together forever but were, to put it lightly, on the rocks as of late. It was precisely why Evie couldn't take me in. Aside from the fact that they lived in a tiny studio, and aside from the fact that Mike had firmly said no, their tension these days was already like a third roommate. Trying to make a relationship work was hard enough, so they definitely didn't need the burden of my homeless ass crashing on their couch.

"Well, if you ever *do* need me to set up pillows and a comforter in that shower, I'm more than happy to," I offered to make Evie laugh.

"I actually could take you up on that. I mean you're sure he won't drop by at all this summer, right? Like, not even once?"

"Trust me, I triple-checked with his mom when I picked up the keys. She said her friends were just staying at this place because he's always out of town. He's at like, some resort for the next three weeks. Then it's off to his house in Hawaii till the end of summer."

"Jesus, how rich is this guy?" Evie asked, sounding both amazed and disgusted. "And what exactly does he do for a living?"

"I actually have no idea," I mumbled, rereading the texts Emmett's mom sent me when I double-checked about him being away.

AUNT AUDREY: Yes he will be in the Maldives for the next three weeks! After that he's got the gala and then it's Maui till Labor Day! House is all yours.

AUNT AUDREY: Please relax and make yourself at home – you deserve it after everything you've been through!!

She wasn't kidding.

I wasn't big on pitying myself, but this last week had seriously put me through the wringer, starting with the electrical fire that tore through my Sag Harbor apartment in under thirty minutes.

Thankfully, I was at the café when it happened. Not so thankfully, the fire devoured almost all the clothes, books and other belongings I'd acquired over the course of my twenty-eight years – something I'd be way more torn up about if my mind weren't so completely focused on this particular week of work.

It was basically my coming out week for the new and improved Stanton Family Market. Evie and I had poured every last penny of our savings into buying the dead company from Dad, and as a seasonal business in its very first year, I had a lot to prove in just a few months' time. So the last thing I needed to stress about was where to lay my head at night.

I needed a place that I could get quick, cheap and close to work.

Hence the summerhouse arrangement.

"Alright." Evie gave one loud clap of her hands. "Let's stop drooling over this place and start unpacking. We can't lose focus – we *do* have a mission tonight."

I nodded dutifully.

That we did, because on top of a surprise fire this week, I also had nearly a lifetime of insomnia working against me. I hadn't slept more than three hours a night for two months now, and while I was generally happy to run on fumes, tomorrow was a different story. Tomorrow, I had to be functional *and* easy on the eyes since I had Hamptons frickin' Magazine coming to do a feature on the café.

According to Evie, I needed to let them photograph my "pretty lil' face" in order to personalize our brand. And while I was normally averse to picture taking, I'd do pretty much anything for this venture, so tonight, I needed my beauty rest.

And since college, there were only two surefire ways to get my restless body a full and healthy night of sleep.

"Dancing and fucking!" Evie declared the moment we finished unpacking the last of my things. "I'm making you do both tonight. You ready, girl?"

I snorted as I rolled my empty luggage into the massive walk-in.

"Uh, no, because that's not necessary. It only needs to be one or the other, and I choose dancing."

"Why?" Evie whined. "Wouldn't you rather play it safe and do both?"

"No, because with dancing, I only have to rely on myself. The other option is never a guarantee," I pointed out. "In case you forgot, I only fall asleep after like... crazy, mind-blowing, *lost-two-pounds-in-the-process* type sex, and that's not always easy to find."

"Aly. It's East Hampton in July. This town is currently a hot bed of A-list actors and pro athletes – you're basically drowning in sexy, physically fit dick right now," Evie said. "Also, if there's anything good about my butthead fiancé at this time, it's that he works in PR. So it's legit his job to hunt down the places where all the yummy famous people go."

"Alright." I laughed as she started digging like a squirrel through her Madewell tote full of dresses for me to borrow. "Well then, if I spot Brad Pitt or George Clooney tonight, I'll totally go for the one-night stand. But otherwise, we're just dancing. Alright?"

"Brad Pitt or George – what the fuck? Those guys haven't been hot since two thousand nine," Evie said with exasperation, tossing a bunch of slinky numbers onto my bed. "And I can guarantee you neither of them have a six-pack anymore, let alone an eight-pack."

"An eight-pack? Does *any*one have those outside of Marvel comics?" I asked distractedly, undoing my topknot and shaking out my hair in the mirror. It was just past my shoulders now – long for my standards, and back to blonde for the first time in ages. Three months into this new look, and I still wasn't used to it yet. But it was finally me – the *real* me – so thus far, I was loving it.

"Yeah, the eight-pack is definitely a rarity," Evie conceded, tossing me a little black dress to try on. "Like a four-leaf clover. But that's exactly why if you find one, you have to fuck it."

"I have to fuck the eight-pack?" I snorted as Evie narrowed her eyes at me.

"You have to fuck the guy who *owns* it," she clarified. "Because he's clearly physically fit enough to fuck *you* like a champ. I'm talking pin-you-up-against-the-wall sex, or bang-you-while-you're-on-top sex."

"I'm sorry – what was that second one?" I grunted as I struggled to wiggle into her skintight dress.

"You know. When you're straddling him but he's holding your hips and like, slamming up into you? It takes a shit load of core strength to go at it like that for awhile, which is why the eight-pack is essential," she insisted as I rolled my eyes. "I'm serious, Aly. You know you want that Superman sex. Especially since you lost your good vibrator to the fire."

"Ugh. Don't remind me."

"I know, it's a tragedy," Evie lamented. "But that just means you deserve a good lay tonight. Get some good dancing in, have dirty, wild sex with some stud, then pass out on this five thousand dollar mattress here. No way in hell you don't get at *least* six hours of sleep after all that."

I smirked, partially convinced.

"Fine. If I find a guy with an eight-pack tonight, I'll go home with him."

"Atta girl!"

"*But* he also has to be phenomenally good-looking with a decent personality," I said as Evie groaned.

"Oh, please – who cares about personality? It's a one-night stand. You'll never see him again!"

"Yeah, well, I need to trust him enough to go home with him, 'cause there is no way in hell I'm having sex with some guy in *Emmett's* house." I shuddered. "That's just... gross. And way too weird."

"Fair enough," Evie declared, sliding my shoebox across the floor at me. "Now hurry up and put on these fuck-me heels. We got eight-packs to hunt for, and time's a wastin'."

∽

CHAPTER TWO
ALY

"Hold up – what are you *wearing* under that dress?"

Evie's question came only once we hit the dance floor at Godsend, the absolute jungle of a nightclub she'd brought me to. Hanging from the ceiling and snaking up the walls were vines upon vines of beautiful flowers and plants, their petals illuminated by the black lights.

At first I liked the lights. Then I realized they lit the white of my bra on fire and made it shine like two blazing suns under my black dress. I was legitimately blinding people on the dance floor. One guy actually passed me, yelped and shielded his eyes like he'd stared at the eclipse. Beyond that, I was getting taunted left and right.

"Hey! Hush!" Evie scolded two girls who shimmied past me and yelled, "*Nice bra!*"

"It's okay, I deserve it!" I yelled over the music, still dancing as I stared down at myself. For God's sake, there were polka dots on the bra. Pink ones. They were so bright they were distracting even me.

"Do you not own a black bra?" Evie shouted over the blaring EDM.

"Do you not recall the fire that ate everything I've ever owned?" I countered.

"Shit, right!" Evie cursed, still grooving as she tossed her honey locks over her shoulder. Peering around the floor, she looked back at me and laughed. "Alright, girl, we've got way too much weird attention right now. You gotta lose the bra."

"Really?" I crinkled my nose. I had far too much boobage to dance comfortably without a bra, but Evie was right – I also had way too many guys staring at me with grins that ranged from leering amusement to flat-out creepiness.

"It's okay, the dress is tight enough to keep the girls contained!" Evie yelled, reading my mind. "Now go, go, go!"

"Alright, alright, I'll be back!" I shouted before heading off to the bathroom.

The first one I located had a line spilling out the door, but thanks to a shot girl who took pity on my radioactive chest, I managed to find my way to an empty employee bathroom on the second floor.

In the last stall, I peeled Evie's skintight dress down to my waist, unclasping my bra and laughing at myself as I whipped it off. It had been on clearance at Victoria's Secret, and for good reason – it was ridiculously over-the-top girly. Even its polka dots had polka dots. But that was precisely why I bought it. Once upon a time, for all the wrong reasons, I was that stone-faced tomboy who wouldn't cry and scoffed at all things pink. I went as far as to wear undersized sports bras to minimize my curves because I felt the urgent need to hide all shreds of femininity. Like it was something to be ashamed of.

I was stupid then.

So these days, I was making up for all the years I forced myself to be what somebody else wanted. These days, I no longer hid my body. I no longer scoffed at "girly" fashion. Gone were the sports bras, over-sized button-ups and shapeless loafers. Replacing them were things I'd always liked but never let myself wear – all the shift dresses, pencil skirts, ballet flats and espadrilles.

And occasionally, the neon polka dot bras.

I snorted at myself as I exited the stall, swinging my bra on my wrist and rather enjoying the feeling of going braless in public for the first time in my adult life. Gathering my hair to the side, I gazed down my front, giving myself permission to admire my heeled feet, my smooth legs and the poor, braless boobs that I'd hidden from the world since the summer they came.

Poor girls. It's your time to finally shine tonight, I decided with a giggle, reaching under my neckline to give my cleavage a boost. But just as I scooped and lifted, I heard a groan.

"Fuck – what are you doing?"

"Omigod!" I yelped in shock, clasping my hand to my chest as my eyes shot up to see whom the voice belonged to.

Holyshitholyshitholyshit.

My mouth fell open when my eyes landed promptly on muscle – hard, naked muscle on a tall, dark, *shirtless* God of a man.

Whoa.

Okay.

What... the fuck?

My eyes fluttered. Who was this guy? Where were his clothes?

How was this level of hotness even possible? In two seconds I already had so many questions, but none of them made it out of my mouth because it was too busy watering over his body.

Holy pecs, Batman.

I swallowed hard as my gaze traveled across the stranger's shoulders down to his broad chest and killer six... no. *Wait.*

My shameless eyes narrowed as they counted every deep-cut section of his *eeeight-paaaack!*

In my head, I yelled it like Oprah.

But seriously. Shit. He had a fucking eight-pack. *Oh, Evie.* Part of me wanted to whip out my phone, take a picture and send it right to her, but I found myself quickly distracted by those insane rib muscles. What the hell were they called? I had no idea, but this guy had them and they made him look stronger than a wild fucking animal. My thighs squirmed against each other as I heard his low voice speak to me again.

"Yeah, you, uh..." I looked up to see him wince and rub his square jaw in a way I found painfully sexy. "You gotta stop doing that," he said with a short laugh.

I blinked.

"Doing what?"

He nodded at my chest with a slight crease in his brow.

"Fondling yourself in front of me."

My eyes fluttered down my front, and only then did I realize my hand had still been under my dress when I clasped my heart in shock. My cheeks lit aflame as I processed the fact that I'd basically just groped my boobs for a good three to four seconds in front of this absurdly hot stranger.

"Oh... my God," I whispered under my breath, fairly mortified as I released myself and slipped my hand out from under my dress.

"I mean if you want to keep doing that, by all means," Eight-Pack smirked, his lean biceps twitching as he hooked his thumbs in his pockets. "It's just I already stained my shirt tonight." He nodded toward his booze-splattered button-up in the sink. "Didn't really feel like busting the zipper on my favorite jeans."

I took a moment to process what he was saying. I gave a dry laugh as I stared at him.

"Was that a boner joke?"

"Yeah, but I don't know how much it counts as a joke when I'm actually hard right now."

"Oh my God."

"What?" he laughed. "Cut me some slack, I thought I was alone in here – I definitely didn't expect a fucking gorgeous blonde to walk out playing with her own tits." He held both hands up when I shot a look. "Breasts. Sorry."

"Huh." I crossed my arms, unsure if the noise I made in response was a laugh or a scoff. I honestly couldn't tell if I was offended, charmed or completely turned on by this guy, but I was leaning towards all of the above. "Yeah, well... I also didn't expect to walk out of the bathroom to find a guy just standing there without a shirt on," I countered. "Pretty sure this is a women's bathroom."

"It's a unisex employee's bathroom," he corrected, his gaze traveling leisurely up my legs. "And I'm pretty sure you're not an employee."

"How do you know that for sure?" I challenged.

"Because I would've remembered you," he replied as his eyes landed back on me.

Ugh, fine.

I had been biting it back till this point, but fuck it, I finally let go of my grin. I was officially charmed, my heart skipping a beat as I watched the stranger's lake blue eyes fall gently onto my mouth. When he looked back up at me, a curious frown pinched his brow.

"What's your name?" he asked.

"Evie," I lied.

"Evie," he repeated.

His stare was still glued on me as my own trailed down the vein snaking from his tricep to his thick forearm. I imagined that vein twitching as he did everything from open jars to roll up sleeves to lift giant weights at the gym. I also might've pictured those forearms flexing as he lifted girls by the backs of their thighs and pinned them up against the wall, but that fantasy was fleeting.

And by fleeting, I mean I forced it out of my head because if my panties got any wetter, they might very well slide off my body.

"Hey." There was a laugh in his voice. "Still with me?"

My eyes fluttered up at his question, and only then did I realize he'd been talking to me during the entirety of my ogling.

"Sorry – what?" I asked hastily.

"Nothing, I was just asking what finally brought you to this club tonight," he chuckled. "Nothing urgent – just your shitty, run-of-the-mill small talk to hide the fact that I can't stop staring at you."

Oh. I raked my little grin between my teeth as our eyes gleamed like fucking stars at each other. God, what was happening? I'd known this guy all of twelve seconds yet the sexual tension was through the roof. I could practically hear the spark of electricity between us. It was nothing I'd ever felt before.

Then again, he is shirtless and beautiful, I reasoned with myself. And his first glance at you did involve extreme boob grabbing, so of course you're both thinking about sex. Dirty... sweaty... bite-his-shoulder, claw-his-back kind of sex. All things considered, totally expected – but for the love of God, change the topic already.

My mind raced as I rewound the conversation back to his mundane question about what had brought me to the club tonight.

"I have insomnia," I blurted, watching Eight Pack lift an eyebrow. "And dancing is one of two things that gets me thoroughly tired."

He tilted his head to the side.

"Come again?"

I blushed at myself.

"Sorry. Going back to your question about what brought me here tonight... I have insomnia and a fairly important thing at work tomorrow morning that involves getting my picture taken, so basically, I need sleep and I'm pretty much here tonight so I can tire myself out," I explained, waiting for that sexy laugh – for him to tease or ridicule me.

But he gave no reaction.

Instead, he studied me, letting silence fill the room for several seconds before flashing a smirk.

"I could tire you out," he said.

The huskiness of his voice went straight to my clit.

Easy, I pleaded with my imagination. I really didn't need more mental pictures of what this guy looked like naked and pinning me down on his bed. Any more squirming or blushing and he'd know that he had me tempted, and I couldn't have that. I couldn't just *hook* up with some random guy at a club. Despite how unbelievably hot he was, and how unbelievably hot he'd gotten *me* in about three seconds, it just wasn't a thing that I did.

"Sorry." A wry smile twisted my lips. "But I think I have to decline."

"Of course you have to," he grinned. "Whether you want to is the question."

"In that case, I plead the fifth."

"Why not just take what you want?" he laughed. "I do it all the time, and let me tell you, it's a great way to live."

I snorted. "I just don't go home with strangers."

He glanced to the side. "Fine. Then I'll tire you out over the sink."

Fuck.

I couldn't help glancing over at the sink as well. One tiny look and I was already imagining his hard chest pressed against my back and his big hands filling themselves with my tits, squeezing them relentlessly till I cried out. I could practically hear his gravelly voice growling dirty, sexy filth in my ear as he gripped my hips and pumped into me from behind. *Yeah, he's definitely huge*, I decided, not even realizing that I'd closed my eyes till his voice made them flutter open again.

"Now that's just fucked up," he said, serious despite a curt laugh.

Tipping his chin up, he drew a hand across his perfect jaw, his face a mixture of annoyance and arousal as he looked down his perfect nose at me. I swallowed.

"What is?"

"You making that lusty little 'fuck me' face right now."

I breathed out a laugh. "Was I?"

"I don't know. Your cheeks got nice and pink and you were sucking on your lip like it was candy. Is that the face you make when you want to get fucked?" he asked, his question flooding me with heat.

"No." I lied. "I just do that sometimes."

"Well, don't do it now," he muttered. "Not unless you want me to pull that little skirt up your thighs and make you come all over my mouth."

Holy...

Shit.

I was speechless as he smirked.

"You're doing it again."

"What? The fuck-me face?" I choked breathlessly, my entire body on fire. "Sorry. Can't really help it when you're standing there without a shirt on and telling me you're going to lick my pussy till I come."

"Christ." His jaw tightened as a low growl rumbled from his chest. "Did I say those exact words?" he asked, arousal thick in his voice.

"No," I sputtered hotly, suddenly embarrassed that I'd dropped the word "pussy" right in front of a stranger. "But you implied. So I deduced."

"Right," he grinned as his eyebrows pulled tight. "Are we fighting, by the way? Because if we are, it's getting me even harder than I was when you first walked out squeezing the hell out of those perfect tits." He laughed as my jaw dropped. "What? You can say pussy but I can't say tits?"

"Now you're just *trying* to rile me up."

"No, you've been riled up. You're just trying to pretend otherwise because you don't want to believe that some stranger at a club is actually tempting you to break whatever rule you have about one-night stands."

I glared at his self-satisfied smirk, letting the silence stretch between us till it felt almost deafening. He broke it with a laugh.

"I meant to ask, by the way – what was the other thing?" he asked.

"What?"

"You said that dancing was one of two things that got you actually tired. What was the other thing?"

Fuck, I cursed, our stares locked tight as I sucked on my bottom lip. *Sex is the other thing,* I answered silently as he gave that low chuckle. *Crazy, sweaty, eight-pack sex. You asshole.*

I wasn't sure how, but he already knew the damned answer, so rather than say it I simply swallowed the knot in my throat. Holding my hair off the blazing hot back of my neck, I tried to reconcile the fact that I was about to do something crazy.

"I can have my driver outside in a minute if you want to get out of here," he murmured, his eyes gleaming at me.

I was still chewing my lip, and it took a good few moments to find my words. But when I did, they came out without the slightest tremor.

"Fine. Call your driver now."

Dirty Deeds
Available Now on Amazon and Kindle Unlimited!

Made in United States
Orlando, FL
03 November 2022

24182811R00181